Dancing with Fate

Book One

UNWANTED
LEGACY

F. J. NAMINI

F. J. Namini

The official website of F. J. NAMINI

https://fjnamini.com

Contents

CHAPTER ONE

BIRTH

MANNEA[1], Ancient Land of Mannaeans, 644BC, Autumn

Her painful scream faded beneath a loud clap of thunder. It was hard to breathe, heavy with the strong smell of herbal medicines. The old midwife looked at the young woman, between her bowed legs, frowned, and her hands curled into claws with the watery blood dripping from her palms. The old midwife's dark, almond-shaped eyes seemed quite concerned, sweat beaded her skin and trickled down her brow, and she wiped it away with the sleeve of her shirt. Amitira, the young woman, had laid naked down on the bed, whimpering from the pain. She was so young, with a fantastic body that reminded the statues of love goddesses.

The old midwife took a deep breath, and her gaze flickered to the women surrounding them. The women's pale skin was painted a sullen red by the whirled flames, which raced each other in the fireplace. One was tired, and another impatient; others wore expressions of boredom.

Mannaean women do not like her, none of them, the midwife thought. She gazed at Amitira again, somewhat more sympathetically. Amitira was fighting hard to regulate her breathing, her golden honey eyes fixed on the ceiling. The firelight played upon her wet olive skin. Her long

---

[1] An ancient territory around the 10th to 7th centuries BC, present-day northwestern Iran south of Lake Urmia

neck, rounded shoulders and small but full and firm breasts had made an excellent combination that was not in harmony with her swollen, big belly. Her breath quivered in short, quick gasps every time she inhaled, her lips puffed out and her dark red hair was wet and matted on her forehead, yet, she still seemed so pretty.

Amitira's long, rising wail brought the midwife to her senses. A new wave of pain had come back, and her screams sounded so terrible. She was pushing herself up, struggling to release herself from the women's strong hands who detained her on the bed. She winced as her leg trembled, blind with pain, lashing out with her foot.

"Breathe, breathe baby… breathe and push!" The midwife said, trying to encourage her.

Amitira twisted, squirmed and kicked the air, then went on yelling like a stuck beast, as she had done before. She grew calm slowly, took a deep, painful breath, and her eyes became fixed upon the ceiling again, whispering the words, apparently meaningless.

Sheedvash[1] stepped forward, her long skirt trailing after her. She glanced at her brother's wife for a moment. Amitira's crying made no sense to her. She knelt in front of the stone fireplace to put some sticks on the fire. The fire devoured the wet branches slowly, and a strong reddish-orange color shone slowly around the bedchamber. Her pale white skin turned red when the fire began to blaze, and reflection of the flames danced in her black eyes, like two pristine stones of onyx that lit up with an orange flare. Even in these grim hours, Sheedvash looked graceful, dressed all in a long black dress that was tight around the waist with silk embroidery on her skirt and chest, a perfect dress for a widow. She was seventeen, slender as a willow, and her straight black hair was worn in a long braid with a silver robe. Her high cheekbones, full lips, and milk-pale skin made her a beautiful Mannaean woman.

Sheedvash gave a long weary sigh, lifted her chin and turned her face toward Amitira. She could hear Amitira's labored breath, rattling through the air. Just for a moment, Sheedvash felt pity for her but then

---

[1] A name was used in ancient Persia meaning beautiful like sun

closed her eyes and remembered how much she hated this woman. The God punishes her by giving the pain, Sheedvash thought bitterly. She turned her face away from Amitira in disgust and got up slowly. She could feel the midwife's eyes watching her, but she did her best to ignore her, went to the doorway and sat on a bench.

The midwife took her eyes off Sheedvash and looked at Amitira's face again. Valuable time was flying like the wind, and they were wasting it. Amitira's labor had taken too long, and she and her baby were in danger.

"Calm down baby! You must help me!" The midwife said apprehensively.

Amitira's eyes were sunken deep into blackness; cold and dull. The midwife did not even know if Amitira had heard her words or not. After a few moments, Amitira finally calmed down and slept on the bed although her wide-open eyes were fixed on the ceiling, and her lips still moved without a sound. The women left her alone, oblivious to the look that the old midwife gave them.

The old midwife had helped many mothers to give birth for years, but she had never seen such a difficult delivery. *Well, this time is different,* she thought. Usually, the family and neighbors wore white clothes, the men sang hymns, and the women helped the mother by the time a baby was born through this land. However, in the Dark Stone castle, their old shelter, risen amidst the blue-grey Orin Mountains, there was no man to sing hymns and no woman liked to help Amitira. It was apparent that if the women had no respect for Taham[1] Beik, the paramount of the tribe and her wife, Chista, no one came to help Amitira.

The midwife slowly began to get up, moving further from the bed. She dipped a soft towel into the brewed peach bark, squeezed and wiped the sweat from Amitira's hot face. She wanted to speak with her, hoping to encourage her in her delivery but Amitira's eyes were fixed on some invisible object which no one but she could see, muttering something

---

[1] A name was used in ancient Persia meaning strong

incomprehensible. The midwife paused, sighed and wanted to go but suddenly Amitira's frail body began to shake, and her breath came faster and faster. Another pain grasped her, and she let out a shrill, high scream.

"This time, you should help me, please baby," the midwife mumbled as she moved close to help.

Amitira struggled to push her back and climbed out of bed. Sheedvash was staring at the rain that was falling fast; not even looking at her. Other women saw the midwife's gaze and came to her aid. Their strong hands grasped Amitira by the shoulders and kept her on the bed. A queer look passed across Amitira's beautiful, pale face, and her eyes blinked open, full of fear. She licked her lips. The midwife sighed. Something was bothering her. Something felt so wrong, so strange but she could not understand what. She had tried to help this unexplained pain but failed. Everything felt so confused. The midwife looked at Amitira, frowning, and seemed to be engaged in some kind of internal struggle. Then she glanced up, a decision had been made. The danger was just around the corner, and they had wasted too much time. She put her wrinkled but strong hands above Amitira's big belly and pushed down.

Amitira's horrific scream echoed through the bedchamber and across the mountain.

*****

The wind gusted along the top of the cliff. Ashvan[1] stood above the cliff, gazing down at the Dark Stone castle, which lay below her, like a sleeping, ugly monster. The castle was built into the heart of the steep side of the Orin Mountains, safely hidden behind the thick granite walls. Above the first floor of the castle was another, higher, and still higher a third.

Night had befallen, wrapping the word in its dark blanket. Lightning flashed, and thunder rumbled. The dark clouds filled the sky, going to turn into a storm.

---

[1] A name was used in ancient Persia meaning Justice

The world seemed a black emptiness of windswept hills and rocky fields in every direction, but Ashvan could not see the mountains and rocks. She stared off into the distance and saw their safe and snug homes, full of the fragrance of ribs, roasted in a crust of garlic and herbs, the kids laughing, and hot stoves to sleep on with their husbands. *People only see what they want to see,* she thought. After her mother's death, people wanted to hold Ashvan responsible for everything and saw her as a leader, which she did not believe in yet.

The freezing drops of rain hit her face. Her delicate body looked more significant and more substantial in her layers of fur and leather. Her pale face flushed from the cold wind even though, the hood of her cloak was pulled down over her face. Her curling black hair moved in the wind, and her almond brown eyes watched the rain dance in the dark sky as if there were nothing else in the world.

She sighed; her breath left her in plumes of white vapor. Horrible stillness reigned over all; everything was too quiet, everything but her stormy mind. She did not want to come back to the castle, where they had taken shelter. Everything that was happening seemed beyond her capacity to absorb. Their men were fighting in the border, and they had heard nothing from them since they left the land of Mannea. Amitira, her brother's Assyrian[1] wife was suffering from unusual labor, which showed no sign of ending. Her sister, Sheedvash had been widowed only a month after her wedding and always was crying silently or staring at Amitira with hate and disgust. Their food and supplies were running low, and all women wanted to know what their first lady's further decision was for the tribe. It felt like nobody knew she was only twenty-two years old. *Mother had died too soon,* Ashvan thought bitterly.

A month ago, her mother died, and the feeling of her loss was unbearably intense. Her mother solved all problems before she got sick, but after her death, there was no one to hear Sheedvash's silent cries, wipe her tears and comfort her. There was no one to endure Amitira's arrogant behavior or to pity a woman like her. There was no one to listen patiently to the tribal people who always muttered complaints or wanted

---

[1] An inhabitant of ancient Assyria

something. There was no one to know how scared Ashvan was, even when her pride would not let her cry.

Ashvan could not take her eyes off the darkness, where Diheh[1] was located. Just three months ago, everything was much different. She remembered those days well. The last summer had been hotter than ever. The sun was a bright, all-watching eye, its light creeping into every corner, bathing Mannea in a warm glow. Newly harvested wheat fields lay in the sun to rest before the next growing season, and the mature grapes hung down, each one a perfect miniature globe of ruby red. Autumn was on its way; they would mark the days by the swelling of the grapes.

In Mannea, summer was the time for celebrations. Women prepared for Sheedvash's wedding ceremony. The flax had been harvested and made into fine linen for her wedding dress. Everything was ready for a big celebration but that summer they had concerns that are more pressing too. The war was on every lip; the king of Media[2] recently had conquered Pars Land, and everyone thought the Assyrians would also suffer a much more crushing defeat. Media would likely attack the Assyrians in the North Mountains, where they had setup combining field strongholds with fortresses.

It shall be in that day that the burden of the Assyrian shall depart off from Mannea's shoulder, Ashvan's brother, Armaz[3] said, who was the most enthusiastic about waging war. He was talking everywhere about farmers who had nothing during the drought season but had to pay tribute to the Assyrians, the women who had been raped by the Assyrians, the children who had been thrown into the fire by the Assyrians and the men who had been lost to slavery.

"It's time for us to take revenge!" The men's scream still echoed in Ashvan's ears.

The long summer days finally ended, Sheedvash got married, and the men joined the battle. The war that was supposed to be over in a month

---

[1] Small city

[2] An area in North-western Iran

[3] A name was used in ancient Persia meaning steady

lasted for three. Two months later they learned their men had stopped during their approach to the north border and nearly two thousand men, median hedge knights and newly trained soldiers of Mannea were fighting with traditional weapons in a chaos of mud and blood, against thousands of fierce Assyrian warriors, who came with long, razor-sharp swords, mace, and flagons.

Almost all the men were fighting in the war, and the women were worried and confused by this sudden change. Before the war, when everyone thought they would be victorious very soon, the people had insisted that they would need to fight to make their peace, but now they believed Armaz, the Mannaean troops' commander, was responsible for starting the war.

"The war was the worst disaster that could befall us!" The women moaned.

However, an even greater disaster was awaiting Mannea, worse than could be imagined! A group of the Assyrian army broke from the ranks to attack Mannea. The new Mannaean army had left the city defenseless, without even a warrior, and the Assyrians could kill two birds with one stone. Their attack would pressure Mannea's men, and they could pillage the Mannaean wealth, desolate their houses, take the fruitage of their vineyards, and slave as they pleased. No one had expected Assyrians.

By the time they realized they were under attack, they had no choice but to flee. Ashvan's mother, Chista, bravely gathered the tribe and they fled north, to the Dark Stone castle for shelter. The castle that their Mannaean ancestors had built on their holiest mountain, Orin. Two months had passed, and they had no news from their men yet.

The brisk cold wind blew her memories away. Ashvan gazed up at the starless sky; the drops of the rain had frozen into ice as they fell.

"It's going to snow all night, I feel it!" Ashvan's fat maid mumbled, not finding a roof to shelter under.

"Maybe!" Ashvan said quietly, trying to hide the growing sense of anxiety that gnawed at her belly.

"Snow, sleet and freezing rain, it will be bloody hard to find dry wood or hunt rabbit for boys!" The maid said.

"It has never been easy!" Ashvan murmured.

"Great. We've burned almost all that scrap wood to keep a fire burning in that Assyrian woman's chamber!" The maid said, frowning.

Ashvan turned to her maid sharply. Her hood shadowed her face, but the maid could see the hard glitter in Ashvan's eyes as she stared at her. Ashvan started to open her mouth to say something, but a scream echoed through the mountain night. She looked fearfully at the castle, and then ran hurriedly down the twisting path, her fury forgotten.

She ran down the steps, toward Amitira's chamber as fast as her feet would take her, her long skirts trailing after her. Nobody had noticed that she had been in; she stood in the doorway, looking at Amitira. She almost fainted, her bed soaked in blood.

"What do you think you're doing?" Ashvan yelled, running toward the bed.

The old midwife glanced at young Ashvan calmly. "It could be too late. She could die if we don't do anything, mother and child!" She said in coldly.

Ashvan looked at the midwife, her face dark and angry but the midwife walked to the fireplace, oblivious to Ashvan, who could feel the other women's eyes, watching her. Sheedvash, pale from fear, stood beside the bed, looking at Amitira, worried for the first time.

"I told you to take care of her!" Ashvan shouted at Sheedvash, the only way to show her dominance.

A flicker of hate crossed Sheedvash's face, and she ran back to her seat, sobbing. The midwife peeked over her shoulder at Ashvan. She drew out from her pocket a small silver container and walked back to Amitira. She took a pinch of yellow powder from the bottle, rubbed it with her fingers near Amitira's nose. Amitira opened her eyes and groaned. Ashvan wiped the big drops of sweat away with her scarf from Amitira's pretty face. She had gotten very skinny, and her eyes appeared larger than they really were. Ashvan did not really know what to do or what to say, so she sat near Amitira's bed and stared at her. Amitira's beautiful face reminded her of before, two years ago when her brother, Armaz, returned home after his journey.

*****

Ashvan had been to see her mother, as usual. It was early in the autumn. In the garden, trees' leaves had turned red and yellow, shivered and dropped off with a beautiful dance against the wind. The maids had thrown a large shawl on the ground and prepared the last clusters of grapes from vineyards for drying in the large basement of the paramount of the tribe's mansion. Ashvan sat on the large porch with her mother, leaned her head against the wall, with tears running down her cheeks.

"You worry quite needlessly, dear. You've just been married to Zarvan[1] for a while; you can still be a mother." Her mother took her hands kindly. "Your prayer will not go unanswered… of its time!"

Ashvan tried to hide her tears from the maids' watching eyes. "I can wait but Zarvan grows more impatient every day!" She muttered in a low voice. "Actually, I think he was trying to find a good excuse to leave me."

Mother smiled, but the smile was tinged with sadness, as her pale fingers caressed Ashvan's hand. "Tell him you love him. Only love can make him happy, not a baby!" She said.

"Zarvan never loved me. He never wanted love!" She could feel that the anger was going to rise in her. "You cannot eat love, nor buy a horse with it, nor warm your halls on a cold night!" Ashvan said in mock disgust. "I've heard these words from him many times!"

Mother ignored the mockery in her voice. "Forgive his mistakes, let him believe love!" She sighed. "For men, love is hard to believe!"

"He hates me!" Ashvan said in a quiet sob.

---

[1] A name was used in ancient Persia meaning meridian

"I think you misunderstand him," mother said in a sad voice.

"Misunderstand?" Ashvan sneered, then peeked at the maids and lowered her voice. "He hasn't shared a bed with me for more than two months!" She said.

They heard doors slamming shut as her mother opened her mouth to answer. Looking at the garden, they saw Armaz came in on horseback, passing the women who were staring at him and with a beautiful young woman behind him. Armaz stood in front of the porch, where his mother and Ashvan sat. He brought up the rear, jumped down and helped the beautiful woman to slide gracefully from the saddle.

The woman was a well-dressed Lady, in a gown of ruby red silk, trimmed with lace as pale as foam, though it was torn and muddy. Her dirty face and messy hair did not detract from her extraordinary beauty. She was beautiful beyond a doubt, her curling dark red-brown hair, dancing in the wind, and her golden honey eyes staring at them. Her face reminded them of the most beautiful statues of the goddesses. She was so young that she still had the exuberance of youth, but she walked with the confidence of someone a decade older and her every move was graceful.

Armaz took the girl's hand and stood in front of his mother who stared at them as they slowly got to their feet.

"This woman is my wife," was the only thing Armaz said.

*****

More than two years had passed; Ashvan's womb remained dry but Amitira, Armaz's proud Assyrian wife, unpopular in Mannea, had gotten pregnant.

Amitira's whispers attracted Ashvan's attention. Her dry lips moved quickly, and her words were meaningless. Amitira's voice gradually became louder and louder and echoed around the chamber. Nobody understood her words; she was speaking in a tongue that they did not know but still was so familiar to them; the same language, which the Assyrian soldiers spoke. The women trembled with fear. Everyone was silent as the dead, and the sound of Sheedvash's crying made the bad situation even worse.

Ashvan gazed at Amitira, feeling helpless because there was nothing practical she could do. She began to caress Amitira's dark red-brown hair gently.

"Amitira! Dear!" Ashvan said.

Amitira heard Ashvan's voice, and with a sudden motion, she turned quickly toward Ashvan and looked at her without recognition. She took Ashvan by the arm, her fingers squeezing so hard that they hurt. Ashvan could see the reflection of the fire's flame dancing in her golden eyes. Amitira's face was so close; Ashvan could feel her hot, feverish breath on her face.

"They are coming!" Amitira said and then stared off into the darkness.

"Who?" Ashvan asked, surprised.

Amitira looked again at Ashvan, frightened. "Those who never sleep, live underwater, and only come out with Magic!" She said, gulp for air interrupting her voice.

"What is she saying? It is horrible! We've escaped from her cruel brothers, but she invites demons to destroy us now!" Ashvan's fat maid said as she shook in fear.

Ashvan stared angrily at her. "Shut up! Don't you see? She has a high fever!" She shouted at her maid.

The maid stopped and remained silent at Ashvan's sudden fury, drawing into the shadows in the corner of the chamber, out of sight. Ashvan opened Amitira's fingers slowly from their hook around her arm and then laid her on the bed.

"Calm down, dear! No one can hurt you," Ashvan whispered in her ear.

Suddenly Amitira's muscles became tense, and she cried out in pain. The midwife came to them quickly. Ashvan looked at her then took

Amitira's hands. "You must help us! You must deliver your baby; your child, Armaz's child!"

Amitira looked at Ashvan. She seemed alert when she heard Armaz's name and Ashvan even saw the smallest hint of a smile playing around her full lips. Her smile lasted only for a heartbeat as pain shot through her belly, and it faded from her face. Ashvan looked at the midwife helplessly. Amitira did not seem to be able to help them, but her voice turned their attention back to her.

"Armaz has asked the god to bless us with a son!" She said through her pain and smiled, blood dripping from her cracked lips. "I'll give him a son, even if I die, I'll give Armaz his son!" The pain made her grit her teeth. She coughed, drew a deep breath and clutched Ashvan's fingers. "Please… ask Armaz's god, ask to bless us… me… our son… aaaaah."

Ashvan felt tears in her eyes. "The god is merciful," she said, then put her scarf on and began to read hymns in a monotonous, half-tearful voice.

The women looked at her; then knelt one by one. Whispering hymns rose all around her. The midwife went closer and stood between Amitira's legs, oblivious to Ashvan's tears.

Amitira's small hands shook between Ashvan's fingers, her fingers tightened into fists, and her nails dug into Ashvan's palms. Ashvan saw the dark blood seep into the linen sheets, which gradually darkened. The long deep breath that Amitira took into her chest released as a painful scream and shortly after that, the sound of a baby crying echoed inside the chamber.

Amitira threw back her head, panting.

"A boy!" A woman who was helping the midwife cried cheerfully.

"God has mercy; finally, it is done!" Ashvan sighed with relief.

"Not yet!" The midwife said glumly, her voice as cold as ice. "They are twins! She has another child."

Ashvan looked at the midwife despairingly. *Amitira could never survive,* she thought.

"Feed the fire, I need more boiling water!" The midwife commanded and put the bloody clothes in the basin.

When the fire flashed again, Ashvan saw pain, fear, and rank disbelief through Amitira's eyes. Another pain grasped Amitira. Wincing in pain, she started to grab the corners of the bed, gasping for breath. The pain was so fierce that she thought her heart might stop.

"Push… push!" The midwife shouted at her.

"I… I caaaaan't!"

It was a terrible cry, a wail of pain.

"If you don't push, your child will die!" The midwife said dryly.

Amitira took a deep breath, breath hissing between her teeth. Her fingers clutched the bloody sheets, but she was too weak to do something.

The midwife looked at her, still waiting.

Amitira closed her eyes and began to whisper through her cracked lips, but nobody could hear her. A cold wind blew out of the north. Far off, they heard the howling of wolves.

"We can't wait…," the midwife said, but Amitira was whispering, her voice as faint as the sound of slithering a snake through the grass.

A gust of wind through the door made the torch sputter, and the flickering reddish light seemed to make the shifting shadows stir as the living passed by. Amitira's whisper rose in a strange spell. "Aya mi shalookh… Aya mi shalookh…!"

The women stood, frozen with fear. Ashvan looked at them, and then stroked Amitira's head, gently. "There's nothing to fear dear, just take a deep breath and…," Ashvan said.

A sudden gust of wind opened the window, and its sound made Ashvan gasp. The cold wind rushed to the chamber. Amitira's body began to shake violently. "Havashi mi dekh shalookh… Aya mi shalookh…"

"God, why is she doing this?" Sheedvash whispered her voice shrill with fear.

From the window came a flutter of wings. A crow landed on the black stone, opened its beak, and gave a harsh caw.

"Havashi mi dekh shalookh… Havashi mi dekh shalookh… save my child, God Marduk pleeeeeease…" The pain stole Amitira's words from her throat. She let out a loud cry, her voice cracked and head thrown back.

Her painful cry mingled with the baby's cry!

CHAPTER TWO

A DAMNED WAR

KARALA, MANNEA –Assyria border, 644 BC, Autumn

The death was before his eyes, he could see it, with moistened eyes, heaving breast, and lips half open.

A gigantic Assyrian man knocked him backward over the ground, and landed on his chest with both hands on his throat, with his horned helmet, he was more like a wild bull than a man. Zarvan gawped at the man's face, his red eyes, half hidden behind his bronze helmet, then at the sky, filled with monstrous shapes and sucked air in desperately as the man's powerful hands strangled him. His breath rattled harshly in his throat.

I'll be dying soon, he thought in intense fear, but he didn't want to die, not here, not at least in this way.

He pushed himself up higher, wincing as his legs trembled with pressure. He believed that death was the gateway to life everlasting, but he did not want to enter upon that life, at least not now. He always imagined a long and comfortable life for himself, long enough to see his grandsons, enjoy the finest of foods, the best of clothing, and the most luxurious of surroundings. He wanted to die in old age, in peace, surrounded by his family. In his dreams, everyone was sad by the time of his death, and his body buried with respect. *But the truth is, a couple more days my body will be a swollen corpse on this foreign land, being torn at by animals, yet no one seemed to care,* he thought bitterly.

For many years, Zarvan and his fathers were significant landowners. He had grown up in a family that they did not take many risks. Asking Ashvan to marry him was the biggest gamble than any he had ever made. She did not belong to a prominent family, like Zarvan, but if you wish to trade, you must offer something equivalent. Ashvan's father was paramount of the tribe, who had been chosen by the people. The people whispered behind Ashvan's father's back, which could harm Zarvan's family's fame but they respected him so much as well, so being a part of this man's family could reinforce Zarvan's hope of to be the greatest lord of the greatest tribe of Mannea.

He could win a fortune in this game, but it had been a mistake for him to come here… a ghastly mistake. Zarvan was not built to fight. A few months ago, this war sounded like an incredible opportunity that gained him popularity but now… *Damn me! Why should I die for those worthless farmers?* He thought bitterly. One more time, He tried again to push the Assyrian man's shoulders back and get him off, but the man was heavy as a horse, impossible to move. Once more, once more,… he struggled to open the soldier's strong fingers with all his strength, but he was helpless in the man's grip. He made a croaking sound, he could not breathe, his hands were numb, his vision blurred.

Zarvan closed his eyes to pray for a vision from God.

Suddenly the pressure was removed from his throat, and life-giving air filled his lungs. Zarvan took a deep breath and opened his eyes, but there was darkness everywhere.

Maybe I'm dead, he thought, but the giant man's body fell off, and Zarvan saw a long, lanky man, with shaggy hair and a crooked sword in hand, was standing over him.

"Are you wounded, my Lord?" The young man asked as he knelt on the ground beside Zarvan, offering a hand to help him up.

Zarvan knew him; he was working for Zarvan's father. He wanted to thank the young man, but a nobleman should never be grateful to his workers, so he just nodded as he was rubbing his neck and stretched his

16

hand to take the young man's hand, but suddenly a stream of warm, gelatinous fluid splashed against Zarvan's face and the young man fell on his chest.

Zarvan stared at him. Half of his head had been smashed, and blood spewed out of his skull. An Assyrian warrior reined his horse up beside them, then set off at a brisk trot, waving the padded mace vigorously above his head. With its every rotation the sunlight seemed to ripple, and some men fell down on the ground like the young man before Zarvan.

Zarvan's eyes followed the Assyrian warrior and remained on the scene of the battle that seemed to have moved beyond him. For every Mannaean soldier, there were two Assyrian warriors on the battlefield. The Assyrian warriors had worn iron helmets decorated with wild animals' curving horns, and the nasals that half hid their nose. They were shouting terribly, seemed to await spilling blood impatiently.

His tribesmen were killed, but he did not dare to move. *No one could win against that strong of warriors,* Zarvan thought. He did not want to die. He looked at his savior again. Only one eye remained on his face, and this lifeless eye was staring at him. Zarvan dragged himself under the young man's body and hid. The man's warm blood poured onto Zarvan's body, but he did not move.

We are almost defeated, Zarvan thought. *I'll leave this horrible place when the Assyrians win the war. The god take pity on my soul!* He suddenly heard a shouting... a mountain shaking roar! The soldiers turned toward the sound involuntarily.

A young man, riding a tall white stallion, galloped down the hill, holding a double-edged sword high. A stout Assyrian man fell with each landing of his sword.

"Armaz!!" Zarvan whispered.

*****

The king laid down on the bed, cold sweat glistening in his gaunt features.

The vast tent smelled of sickness, a cloying odor of rotten meat. The king's eyes were closed and his face pale as milk. A deep wound showed the king's rib bones; it was black and glistening with corruption and smelled horrendous. A healer was seated next to the king's bed, cleaning the wound carefully. He was removing the infected areas slowly. He had tried to close the wound many times before, but it had turned into an open, bloody lesion that would not heal.

The king's breath rattled harshly in his throat. The healer finished his work, but he did not dare to get up. He began to gather up his jars and bottles slowly as he peeked up anxiously. Cyaxares, the crown prince of the Medes Kingdom, sitting near his father's bedside, waited for minutes, but the healer's silence had stretched unbearably long, so the prince grabbed the healer's hand in a surprisingly firm grip.

"Say!" Cyaxares said sharply.

The healer raised up his head. Cyaxares was stout, round of shoulder, a head taller than the tallest man in his army. His dark brown beard was shot with white, making him look older than his thirty -two years. He wore a heavy brown cloak, worked with golden threads and warm bear furs.

"The wound has festered badly..." The healer could see the hard glitter in Cyaxares's kohl black eyes as he stared at him. He swallowed. "That shows the Assyrians commander had fought with a poisoned sword...," he added fearfully.

"You said that before!" Cyaxares shouted, eyes wide. "Tell me, can you heal him?"

His question made the healer's blood run cold. "Only God can heal the great king!" He said, waiting with bated breath.

Cyaxares released the old man's wrist. "Get lost!" He said in a cold, hard voice.

The man could not believe that he was forgiven. He got up. A soldier came forward to lead him out of the tent. Cyaxares glanced at an armed man, standing in the corner of the tent.

18

"Everybody here?" Cyaxares asked.

"Yes, Your Highness, they are waiting outside the tent," the young man answered.

Cyaxares moved his hand slightly, and the guard of the king realized that he must go.

Cyaxares looked at his father. Every time the king inhaled, his breath quivered in short, quick gasps. The great king always managed to look imposing, but he looked weary and miserable now, his eyes sunken and his skin sallow, a face that only drew compassion from others now. The king loved expensive floral perfumes the most, but now the tent was filled with the annoying smell of his rotten body.

Monarchy is untrue, glory is meaningless, and destiny is very cruel! Cyaxares thought. He sighed, but there was no time for sorrow. He should waste no time. He had to return to the capital city, Hegmataneh[1]. He was true heir, so he needed to be there before his brothers, who had no claim to the throne. His father must be there, alive or dead. The great king's death and the good news of Cyaxares's Kingdom must be announced at the same time. First, he had to get rid of this damned war.

With calm but firm steps, Cyaxares got outside the tent. The eight army-commanders of Mannea's eight different tribes, along with his army commander were there. All bowed their heads respectfully. Cyaxares strolled towards them. The king's tent sat beneath a jagged outcrop of black rock, atop a hill, where less than two thousand feet below, the Median and Mannaean army fought together in the foothills, alongside Mannea's bloody red banners. Cyaxares could hear the whicker of horses, the clash of swords, and the cries of men.

Cyaxares's face was attractive, with an imposing look. Even the middle-aged commanders became nervous against his gaze. He stood beside the king's white warhorse that was tied to the mast, near the tent. He raised his hand up to caress the horse, but no one could touch the king's horse but the king. The horse neighed loudly, pawing the ground. Cyaxares took a step back, silent and thoughtful. He glanced up at the

---

[1] It was the capital of the Medes, around 700 BCE

darkening sky. The clouds were gray, ominous and threatening, the sky wished to rain. The eyes of the crown flickered quickly about the mountain, resting for an instant on each face. "We have to go for a peace negotiation with the Assyrians, so you must retreat!" He said, quietly and calmly.

"What? Retreat? After days of fighting? What can I tell my soldiers?" A young newly made commander, spoke up, his voice heavy and blunt.

Cyaxares turned to him. The young commander's long black hair stirred in the wind and his amber eyes boldly stared at Cyaxares. He proved to be a Mannaean with pale skin and a carefully trimmed black beard. He had donned a night-black armor, with the winged lion picked out in rubies on his breastplate and a fur of a lion on his shoulders.

"Tell them their king is wounded!" Cyaxares said.

"That is completely ridiculous!" The young commander said.

All the other men stared at Cyaxares and the young commander in silence and horror.

"Ridiculous?" Cyaxares said after he paused for a few moments. "What do you mean by that … young Commander? I guess you know your king has been wounded."

"My men are wounded too, but they are still fighting!" The young commander snorted.

"Don't be a fool," Cyaxares shouted, anger rising in him. "Look at the hills, young man!" He eyed the young man with a sour smile. "We don't fight, we've almost been defeated!"

The commander took a step towards the valley. The long V-shaped valley spread beneath him, awash in blood and cries.

"You look, my Lord! Look at your men, your soldiers; they have remained faithful to you. We are far from lost. For every man we have lost, two showed up to take his place. Give me the chance to try my own steel against these monsters…"

Cyaxares finally ran out of patience and lost his temper. "Get your forces out of this damned valley. This is the king's command!" He yelled, furious.

The men were still undecided.

The commander looked up sharply. "Every man has choices. They might have refused to kneel!" He looked all around at the commanders' faces, in the chill silence of them; he breathed deeply.

The commanders could hear the crown grinding his teeth; a vein bulged, blue and swollen, in Cyaxares's neck.

"Every Mannaean man must remain loyal to his rightful king, even if the lord he serves proves false!" He declared in a tone that brooked no argument.

Finally, a middle-aged tribal commander took a step forward. "We are subservient to you, Your Highness!" He promised.

The other men looked at each other slightly and then took one step forward. "We are subservient to Your Highness!" They said together.

The young commander stared at them for a moment, then blinked and looked away, at the scene of war. His soldiers fought bravely against the giant Assyrian men. Their actions were outstanding, more than their king could have hoped for or imagined.

Why couldn't the king understand that his troops have left everything, their wealth, wife, and children, even their lives... only to fulfill their promise? How could he ignore all this great devotion? He thought.

"We do not fight for the king; we fight for our people until every man of us is dead!" The young commander growled as he stared at the crown. His feelings were obvious all over his face. He took a few steps back then in the blink of an eye, he opened the bridle of king's horse and jumped on the bareback horse.

He rode down the hill faster than the soldiers could react. The white warhorse that nobody could ride except for the king was galloping forward obediently. All of the commanders had become a slack jaw and staring eye.

Cyaxares' fingers opened and closed. "What's his name?" He asked dark with fury.

"Armaz, Your Highness!" The king's guard answered.

Armaz's mountain-shaking roar echoed through the mountain. The soldiers turned toward the sound involuntarily.

A young man, riding a tall white stallion, galloped down the hill, holding a double-edged sword high. A stout Assyrian man fell with each landing of his sword.

"Soldiers," Armaz yelled as he brought up the rear. He stopped on the rock above the battlefield, surrounded by his soldiers, who looked at him, apprehensive about what might come next.

"You are soldiers... not warriors!" Armaz's voice was the loudest among them. "Yes, warriors know how to fight but to please their commanders. You fight for your people, for your land. You were not made for the battlefield, but you love your land so you will stand shoulder to shoulder. The Assyrian warriors too need to be obedient to their commanders, without thought or hesitation; ... you need to get your land back, your freedom... so you will win this battle. Do you hear me?"

"We do," the Mannaean soldiers shouted. "We hear you, Lord."

Armaz raised his sword above his head; it glowed with a light that was followed by the crash of thunder. The Mannaean men turned to the battlefield.

"Kill all of theeeeeeeeeeem!"

Armaz's voice caused quite a stir on the battlefield. The excited men rushed forward precipitously.

The Assyrians terrible war music was off, and the Assyrian warriors seemed perplexed and confused. Armaz was at the forefront of his men, swinging his sword left and right to knock away every enemy in his infantry's path. The Mannaean men fought with redoubled force, and the Assyrian troops retreated. They were afraid of the Mannaeans, not for their skills in fighting but for their courage and gallantry.

Metal screamed on metal in the Mountain's heart. The men, crying in pain, clutched their grievous wounds as they tried to stand up and continued to fight.

"Go!" Armaz ordered, and again waves of men rushed forward, their cry lost beneath another thunder crack that rolled overhead. Armaz was riding ahead, his sword stained with blood.

His enemy, the chief commander of the Assyrian troops, swiveled in his direction as his heavily armored horse sniffed miserably. Both swords met in the air with a resounding clang. Armaz thrust his sword downward, and a red point burst out through the commander's ribs, piercing leather. The man was dead before his sword hit the ground.

The bloody red Mannaean banners were afloat in every spot on the battlefield. Armaz moved among the flutter of flags as his soldiers ran, leaping toward the Assyrian warriors, whirling the blades around their heads. In just a few minutes, the Mannaean men pushed the Assyrians forces back from the valley.

Everything seemed to be changed. Despite the Assyrian warriors' gained strength, they were retreating. The Mannaean men turned over a new leaf, hoping to win, but the sound of horns was heard from the top of the hill.

The Mannaean men looked at each other in complete bewilderment. The buglers were playing the melody of retreat when the Assyrian's army was fleeing!! The Assyrian soldiers realized their uncertainty and confusion, and they became ready to attack.

Armaz looked at his men to see all eyes were fixed on him. There was no time for hesitation. He could not betray his men who trusted him.

"Attack, the victory is ours!" His voice was louder than the sound of horns.

The soldiers turned to raid, oblivious to the sound of the horns. The roar of Assyrian cymbals and the sound of horns slowly faded in roaring screams of the Mannaean men.

*****

Arsen[1], the Lord Minister of the Assyrian King, was looking at the battlefield carefully, monitoring Armaz's actions. He was a middle-aged man, past fifty, who had spent forty years in the battles of the Assyrian army. His armor was thick and shiny but in some places battered. It was never polished since the war signs on his armor were a mark of pride.

"Bring me the sniper… Ebigil!" Arsen said, kept looking at Armaz.

Only a few moments later, a tall man ran to the Minister, with a bow in hand. He was grey-eyed and slender as a knife, sheathed in his black armor. Everyone called him *eagle eye*. He had been the best sniper in the Assyrian army for over five years, and no one could say there was a better sniper. He knelt on the ground to show his respect.

"Do you see that young man? The young man, riding the white horse… the bravest man among the Mannaeans!" Arsen said as he allowed Ebigil to get up with a slight movement of his hand. "I want you to kill him, with an arrow. Only one arrow, no more!"

Ebigil got up promptly and looked at the battlefield. His little round gray eyes were as sharp as an eagle, and he raised his eyes to gaze at the enemy. Suddenly his eyes gaped wide. "Armaz!" Ebigil muttered, low under his breath.

The memory of that rainy night was still clear in his mind. That night, it was fully dark when they were fleeing from the castle, this man, and Lady Amitira, but Ebigil could remember his face well. *I am at it again,* he thought to himself. That night, like today, Ebigil was asked to kill Armaz.

"Why do you stand here dazed? Do your job!" Arsen snarled, piercing Ebigil with his brown eyes.

---

[1] An Armenian name meaning masculine

"Yes, your Honor!" Ebigil answered fearfully.

Arsen turned his eyes to Armaz again. "Tell the commander of the horsemen to attack him, as soon as he falls down," he said to his guard. "Do not forget, only an arrow!" Arsen warned Ebigil again.

Ebigil nodded. "Yes my Lord!" He said obediently.

Ebigil went ahead, leaned heavily on a rock and closed his left eye. He drew the string towards his face and waited for the perfect time. He did not know why he should determine this young man's fate. He did not want to kill him for any particular reason, but that was not a feeling to share with the Lord Minister.

Ebigil could see the hard glitter in the Lord Minister's eyes from the corner of his eyes. He had to hurry. He had delayed too much, and he lost the opportunity to shoot. He knew he had no choice but to obey. Ebigil's finger clenched and the bowstring thrummed. He held his breath and slowly released the string.

The arrow landed directly into Armaz's chest, so strong that he fell down immediately. The Assyrians horsemen were waiting for this opportunity, and a dozen giant men attacked him galloping toward him at a furious pace, yelling like rutting beasts. Armaz's sword slashed right and left, and two horsemen went down. The king's white warhorse reared and kicked a man in the face as he was trying to hit Armaz, but the others attacked hard. The maces beat the horse, and it slightly bent at the knees. Armaz raised his blade, too slowly, too weak to move with much force.

Armaz wounded, shivering wildly, but the Assyrians did not stop and stabbed him ruthlessly. The Mannaeans struck dumb. The buglers played the melody of retreat again. The Mannaean soldiers appeared confused and groggy, not knowing what to do. Some took a few steps back, but most men could not leave Armaz alone.

Arsen raised his hand. His special guard touched his horse with his heels and galloped toward the battlefield at a furious pace, where Armaz had stood. He jumped down from the horse, lifted the sword high above his head and took off Armaz's head with a single sure stroke. Blood sprayed out, and Armaz's body fell down beside his dying horse. The guard lifted his voice in a triumphant halloo as he held the head up and the others Assyrians began to howl after him. The sound of their voices mingled with the whicker of horses, the clank of steel, and the groaning of fearful retreat music.

The Mannaean men started to walk backward and the valley filled with the Assyrians, screaming in happiness.

Zarvan pushed aside the young man's body and got up. It was the best time to escape from this horrible hell. He looked at the Armaz's pale face for the last time as he ran. Armaz's eyes looked as if he was still concerned about his men. Zarvan no longer watched, but dashed toward the hill, along with other men.

The fighting was over, and the only sound was the Assyrian commander's endless yelling, as he stood in the middle of the battlefield, still showing the severed head triumphantly.

CHAPTER THREE

THE DAUGHTER OF DEVIL

MANNEA, ancient Land of Mannaeans, 644 BC, Autumn

After hours of suffering, now Amitira slept in peace. She had died before she could hold her babies in her arms. She lost consciousness when her daughter, the second twin was born. The midwife brought the child to her mother happily just after Amitira died.

The incense had sweetened the air. Amitira's face looked too pale in the candlelight. No one was in her chamber but Ashvan. All had left them hastily. The midwife wrapped the babies in a blanket and took them out of the chamber. The tribal people believed that the mother's ghost might return to take her children. Ashvan did not believe them, but she preferred to be alone. Her mother had taught her how to sing hymns for keeping the ghosts calm, but Amitira's face was so quiet, and Ashvan didn't know if she would like to have this kind of mourning or not.

Amitira had never spoken of dying. She was still too young to think about dying, although, she did not talk much to anyone. Armaz's Assyrian arrogant wife had learned her husband's mother tongue quickly, but she did not speak a word in this language.

Armaz and his mother, whom Amitira worshiped her like an idol, were only people that loved her and were close to her.

Armaz's mother accepted this unwanted bride warmly and loved her as much as her daughters. She always said 'Nobody knows Amitira well; she is very kind-hearted.' However, it was so hard to believe, given Amitira's arrogant behavior. Of course, they did not dare express their true feelings, even Taham, Armaz's father who did not like her at all.

Chista, the paramount of the tribe's wife, the first lady of Mannea, was like a mother to all the tribal people and she was honored and revered. The people of Mannea respected Amitira because Chista was worthy of respect and when Chista died, there was no reason to respect Amitira, especially since the Assyrians had attacked them and took their homes and husbands. The silence was Amitira's only response to the people when they were whispering about her; in fact, almost no one had heard her voice after Chista's death. Now the women had a new reason to hate her, they said Amitira feels nothing for no one, even Chista, who had expressed an outstanding undeserved kindness to her but Ashvan had seen Amitira's mourning for Chista.

"That cold night," Ashvan whispered.

Midnight had fallen on the mountain, like a rich velvet blanket. Ashvan woke anxiously in the darkness of her chamber, still panting. She slid her hand between her wet thighs.

"Oh God…," she mumbled. She cleaned herself and tried to go back to sleep, but sleep would not come again. She closed her eyes; tasted a delicious torsion of her muscles from deep down, the joy of having sex with a strange man, her first real sexual pleasure that she had never experienced with her husband.

She closed her eyes, hoping to feel that sweet feeling again but suddenly she opened them.

"You should be ashamed of yourself," she murmured.

The fireplace was full of hot ash and a small black log with a faint orange heart burning within, but her chamber seemed unbearably hot. She needed fresh, cold air against her cheeks. She clambered out of bed and grabbed her dressing gown hanging on the chair. The castle was asleep as she went out. She was just outside the great entrance gate of the castle. The light had drained away, barely enough even for shadows but Ashvan made herself take quick steps, not wanting to think about what had happened.

She went down to the bottom of the mountains, with no specific purpose and unconscious, where her mother was buried in a common grave beside a big boulder as a sign. Ahead loomed the snow-covered field and Ashvan heard a voice, vague and unclear. Her ears became sharper, and she paused for a moment to glance at a shadow that stood along the boulder, candles glimmering round her. The light of the candles turned Amitira's red-brown hair and left her face clear.

Ashvan gave a little gasp.

Amitira whispered spells and danced nude on the grave. Her spells grew worse, more frequent and more violent. She was spinning, mimicking the repetitive circles as she focused on the moon, her breath coming hot and fast, steaming in the cold air.

Suddenly she stood, her eyes brimming with silver tears that shone brightly in the moonlight. She screamed in some queer foreign tongue. Her scream seemed like the kind of strangled cry that belonged to those from another world. She raised her hand to her chest, and it came away bloody.

Ashvan's heart was pounding in her chest, but she tried to ignore it and slowed her breathing.

Amitira knelt on the grave. The blood flowed like a lazy river on her breast onto the snow-covered grave.

"Your people say that they can find peace in the grave, but I want you to fly, far, so far from this cold soil, where I will come after my death," she said.

Ashvan looked at her dead but beautiful face again. She guessed silence was the only thing that the ghosts needed. "Soil likes dead, dead likes soil, I must think of the living," she said, thinking of what will the response of Armaz be when he realizes that his wife is dead. "I don't know how Armaz can bear Amitira's death?" Ashvan knew her brother just worshipped his wife.

Ashvan saw a golden sunrise through the gap in the curtains. The snow had stopped, and now there was a hope of finding food.

"I suppose we should be thankful!" She whispered. Ashvan had stayed awake all night, and now she fell into an exhausted sleep.

*****

The silence was broken by the sound of a squabble. Ashvan awoke with a start, dizzy. She became wide-awake when she heard the shouting, distant at first, then growing louder, many voices yelling together. She could not make out the words.

The snow had drifted down all night in ghostly silence, lying thick on the ground, and the snow-covered ground shone with the sun's touch. The castle yard was full of angry women, who surrounded Sheedvash and the old midwife, yelling. The babies were crying in Sheedvash's arms as she held them firmly.

"Have you completely lost your mind?!" The old midwife said, her voice full of disgust. Her angry eyes did not trouble the hard looks on the women's face who stood in the yard.

An ugly old woman came forward, shrunken and wrinkled, although the people said that she had been young and beautiful once, back when her husband had left her. Her dark brown eyes were fixed angrily on Sheedvash's face. A big round brown mark on her forehead, a sign of her lying prostrate on the stone floor of the temple of God, looked more obvious on her face, red with anger. "I hope you do not intend to keep that girl!" She said.

"What are you talking about?" Sheedvash said, surprised. "She's my niece!"

"She is the daughter of the demons, not your brother!" The old woman gave an indignant sniff.

Behind the old woman, another woman stood wrapped in a black cloak. "Believe me, that woman had slept with demons... her child is a soulless evil!" She said with a flat, emotionless voice.

"It was obvious to me that demons sent her here," another stern-faced woman in a gown of old velvet said, her voice was thin and sharp as a whip. "Her malevolent presence destroyed our land. Last year, we were troubled with drought, and this year her land's bloodthirsty men attacked us."

"If she had a malevolent presence for everyone, she was a good omen for you." The women turned towards Ashvan who stood on the gate of the castle, looking them angrily. "My mother gave you a house near our home because Amitira was pregnant and needed a nursemaid; otherwise, you had to move from Mannea after your husband's death with your young child, wasn't that it?" Ashvan shouted.

"Your mother gave me money for working in her house!" The woman said quietly, trying to hide her embarrassment.

Ashvan raised her eyebrows. "YES, but your salary was more than you had been used to, more than enough to support yourself!"

The woman's mouth tightened into a hard line, but she said nothing.

"This is not her idea; we all say the same thing!" A young woman said.

Ashvan looked at her sharply. "And what are you saying?" She shouted.

"That baby girl possessed with a devil."

Angry voices rose around Ashvan.

"The women who were in Amitira's chamber saw she was calling evil spirits!"

"That baby will bring more disaster for us! We cannot endure another disaster!"

"Yes, she brings misfortune to everyone here!"

"Demons can be killed only by cold iron!" The ugly old women said dryly.

Ashvan turned to her sharply. "How dare you? Do you know what you're talking about?" She stepped to the old woman. "Do you remember last winter? My father was coming to your home to heal you, every day, even during storms!" Ashvan yelled, then stared at the women's face angrily. "Is there anyone, who can say that my father has not gone to her house to heal her illness? Is there anyone, who can say that my mother has not helped her in her time of distress? Who could deny my parents' love for their tribe?" Ashvan's eyes brimmed with fury. "How you can be so ungrateful?"

No one spoke for a few moments.

"You told the truth. None of us can deny our paramount of the tribe or his wife's affection, but she isn't their granddaughter. She is the daughter of Devil!" The old woman said with a sharp, cold voice.

"Have you completely lost your mind?" Ashvan said, shocked. "Last night Amitira was feverish and weak from loss of blood; she suffered from heat delirium. You want to kill an innocent child just for her meaningless words?!"

"This child has the demon's gift!" The old woman insisted, in her deep voice. "Demons have marked her face!"

Ashvan stared at her; she did not know what she was talking.

"Have you seen that girl?" Asked the old woman. Her face twisted in a mockery of a smile.

Ashvan stared at the woman for a moment then turned to Sheedvash, as confused as she was angry. She looked at her sister; studied her eyes.

The eyes do not lie. Sheedvash believed them, Ashvan realized.

She threw aside the blanket. The newborn girl's legs kicked in a tiny jagged motion, finding nothing but air. Her head was a crazy mass of red-brown curls, her eyes melted gold, more brilliant than anybody could have dreamed. She looked so light, seemed so perfect, like a tiny marble statue. Ashvan had never seen such beauty, but… but there was a strange birthmark on the corner of her right cheek. A birthmark that was exactly like a skull tattoo! Ashvan's blood ran cold. She stood in silence, struggling to keep control of her emotions. Finally, she took a deep breath, held the child in her arms and turned to the women.

"This child is Chista's granddaughter. My mother didn't reject others because of their appearance. She is Chista's granddaughter. Her face is not important because she has Chista's heart in her chest and she will be a source of pride and blessing for Mannea," Ashvan said, staring at them. "Now, if you want to kill her, you have to kill me first!" Every muscle in her body looked tense, like a mountain lion ready to attack.

The women stood, rooted to the ground. Everyone was very silent; Ashvan looked triumphantly at them. The old midwife smiled as she was looking at Ashvan. *She proved herself as a worthy successor*, the first lady in Mannea, the old midwife thought.

Suddenly they heard excited shouts coming from the valley. They turned their faces and saw some boys waving their sticks, shouting, and running up the road. It was difficult to understand what they were saying, but women rushed at them, assuming hungry wolves attacked the boys, who had gone to the mountain to hunt rabbits. One boy got ahead of others.

"The men are coming... the men are coming!" The boy shouted, breathless with excitement and joy as he reached to them.

The women began to stir, like waking from a dream. They looked at their neighbors incredulously, but gradually the sound of rejoicing swept over them. They cheered and ran toward the valley.

"Did you see?" Ashvan whispered, faintly to herself, looking down at the woman who ran through the winding trail led down to the valley. "This child is propitious like everyone in this world!"

"I did," said the midwife.

"Mithra[1]!" Ashvan said. "I named the child Mithra."

---

[1] In Persian mythology she was a goddess of light and friendship

The midwife blinked in disbelief. "But… it's the name of the most honorable goddess for this people!"

Ashvan strolled to the midwife and placed the baby in her arms. "I believe she is a goddess come to earth," she said, with certainty.

*****

The grave was hidden under a blanket of snow. Taham's fingers brushed across the cold soil as gently as if the ground had been a living flesh. He could see Chista's kind smile in his mind, a sweet smile that had changed his life forever. He remembered thirty years before...

*****

The Mithra's temple was hazy with smoke and heavy with the smell of incense.

The temple was more elaborate than everyone's expectation, mysterious and underground, engraved in rock, overlooking Chichest Lake. Daylight, the sun's rays, even the moon, held no way in this place. When they came to worship God Mithra, time would just stop, and disciples could do it all day. The windowless granite walls surrounded them. Inside the temple, you could feel a mysterious brutal force that guided the life against the spiritual inclinations, an invisible force, crushing your body, squeezing the life out of you. In fact, self-annihilation was the purpose of Mithra's disciples, ignoring the mortal living to reach the pure, eternal life.

Khonyagar[1] played steady rhythmic music. "Hey, hey, hey…" Some of the devotees were on their knees moving their heads down and repeating the short mantras in rhythm. They could hardly see each other clearly in the darkness of the temple, so they didn't need to because they required wearing a face mask.

Taham clutched the cup into his hand, tossing the glass off in a gulp. The strong wine, mixed with Ephedra sap, made his head spin. He

---

[1] Instrumentalist

laughed hard and raised his hand. "Hey boy, bring me more wine," he said.

A young man, his face hidden behind a black mask with a beak, was serving others. He kept hurrying forward and held his tray in front of Taham. He banged his empty cup on the plate and grabbed another. The young man's eyes stared at him behind the mask in disgust. Taham leaned forward to whisper in the man's ear, but he did not trouble to lower his voice.

"I strongly advise you little raven… don't look at a lion like that," Taham said as he tapped a finger to his golden mask with the golden lion mane.

Taham was drunk, but he was alert enough to know Ravens were the lowest in the cult of Mithra's chart. Every Raven had a chance to improve his lot; he must be directed toward being pure and holy by serving other men and difficult graduated tests. The devotees in the higher lot were more faithful and stronger, and the crows had to respect them. The young man went and hid in the darkness. Taham grinned, waving his hand in farewell.

"I'm a lion," Taham said again loudly as he took a sip of his wine. He leaned against the wall, closed his eyes. "I'm a lion," he repeated. Everyone could almost hear his laugh. There was undoubtedly a mocking, jeering note in his laughter.

The temple was a small rectangular subterranean chamber, on the order of seventy-five feet by thirty feet with a vaulted ceiling. An aisle ran lengthwise down the center of the temple, with a stone bench on either side, three feet high on which the cult's devotees would recline during their meetings. At the back of the temple, at the end of the aisle was a statue of Mithra, the God of the holy kingdom, accompanied by a snake, a raven, and a scorpion.

Taham looked at the men, they sat on benches, with half-closed eyes behind their masks, he did not know anyone.

"There's the temple of Mithra… where we should find the holy LOVE…" He laughed. "In the holy love, nobody knows others…," Taham mumbled and gave another drunken laugh.

Somebody nudged him in the ribs and Taham opened his eyes. Javid[1] sat next to him. He was Taham's only friend, who had introduced him to the temple.

"Come to yourself! You are in a holy temple, not a pub," Javid muttered, low and angrily under his breath.

"Take it easy! I'm fine," Taham said, his breath smelling strongly of wine.

Javid raised his head and stared at him. Taham could see the hard glitter in his eyes beneath his silver mask as he stared at him. "You have drunk more than enough through the night. Get up and go home! The ceremony will begin shortly, and you'd better not be here," he said.

"Don't worry my friend! This little lion could have better behavior, I promise!" Taham said as he tried to stand and improve his appearance, but his foot slipped through a gap. He leaned back against the wall as he continued to laugh drunkenly.

"Are you deaf, fool? You are totally drunk; go home!" Javid said.

"Do not be afraid!" Taham leaned close and whispered, "Go back to your place, it's not good for you to speak with your beneath!" He was so drunk that he could not speak lowly. Javid looked around out of the corner of his eye to see some others were watching them.

"Sit your ass down and shut up!" Javid whispered as he stood up and rushed away.

Taham's eyes followed him, and he smirked in triumph. The constant drumming indicated that the ceremony would open soon. One of the devotees had passed a graduate test, and the Holy Pater would give him the crown.

Everyone gathered around the altar that the paters stood on behind it. The Paters had the place of highest honor in the Mithra's temple, the God's deputy on the earth. They wore clothes like God Mithra, a long, sheer white scarf that wound around their body. The veil started

---

[1] A Persian name meaning immortal

wrapped around their neck, then around their chest, and then back, draped over the crooks of their arms, falling to the floor. They were the only ones in the temple who did not wear masks.

A man, with a red mask, came forward with resolute steps and knelt in front of Holy Pater. The Holy Pater was the mentor of mentors, the oldest men among Paters, the political and religious leader of the disciples, holding the title of High Pater who had been chosen by other paters. His white skin had tones of pale pink, his eyes were deep brown, and his lashes were snowy white. His long silver hair fell down his back past his buttocks. He was really skinny, his ribs showing. This was clear to everyone because he was not wearing any clothes, just a deep white shawl that wrapped his waist. His wrinkled face gave him the appearance of age, yet his body seemed to be strong and fit.

He came forward slowly and stood in front of the man, leaning on a gnarled black cane that was as tall as he was, with a large knot at the end. Javid was beside the Holy Pater.

"What we offer cannot be bought with gold. The cost is all of you. Men take many paths through this vale of tears and pain, ours is the hardest. Only a few have made for walking along this path," Holy Pater said, his voice echoing through the temple. "It needs an uncommon strength of body and spirit, and a heart, hard and strong."

The Holy Pater gave Javid his cane, from a silver plate that was on the altar platform, took a crown with both hands to show his respect, and then slowly brought the crown to the young man but the man raised his right hand. "I would choose a holy love over the crown!" the man said in a loud voice, by their ancient custom.

Suddenly, a laugh broke the silence like a clap of thunder on a hot summer. Everybody wondered and looked back. Taham threw back his head and roared with laughter.

"This ceremony is a complete farce, from the beginning to the end. This poor young man has no choice but fucking holy love!" Taham said as he burst out laughing again. "Imagine that, if he accepts the crown…" He could not finish his words, half laughing, half hiccupping.

Javid almost burst a blood vessel when he saw Taham, but the Holy Pater took back the cane and went to Taham very calmly. With his every step, the men stepped back, bowing their head. Taham was still sober enough to know that he should stand for the Holy Pater. Although he was still laughing uncontrollably, he leaned his hand on a wall and stood. The Holy Pater grinned when he saw Taham was struggling to hold straight.

"I think holy love doesn't have a place for you, boy!" The Holy Pater said.

"I know holy love place, my Holy Pater..." The strong wine was making Taham's head spin, "Its place is here...," he said, pounding his chest with his fist. "Not in a temple...," groping for words that did not come.

The Holy Pater gave him a scornful look. "You are a black-hearted bastard!" He said.

Taham's face twisted in sudden fury and he stood before the Holy Pater, staring at his emotionless brown eyes.

"I... I lived with your holy love enough, a lifetime, even before any god had heard me. I have lived in the people's stable, eaten garbage. I don't have parents, relatives or friends; I've been alone for my whole life. I had to fight to live; kill to not be dead..." He laughed. "You see? We're the same but with one difference. You feel you are protected by your delusions and have a right to commit your violent acts because it's justified by your god; you kill and hate in the name of God's LOVE..."

The Holy Pater raised the cane high over his head and smashed it on Taham's mouth at an incredible speed. Taham's last words were lost in his bloody mouth, and his massive body fell down. A jarring impact drove the breath from him. His mouth was full of blood.

"Beat him bloody!" Holy Pater yelled, his voice ringing harshly.

Taham's body was crushed beneath the kicks of dozen angry men. He was savagely beaten, but strangely, he felt no pain, just screams echoing inside his head. He did not realize how long they hit him. It might have been minutes or hours. Finally, somebody took him around the throat and lifted his body up. All he could distinguish through his swollen and half-closed eyes was a shadow of Holy Pater.

Blood ran down his cheeks, dripping off his chin. The last thing he heard was Holy Pater's sharp order. "Do your duty!"

His body was dragged over pebbles and thorn, and they took him to a precipice.

Finally! He thought with a repulsive joy at the last moment.

*****

"Father! Father! He woke up!" It was a beautiful voice with a beautiful tone.

Taham tried to open his eyes, but it seemed almost impossible; his eyes were two narrow slits. He could only make out the silhouette of a woman and then, a little later, a shadow that came to him.

"Do not worry son, you're safe!" An old man said as he sat beside his bed.

The man inserted a curved copper funnel through the feeding hole over his mouth and poured a slow trickle down his throat. Taham swallowed, scarcely tasting. The man removed the pipe from Taham's mouth. Taham felt a sharp pain in his stomach and moaned, but he was already spiraling back to sleep.

*****

Taham slowly opened his eyes. After two months, he could easily open his eyes and see the room that he was bedridden. His bruises had healed, but there was still a deep cut on his forehead, which had divided his right eyebrow.

I should leave here, Taham thought bitterly. He tried to get up, but he let out a gasp as the pain drove through his ribs and he fell back down on the bed. He lay on his back, staring at the cloudless blue sky through the window, trying not to feel the pain that snaked up his right ribs every time he moved.

He could escape from the clutches of death by a miracle, but he was not sure he should be grateful. As time went by, his broken bones became stronger but staying here weakened a hard wall of hatred that he had built around his heart.

I should leave here, Taham thought again, took a deep breath and tried to stand up.

"What are you doing?"

Taham turned back. A young woman was standing in the doorway, holding a plate of food. She looked at him with a frown. She was a little overweight and not very pretty, wore her thick chestnut hair in a ponytail that made her round face look even plumper; the kind of girl who would not catch many eyes but every time he looked at her, he felt the presence of soothing warmth at his heart. Chista's happiness, kindness, and intelligence made her more attractive than any pretty girl.

Chista's big brown eyes were still fixed on Taham, waiting for an answer.

"I should go!" Taham said as he continued to try getting up.

"Have you lost your mind? You must…," Chista said.

Taham suddenly fell with a groan of pain. Chista stopped talking and ran towards him. "Are you trying to kill yourself?" She asked, putting the plate on the table and rushing to help him.

"I'm fine! I'm fine!" Taham said. He leaned against the wall, breathing hard and trying to hide the Mithra's cult tattoo on his arm. "I have to go!"

"Why? Is someone waiting for you?" Chista peeked through half-closed eyelids to see what his reaction was as her hands guided him to bed.

"No… no…" Taham looked into her eyes. She was waiting for an answer, but her worried eyes bothered him. "Why has your father brought me here?" He asked angrily.

"I said you a hundred times." Chista was surprised. "My father is a healer. He was returning from visiting his patients, and he found you while…"

"I was beaten, bowed, and broken sufficiently!" Taham's voice was uneasy.

His words came as no surprise to Chista "Yes, you know that!" She said.

"Didn't you ask yourself, who did this to me, and why did they want to kill me?" His voice was acidic.

"Friends or worst enemies, debtor or creditor, relatives or strangers, what difference does it make? We shall try to keep you alive…," Chista said.

"Why?" Taham interrupted her angrily.

"Because your life is valuable!" She said, staring at him with her kind, beautiful eyes.

"Valuable!" Taham murmured with a hint of mockery then gave her a stony stare. "You don't know me!"

She came to him and slowly raised her hand to run her fingers through his thick brown hair. He felt the blood rushing to his face.

"Why do you like to pretend you're a monster?" Chista said as she caressed his face, looking at his eyes directly. "I prefer you as you are. The owners of these innocent eyes cannot be a monster!"

Taham was restless and nervous. He closed his eyes and took a deep breath painfully despite his broken ribs. "I should go!" He said again.

Chista dropped her hands and looked at Taham's face. "Why?" She bit her lip. "I guessed that you might…"

Taham stared at her. His eyes revealed his feeling, but he put his head down.

"We are from two different worlds…you, your kindness, your father full of grace, everything is strange to me. I grew up with hate and anger; I know nothing of love. Love scares me. I was scared when the cult men began to beat me, but not more than now …I do not know what to do, I…"

Suddenly Taham felt Chista's lips pressed to his. He was afraid. He had learned in the temple that touching and kissing a woman was an unforgivable sin, the worst thing a disciple could do. They believed mortal love was the most significant barrier for men to reach true light, but Chista's lips filled him with a warm glow of joy. Her touch, the heat of her soft body, and her smell sent waves that pulsed through him and his raw nerves gradually calmed. His caresses were clumsy, his kisses nervous.

"I do not know how to love!" Taham said, through his kisses.

"Don't be scared! Love is a contagious disease spread all over the world; everyone gets infected by it," she whispered in his ear.

*****

Taham's shoulders shook with silent sobs, his cloak flapping in the wind noisily. The map of wrinkles on his face told of his most incredible journey. His eye lines said of laughter, of warm smiles and affection, his forehead told of worries. Only fifty, he might have passed for seventy, grey-faced, with crow's feet around his eyes, and hair as white as chalk.

His fingers were painfully cold, but he could not keep his eyes from Chista's grave, could not stop his hands from reaching out to caress the frozen soil. A touch of a hand on his shoulder brought him to his senses, and he raised his head. He saw Ashvan.

She had gotten Chista's beautiful eyes and her attractive look. Taham wiped the tears away with the back of his hand. There were tears in Ashvan's eyes as well. She had never seen her father's tears; she wanted to soothe him but did not know how. She looked at her father, his forehead crossed by a long white scar, which divided his right eyebrow. She knew her father looked rough, but he was the kindest man that Ashvan had ever seen.

"She liked that scar on your face, I think," she said without thinking.

"Yes." Taham agreed but recalling gave him a chill, as it always did. "She saved my life and gave me unconditional love…," he smiled sadly, "… but I left her to die alone!"

Ashvan could see the grief on her father's face. "Mother would love you until the last moment of her life." A sad smile touched her lips. "She always said love is, he gives you a piece of your soul that you never knew was missing." Her fingers slowly caressed her father's hand. "You were in her heart and soul when she died."

Taham looked at her beautiful eyes. He got up and nodded, let his daughter took his hand and led him to the tribe. No other words needed.

Ashvan turned and threw a look at her mother's grave. A little sapling had grown on the grave, right where Amitira's blood was shed over the soil.

CHAPTER FOUR

MITHRA

Ancient Land of Mannaeans, 628 BC, Autumn

All the Paters of Mithra's cult were gathered in the crypt, seated on a moss-covered stone. Fresh torches burned in the iron sconces along the walls and showed damp and mossy walls. The disciples gradually were filling the crypt and their figures producing giant shadows eerily dancing along the walls. At the center of the abandoned crypt, a big pool was seen, where the water was deep, black and cold.

The Holy Pater was first on the crypt, before everyone. He was over seventy years old, older and more potent than all Paters. During the fifty years of his life, he had passed all the cult's exams and gained the top first position in the cult, there was just a handful, which could completely pass those exams and he was the best between them. He was famous for being brave, strict, and violent.

The old Holy Pater leaned his head on his cane, a cane as long as his height with a large knot at the end that he took it in the ceremonies. His silver hair that he kept neatly trimmed and a long silver beard made him look like an ancient statue of the angel of fury, under his great snowy brows, his sparkling with wisdom brown-green eyes were set.

The Holy Pater widened his eyes a little, leaned closer and weighed the dark water carefully with his eyes. If any of the Paters looked at him, he saw a look in his eyes that he had never seen before, uneasiness, even a hint of fear. The Holy Pater had been attended through many rituals, some led to victory, some death! Even now, that the temple needed more disciples and for this cause, the challenges were easier than before.

These thoughts gave him a chill. Today was his favorite disciple's challenge day. The temple of Mithra, where he had been chosen to serve, didn't allow him to get married and have a wife and children when he was young, he had full faith in the temple's teachings, but now he was tired, tired of the dry beliefs, and wished to have a son. This may explain why he had paid particular attention to his new disciple. A brave young man, who was so mysterious and attractive that could even get the Holy Pater attention. He could sense something else in that young man.

"It will be difficult!"

A deep voice of a younger Pater beside him brought him to his senses. "Yes!" Holy Pater said, frowning. He felt guilty about choosing this horrible location for this challenge, but that was not a feeling to share with others.

"That black hole makes everyone disappear; I have seen its appetite before!" The younger pater said with a sharp, cold voice.

The old man looked off into the darkness of the water, hidden behind a stern face. He only could pray his disciple would be as brave and strong as he appeared before.

A man with a red mask lifted his horn to his lips and blew. The sound rattling among the crypt and bouncing from the vaulted ceiling. The young disciple came with his superior. He wore a black raven mask. The superior tied the young man's hands behind his back and his legs with sheep gut rope. The old man's heart pounded in his chest.

"In the name of Mithra!"

The superior cried as he threw the young man into the pool. Dark water with a terrible sound opened its mouth and instantly devoured him.

The long moments passed; the old man was staring into the water. The torch flames fluttered on the surface of the water impatiently, like the old man's heart. That was showing that the young man was struggling into the water to open his hands and separate the stone from his legs. The old man's eyes were fixed on the water, becoming more and more worried about the time that was getting thick!

"Mithra did not fail me, nor will he. Mithra will help me save my soul," the old man was whispering contently and rapidly the spells but the moments was passing with no result. He looked at the pool; it was deep and dark and still, seemed to be motionless forever. He realized, with a sick sense of helpless terror that he did not believe any god who hears his prayers, but suddenly the young man's head broke the water gasping for breath as he was holding the mask firmly to prevent it from falling. Everyone gave a cry of joy, and the old man took a deep sigh of relief.

The young man sat on the floor, panting. His wrists were bloody. His superior came to him and released his hand to help the young man, but he stood immediately needless to assist and went to the paters as his breathing was returning to normal. The Holy Pater got up, smiled and looked at his disciple with pride. He gave the cane to one of his disciples' hand and took the crown from of silver plate. He moved forward a few steps to put the crown on his young disciple's head, but the young man raised his hand.

"I choose a holy love over the crown!" The young man said with a soft but steady voice.

The Holy Pater set aside the crown. "From now on you'll be a Nymphus[1]!" He proudly announced.

The men cheered, and wine, mixed with Ephedra sap was poured into the goblets. The young man raised the cup to his lips but did not drink it, then dropped the wine to the floor without drawing attention. A group of men wrapped in black sarongs, sashes and head scarves with bloody red masks, performed the cow-headed warrior dance in front of a row of empty seats, that had been left for the god, to scare away evil spirits. The sound of the bronze ring, tied to their feet, resonated deep in the

---

[1] The second degree of initiation is called 'Nymphus' or the 'Bride' in Mithraism

chill silence of the crypt. A hunched man, radiated evil with a sinister glee came forward; his movement stilted and unpredictable. The ceremony itself would last until dawn. The young man looked around, went to the holy pater, and dropped to his knees.

"Well done!" The old man said, trying to hide his love. "Then you shall be Nymphus. Wear that face, obey and you will see you will be truly worthy to serve Mithra in every face," he said, and hoped that it was true.

"Thank you Holy Pater…but… but if you let me please to go," the young man said with a low voice.

The old man knew that his disciple always leaves their concourse before the rest of men, so nodded.

"Yes! Yes! You must be very tired; go, my son, go and rest," the old man said.

The young man bowed his head, took a few steps backward, and quickly went away.

Outside, the wind whistled and moaned through the mountains; she looked around. The winds were frigid here, rain fell and froze, barren and dark with not a star shining through the mist. Nothing stirred and nothing spoke, only the howls of wolves and her breaths cut through the still air.

SHE began to run. She was feeling more substantial than usual, but she continued to run. She should get rid of the muffler that she had wrapped around her body.

Under the hill, she stuck fingers in her mouth and gave a short, sharp whistle. Only moments later, a white horse broke out from the tree line, a white mare. The mare's snowy white coat was as fluid as water, stocky limbs moving faster than would have thought possible, her mane was dancing in an arching spray. Her head was extended forwards but her ears flat back, puffs of moisture escaping from her nostrils.

Mithra's hand lovingly stroked the horse's neck. She took the reins of her horse and pulled her towards the rocks, where the straight edge of the cliff was formed by a natural fracture and created a rock shelter in limestone.

Mithra hurriedly took off the mask from her face and her still-damp hair dangled around her beautiful face. She unsheathed her dagger, ripped the muffler shawl that she had wrapped around her chest, down to her navel to hide her firm breasts and threw it down. The night air was chilly on her bare skin. Her body, the hollow of her throat, the round ripe breasts, the lush curves at waist and hip in the dark purple light before dawn epitomized a statue of a goddess.

She pulled out a blanket from the saddlebag and draped it over her shoulders. She sat down and took a breath of relief. She could have sworn that damn muffler weighed a ton. It was heavier than she thought, much more massive than the stone that had been tied to her foot and it nearly killed her. It took a bit of courage, but I did it, Mithra told herself, and then a smile spread across her face. No man has ever had cause to question her courage. Mithra wondered if Holy Pater would be so eager to see his own disciple successes if he knew Mithra is a woman. She sneered.

She got up to return to Diheh. She must hurry; they should not find out about her absence. She grabbed her clothes. She wore the Mannaean men outfit, white linen tunic, a fur-trimmed gray cloak across her shoulders, leather pants and a heavy belt of silver. She sheathed the dagger at her waist, mounted on the horse put the spurs to her horse and trotted briskly toward the Diheh; the hour was close to dawn.

After one hour ridding, through dense forest, peering through the mists, she glimpsed the wooden roofs of the houses in the distance. Mithra brought up the rear. She looked back and scanned the way she had come cautiously. The wind was moving, through the mist of this fall morning, the scarlet leaves were little more than a red haze. There was not any living creature other than leaves that were trembling in the wind. She slid from her saddle, best she went the rest of the way on foot.

She went through a damp and muddy path to the biggest house of Diheh, the paramount of the tribe's mansion. She opened the heavy bronze door and peeked carefully from behind the door. There was a brook, among the paved path that led to a white mansion. The soothing sound of the running water was like a caress for ears. She could see the building in the dim light. A white mansion with a covered patio, that the many arcs on it had formed a beautiful ceiling. A raven that flew overhead and gave a scream made her clench her teeth.

The large, two-story building was in profound silence. Though Mithra knew no servants live in the building and that there was no one to hear her, she instinctively hid, stood still, and began to listen. White Mansion had never had a servant despite its impressive size. Ashvan always was complaining, is it not really beneath the dignity of the paramount of the tribe that his daughter do house works all?! And Taham still was frowning at her attitude, reminding that they didn't have feasts and he didn't like people who feel born only for expense and enjoyment, but Mithra knew well, her grandfather preferred to be far from prying eyes and what people said about them.

Mithra entered the garden, made no sound as she went slowly toward the stable in the backyard.

"I was starting to think you may never return!"

Mithra startled nervously, turned her back. Sheedvash went out of the bower, a lantern in one hand; moved forward for a better look. The light shone on Mithra's beautiful face, she touched her hair and covered the birthmark on her right cheek; a strange birthmark like a skull. Sheedvash knew well how Mithra hates others attitude about her birthmark. Mithra paid her aunt the least bit of attention, turned her face and made her way to the stable.

"How big a fool you are; how do you suppose I would not notice your nightly absences!" Sheedvash said behind her, the mockery was indeed her words.

Mithra took her horse to the stable oblivious to her aunt, but Sheedvash followed her, stood in the doorway.

"Why can't you live a normal life?" Sheedvash said from the doorway. She spoke softly, yet firm.

Mithra took off the saddle of her horse without a word. It seemed all her consciousness was concentrated in work.

Sheedvash ignored her attitude. "I told Father nothing yet… I want to help you…"

"If I need help I will ask for it!" Mithra said her voice rang harshly.

Mithra was busy cleaning the horse's body; Sheedvash stared at her; her curling dark red-brown hair dancing as she moved, and her golden honey eyes staring at her horse. Her beauty was incredible as much as her MOTHER. A cold fury boiled inside Sheedvash.

"You're right. You have no need me; all you need to do is be like your mother." Sheedvash's smiling eye was bright with mockery. "I suppose your mother also trapped my poor brother in one of those night jaunts!"

Sudden fury twisted in Mithra's belly and her fingers coiled into a fist, "So you need to go for jaunts some nights, try to catch yourself a poor man." Mithra kept her voice low, but Sheedvash could hear the fury in her tone.

Sheedvash's mouth twisted in anger. "I think not." She tried to swallow her tears. Last night, her father in just a few sentences explained to her, for empowering the Land of Mannea; they need to make an alliance with the Median Empire, and she should be ready to marry the king's cousin. "I'm getting married soon, and I'll leave this house." Sheedvash looked at her and sneered. "You see; you will soon get rid of me!"

Mithra was surprised, but her aunt's wedding was the last thing she would have wanted to know, so she showed no reaction. She went to the mass of dry hay that was stored in the corner of the stable and raised her hand to lift a bale of hay. Sheedvash suddenly realized the wounds on her wrists, came forward quickly and took her hand.

"Did you wounded…?"

Sheedvash could not finish her words; suddenly Mithra caught her wrist with incredible speed, her strong fingers digging into her aunt's skin like an eagle's claws. It took her a moment to notice her involuntary reaction. The crows were circling above the stable, cawing. Mithra released her, stepped backward as her body was trembling.

Sheedvash looked at her in disgust! She saw Amitira before herself, not Mithra, a beautiful bronze statue of a goddess, curly brown-red hair, soft face with rounded cheekbones, slim nose, olive skin and above all, honey golden big eyes that stared at her with pride, unfortunately, Mithra looked exactly like her mother. "You're evil! No one should love or respect you. You are like your Assyrians relatives, cruel and savage…," Sheedvash said as she was staring at Mithra with hate.

Mithra went backward again. *The temple and its challenges would have damned me down to seven hells; I'm always ready to defend,* thought Mithra. The crows were cawing louder. "Get off my back!" Mithra muttered, low under the breath; her lip was trembling. She ran away from the stables towards the mansion. Sheedvash heard her steep steps until there was nothing but the sound of the cawing.

Sheedvash rolled off feeling more ashamed than furious. *What a wretched creature I've become.* She sighed, leaned forward and wanted to stroke the horse's neck, but she pawed impatiently at the ground. Sheedvash stared at the horse for a moment and then came out of the stable. She slowly walked up to the front steps of the veranda, but she could not enter. She sat on the stairs and dropped her head into her hands.

She felt sorry for her niece. She knew well it was not Mithra's fault, but every time she recalled her loneliness painfully, Behbood[1], her loving husband, she could not protect her heart against the onslaught of hate. In fact, she felt a mixture of intense love and immensely hate and she did not know how to cope with those mixed feelings. Sheedvash wiped her tears, leaned her head on the wooden porch, stared off into the sky, and her thoughts flew. She remembered the day after Mithra was born, sixteen years ago…

*****

Tribal people were all ready to go but the paramount of the tribe was at his wife's grave, and others were waiting for him.

---

[1] A name was used in ancient Persia meaning the best

Ashvan had gone to her father while Sheedvash was looking for somebody who can help her. After Ashvan's speech, the story of Armaz's courage that was told to people, and her father's presence, the people seemed beholden enough, and there was no talk of Mithra's ominous birth, but still, no woman in the tribe was ever going to accept Mithra to feed her. Sheedvash was going to her friend, she was the only one had remained; she had given birth to a stillborn child, and Sheedvash hoped she could find the courage to feed Mithra.

The young woman was standing near their cart; her husband was sitting on the wagon, wounded, deep scars were seen on his face. Sheedvash glanced at the man and took her friend's by hand.

"I need your help," Sheedvash said with nervous eyes.

Her friend looked at her curiously, as she was holding her husband's arm tightly.

"I know you have lost your child and… maybe… It is difficult to hold another child in your arms, but as you know my brother's wife has died, and her child is hungry," Sheedvash said, hardly daring to hope.

"Armaz's child?" The young man asked hastily.

"Yes." Sheedvash turned to him. "Her mother has died birthing her, and for that, we could not find any woman who wants to breastfeed this baby!"

"No one wants to feed his child?" The young man was like a bear with a sore head. "What kind of people are they? Armaz decided to throw caution to the wind, and he bravely ran through our enemies heart." His voice was hoarse with remembered grief. "Bring her unto us; my wife will feed her," the young man said.

Sheedvash looked at her friend's face. "Bring her!" The young woman said.

The baby was crying impatiently in Sheedvash's arms, she redoubled her pace, going to her friend but suddenly the baby pushed aside the blanket over her face; her honey eyes were looking at Sheedvash. Sheedvash's steps gradually loosened. The hatred that was boiling in her heart revealed itself again. She had a lump in her throat when she approached her friend's cart. They went to a nearby tree, which made a sheltered. Sheedvash noticed many crows chirping in the trees.

"Give me the baby!" The young woman said as she was looking at Sheedvash, who grew hesitant.

"Before you feed her it's better to see her face; she has a strange birthmark on her cheek!" Sheedvash said.

"I don't mind what they say!" The woman said calmly.

"I was there..." Sheedvash hesitated for a moment, then added hurriedly, "Her mother was saying strange spells; her voice was terrible!" For a moment, she felt ashamed of what she was saying, but hatred overcame to shame, "The people had not been far wrong. You are young, you can get pregnant again but... maybe those people were right, and you cannot be a mother again."

The young woman's face was shadowed with fear. She drew her hand slowly back, but she was uncertain yet. Sheedvash chewed her lip. A crow flapped its wings above them on a branch and cawed loudly.

The young woman glanced at the crow. "Just remember to say nothing to my husband," the young woman said.

Sheedvash nodded and stepped to the caravan; the baby bawling in her arms and her crying made Sheedvash feel absurdly guilty. *The god might send you down to hell for that evil you've done,* Sheedvash thought, turned to her friend. "I want you to...," said Sheedvash abruptly but she could not finish her words.

The young woman's fingers tightened around her wrist. "Don't ask it, please, I can't," she peered at her husband. "I love him, and I want our marriage has been greatly enriched by our children, please!"

It was too late; Sheedvash had burned her bridges behind her. She went hurriedly to their cart; sweat was trickling down her face, despite the frigid wind. She put the baby in Ashvan's big maid arms and took refuge in a corner, pressing close against the rock.

Her father came; his eyes were red from crying. Everyone stood up to respect the paramount of the tribe. The caravan was ready to go.

"Your friend also didn't accept her, is it?" Ashvan asked Sheedvash as she held Mithra in her arms. Sheedvash said nothing. "She is hungry!" Ashvan's eyes were full of pity. She wished her breasts were heavy of milk to feel the movement of those beautiful small lips on her skin. "It's a terribly cruel thing to do to a newborn baby!"

"They are afraid! All are afraid of this baby!" The fat maid said. "No one wants even to see her. In another hand, the boy loved by people. People say the boy and girl are the opposite. The boy has been born along the worship of God and girl when her mother asked help from the demons. Even their faces are also different; the boy is white as the full moon and girl…"

"Shut your mouth!" Ashvan's voice was angry, as well it might be.

"I'll speak to them," Zarvan said, sitting on a boulder, still in his bloody clothes. "I've fought for them; they must listen to me and feed this baby!"

"You cannot force others to breastfeed this baby," Taham said calmly. "We should get Diheh and find our herds; we can feed her with goat's milk."

"I'll soak a towel with warm water, and give her suck to it, it keeps her calm!" Ashvan said. She looked at the baby, who was crying non-stop. "You are a lovely girl, I'm sure the god will save you!"

The holy Orin Mountain spaced a one-day's walk apart, after hours walking, the great downhill, which led Diheh, loomed in the distance. They were tired, had been walking for hours but at least they were not afraid, and they were moving faster in the hope to find their own land.

Taham looked at the downhill. *Why do I have such a bad feeling?* He thought. Taham put his heels into his horse and galloped to the city. He encouraged his horse to go faster with his shouts. It was heavy rain, turning roads to mud, He following the muddy, slick path until he saw the city. He reined up very suddenly. The trail led him through a burned city. The town walls were smashed, half the homes and shops burnt, charred roofs were all that remained and the ashes swollen by autumn rains, everything had plundered. One by one, people arrived at the gate of the city. The women were crying; no one dared to take a step forward.

Taham took a deep breath; his throat was dry. He suddenly found it exceedingly difficult to speak, but he made himself say, "Everyone wants to appear brave, but nobody really is. I'm afraid, like you, more struggling and difficulties await us but I love this land, this city, I will stay here and build this city back to what it was before!" He looked at people. "Come and follow me if you love this city." Then he spurred toward the gate. Zarvan and Ashvan followed him and after them, the tribal people one by one, wordlessly.

*****

Taham and Ashvan were strolling down the streets and Zarvan, Sheedvash and the maid were following them. The baby was crying in Ashvan's arms, a thin wavering cry, but there was no flock, at all! A thin fearful sound emerged from the baby's throat.

"She's going to die!" Ashvan said in a quivery voice.

Starvation would kill her, Sheedvash thought with horror. "Father…" She had to confess.

"Shush!" Taham suddenly stopped and stared at the temple of Mithra.

Their eyes followed him as he was going towards the temple. In front of the temple's gate, a woman was sitting on the ground, leaning to the goddess Mithra's statue. A crow cawed, flapped its tarry wings and watched them with its beady eyes over the statue's shoulder. Ashvan went forward, glanced at the woman curiously; the woman's face gave her a chill. One side of the woman's face was in burn scars. She had one empty eye socket, and her nose had a chunk missing. The sunset light painted her burned face with orange shadows, so she looked even more terrible.

"An ugly one-eyed woman, a crow on top of her, in front of the Goddess, Ominous signs altogether," the fat maid was trembling. "A disaster is the best we can hope for!"

No one answered. A chill wind was blowing.

The woman seemed not to notice them. She was staring off into the distance, and they saw the dread on her face. She looked alien to them; her dirty, thin clothes were telling them she was not from Mannea. They did not know who she is, why she was here in such ill-time, although the answers were not so crucial for Taham; he had more pressing concerns. His eyes were fixed at a sleeping child in the woman's arms. He moved closer, but the woman paid no attention at all to him. The infant girl in her arms didn't breathe, the baby's face was so bruised and swollen that she hardly looked human, she had died, but the woman had pinched her nipple and led it into the baby's mouth; waiting for drinking milk from her swollen breasts.

Taham gently pulled the baby out the woman's arms as he peered at her uncertainly. She still looked into the distance with her only eye.

"Put the baby on her chest!" Taham said to Ashvan quietly.

It took Ashvan a moment to comprehend her father's words, but when the understanding came, made her gasp. She stepped back involuntary, but Taham grabbed her arm to prevent her. He looked at the baby, who was crying weakly in Ashvan's arm. "We have lost our herd. We should feed her afore; she dies," he said to Ashvan.

Ashvan had not dared to leave the baby in the woman's arms. "If…" Ashvan blinked at her father. "She could be a demon, called up from hell, not a woman."

Taham's anger overwhelmed his sense. "Are you telling me the old nanny's stories? PUT THE BABY ON HER CHEST! She can feed Armaz's child!" He growled.

There was no use to argue. Ashvan went forward and put the baby on the woman's chest. The baby nuzzled blindly against the woman's breast, searching for milk, making a sad little whispery sound but started sucking hard on her nipple, when she found it. Just the baby's sucking could get the woman's attention. Her mouth twitched on the burned side of her face and made a scary smile; she clasped the baby, leaned over, smelt and kissed the baby with great love.

Everyone did a double take when they saw the woman's behavior and Taham took a deep breath of relief.

"Surely I would never have dreamed that kind of fate wait for someone...," Zarvan whispered and looked at Ashvan, "Maybe the people are right..."

*****

She was in a field of green wheat, the stalks waved lazily in the wind. She ran; her hand along the edge to feel the roughness of wheat cluster and held her face upward to feel the warm light of the mid-summer day. The air smelled the wet soil just after the rain, and the birds fly in a cloudy sky. A terrible scream made her stop running; there were a million crows around her with grievous eyes and ink-stained wings. Her hand was covered with blood, the blood goes on forever, and after a while, her hands became wings, as black as coal. She felt herself free; she could fly above a sea of blood...

Heart pounding, Mithra jerked awake and found herself in her bedchamber. "A dream... only a dream," Mithra said herself and stared at around her bedchamber, to be sure. She sat on her bed. Her throat was dry. *The fighting to the death into the cold water never made me any harder or braver,* she thought, sighing, *at least against the crows!* She wondered what the Holy Pater would say if he could see her now.

Mithra peered out over the balcony; the dawn sun peeked through a thick screen of clouds, painting the sky an elaborate mix of bloodied reds and vibrant oranges. *It's chilly,* she thought. The scent of rain hung in the air as she watched the sky darken and the colors fade away as morning fully arrived. Pinks, yellows, and reds disappeared first. Blue soon followed, overtaken by the grayness climbing over the mountaintops.

Mithra got up and walked to the window. She had slept only half an hour, but dawn was her favorite time. She preferred to go out of the house when the new rays of the day are still struggling to bright the day, and almost all the people were asleep. She slipped the pants on and went out. She made no sound as she was going to her brother's room. The room was dark, but she noticed Mahbod[1] sprawled under the covers asleep.

Mithra shook her head. "Sloppy, careless, lazy, more trouble than worth!" She whispered.

It would have been a good time to sneak away and went to the herd. Taham hated the old aristocrats as much as indolence, so his grandson herded the paramount of the tribe's vast flocks of sheep; an unpleasant task for Mahbod that Mithra was doing that eagerly instead of him.

In the stable, Morvarid[2], her white horse neighed with joy when she saw her.

"You are tired, girl, huh? But I'm sure you like to go out, like me. Today I'll take you to a special place, where is none but ourselves," Mithra whispered in her ear as she stroked the horse's head with love.

Taham's big barn was just ten minutes away from Diheh, and Mithra arrived before the sunrise. The herd's dogs greeted her with a chorus of barking. Mithra opened the door of the huge barn, caressed the soft fur on top of the dog's head and scratched their ears. "Good boy. Good, good dog." Black, her best dog, stuck out his tongue and licked her ear. Her face twitched, her eyes filled with joy and laughed heartily, what no one could see in Dihe. Sheep make quiet bleating noises and move about slowly, grazing on the thin grass that grew between the sheepfold and thatched stable.

"Nap is over, move on," Mithra said then peered around. "I want to guide you to an appropriate pasture and a watering place. Come on, it is a long road ahead!" She gave a long slow whistle, and the dog led sheep down the path toward the mountain.

She did not take the main road; instead, she struck off toward the north, following the river, until its spring on top of the hill. The lands, she traveled through were rough rocky terrain beneath a vast blue-grey vault of the sky. The road was prone to vanishing amongst the scoured

---

[1] A name was used in ancient Persia meaning beautiful like moon
[2] Meaning pearl

falling pebbles; everybody but Mithra surely would have lost the way and glide down to the bottom of the valley. There was nothing around, just mountain and sky and rock.

At the top of the Alaberia Mountains, no land could have been more different from Mannea, with its mountains and high meadows and shadowed vales, Alaberia had a unique and pure beauty. *We'll go there,* Mithra thought.

*****

Ashvan loved Mithra. Unlike others, she was believed that Mithra had brought lucky for her. Only a month after holding Mithra in her arms, she felt a whelp in her belly. She did not have any sign of pregnancy, but she knew another being has resided within her, two heartbeats within one body. She felt her beautiful presence even before the child formed. Nahira[1] was born ten months after Mithra. Zarvan didn't stop making excuses for his nightly absences, he was complaining again, this time for having a son but now Ashvan was resigned because he was not the most critical part of Ashvan's life anymore, Nahira was her joy, her hope, her everything.

Mahbod rubbed his eyes for a moment, evidently only just awake. He came out to the triangular balcony that opened off his bedchamber and stood with one hand on the rough stone balustrade. His long black hair stirring in the wind. He was Mithra's twin brother, but they did not look alike. Mahbod was slender, with his father's coloring, the fair skin, black hair, and brown eyes, so dark that they seemed almost black.

Mahbod gave a smile, and his face got much more attractive. "Hi, aunty Ashvan!"

Ashvan frowned and shook her head. "Once again! You should have been at the meadow not Mithra; you are too lazy!" She said.

Unlike Ashvan, Nahira, who was coming behind her mother, smiled happily when she saw Mahbod was going down from stone steps and ran towards him while wrapping her arms around his waist to hug him

---

[1] A name was used in ancient Mannea meaning safe

tightly. Mahbod gave his cousin his sweetest smile. "It's not my fault, it's hers. She wants to be seen so strong, so brave, so..." He kissed his aunt's cheek. "Mithra doesn't need to be allowed to go herding; she is an annoying, self-absorbed guy, oh... as much as smug."

"It's true," Sheedvash said as she was coming out.

Ashvan knew that Sheedvash loved Mahbod much more than Mithra. "How could you say all this? She has gone to the meadow instead of her brother; it is obvious Mahbod woke up now!" Ashvan growled. "I don't know in this family who has given unto you this laziness!"

"I don't know who has given him this laziness as his inheritance, but I know very well who spends most of his time with him," Taham said with bitter sarcasm.

Ashvan turned her head; her father was coming down the garden path. Taham was dressed, ready to go out. Ashvan chewed her lip, trying to ignore her father's taunt. Zarvan, who does not have a son, liked to spend much of his time with Mahbod.

The old man was angry, and nobody dared to speak to him but Nahira. "Good morning Grandpa!" She ran toward him and held him in a tight, quiet hug.

"Careful little lady...," Taham said, placing a kiss on her hair. Taham was exhilarated as Nahira went up beside him.

Nahira was not considered beautiful, nor was she considered pretty; she was merely a plain girl, pug-nosed, with freckles and a mane of thick black-brown hair that tumbled down past her waist. "I was wondering who I look like!" She sometimes said, laughing. "Everybody in this family is beautiful but me." But her beautiful brown eyes looked remarkably like her grandmother, Chista, and her prominent lips looked more like Taham; however, no one doubted that Nahira was a lovely girl, with a kind face and warm personality that made her somehow more appealing than pretty women.

"So people tell the truth," Nahira announced, giggling. "The paramount of the tribe is changed, grew older perhaps..." she shrugged her shoulders, "and with an untidy beard and long hair ..."

61

Taham smiled his slimiest smile. "Well, tell me more! What else have you heard about me, Nahira?" He asked.

Nahira stopped beside him. "They say; the old paramount of the tribe easily becomes grumpy...," she laughed mischievously, "... but he's truly the most knowledgeable, friendly and eager guide we have ever..."

The old man loved to hear it. He turned toward her with a gleeful smile. "Who else but you can wheedle me by words, my beautiful doll?" Then glanced at his children with a laughing face but his laugh vanished when he saw Mahbod.

"Where are you going?" He said, frowning to Mahbod, who was returning to his bedchamber. "The farmers have begun to plow lands, go there and inspect their equipment. If a tool is rusty, throw it away. If a tool..."

"They need to make some haste; I must be bathed and dressed!" Mahbod said as he kicked the door shut.

Taham shook his head. "Sloppy, careless, lazy, more trouble than worth!" He murmured.

Sheedvash was carrying her father's breakfast on a tray. "I waited to pull the fresh loaves from the ovens, Father. The bread's still hot."

"Leave it in my apartment; I am going to visit some patients," Taham said and directed his steps towards the stable.

"He's always been this way, but it's getting worse as he gets older!" Sheedvash said.

Ashvan went to Sheedvash as she opened her hands to embrace her sister. "So you want to marry and leave me alone!" Ashvan said in a tone that was equal parts of sadness and happiness. She kissed Sheedvash as she held her tight. "I hope you're happy!"

"I can't remember the last time I was happy because it was so long ago." Sheedvash sneered. "Especially now, I can't feel happy for an unwanted marriage!" She sighed. "But I can at least help to take down the people who deserve to be taken down!"

Ashvan frowned. She took her sister's shoulders and looked straight into her eyes. "What are you talking about, dear? You're only thirty-three years old. Nobody can go back, but anyone can start today and make a new ending," she said. "You should live your life, and it's the best time; start a new life to be able to forget everything."

"Last night I dreamed my husband was alive again. We were running down the river. We were so happy …" She looked at her sister, the anger burning deep in her eyes. "He might be alive, and I could be happy but …" Her words lost in sobs.

The light breeze touched the leaves, and they danced in the air; Sheedvash's brown hair flew in wild directions. Ashvan reached up and tucked her hair behind her ear. "The past should not hurt you anymore, not unless you let it," Ashvan said.

Sheedvash sneered through her tears. "Words are wind!"

Ashvan wanted to comfort her sister, but she did not know how. "Leave the past in the past, you should prepare for your wedding day!"

"Don't worry; I can pretend I live while I'm dead, just like always," Sheedvash whispered, turning to the stair.

*****

A thick blanket of clouds had covered the sun, and the sky was gray-white and sunless.

After a long ride, Mithra made camp atop a hill.

The meadow flowed like a sea of green over the hillock and interspersed with beech and oak trees. Sheep and goats wandered freely, in search of grass. It seemed like they were swimming in it. The cold wind whisked across the rolling hills of the meadow and brought the bitter penetrating smell of yellow yarrow flowers. Morvarid was dipping her snout in the lush green grass that grew around the oak tree.

Mithra glanced at the dogs; Black stand almost statue-like on the crest of the hill while the others tumble about, pulling one another over. Black with his solid, muscular build, a thick black coat, a large head, and a black nose was more similar to wolves. Mithra added thin, dry twigs in fire and leaned against the oak tree; the smell of wood smoke drifted through the air like incense. She had come to the mountain, looking for solitude, to escape everything and everyone, but now she felt alone, even the fire seemed cold and unpleasant.

Even in the crowded, I am alone, Mithra thought. I don't know who those other people are. Some are kindly, most are fearful or nasty and irony; it seems as though they are in the same world as me, but I don't know who is a friend, stranger or foe. Even in my family, all these affection emotions around me and none of them to me or about me. I feel... no one knows me or wants to know me, what I really am. She sighed.

A north wind swirled through the trees, sending yellow leaves flying from the highest branches, she found the blanket and pulled it up high enough to cover herself to the neck, then raised one hand to push her hair back from her eyes. She had spent a sleepless night; the sounds of the meadow, the howling cold wind and the sound of a woodpecker that kept a steady beat as he drilled a hole made Mithra's eyelids felt heavy...

She awoke all at once, every nerve tingle. The dogs began to bark, she guessed a wolf was attacking the sheep. She grabbed her stick and rush to them, but she saw Black came running back to her as he was barking furiously. She backed away. A giant man suddenly attacked her with a terrible scream. Mithra did not expect an attack, and before she could move, the man crashed her to the ground with bone-jarring force. He threw back his head and screamed, while he sat down on the ground and held his hand to her chest. He unsheathed his dagger, but for a brief instant, his dark eyes widened before he landed his blade.

"You are a woman!" He smiled. His smile showed his yellow teeth in the thicket of the enormous black beard.

Mithra struggled against him, shooting her right leg out but he was nailing his hand to her chest as hard as he could.

"Shh!" He said, his raw voice brutal against her face.

He drew his dagger down, from her neck to her long hair. He was stroking her hair with his dagger tip while it was scratching her thin skin. The man's greedy eyes moved slowly from her olive-skinned neck on her breasts. His breathing became very shallow. Mithra was feeling his erection against her belly; her hands grasped the grass of the hill tightly. The man stared at her, oblivious to his surroundings. Mithra did not move; instead, she waited for an opportunity, and her dog gave her this opportunity. Black sank his sharp teeth into the man's leg, the only part of his body that was naked.

The man cried out in pain and turned back. Mithra slammed her knee between his legs and wrenched free. She shuffled to the side and observed him, alert to every little movement of his fingers. The dogs were barking around them, and Morvarid was struggling to separate itself from the tether strap.

The men lifted his dagger high over his head and rushed forward, roaring. Mithra slammed the heel of her hands into his chest, so hard that he fell back a step. She kicked his hand, and the man's dagger went flying into the grass. He drew his fist back, and it plowed into her face, a sudden gush of pain jolted throughout her face, it was like hitting a cart head-on. Her tongue was soaked in the taste of blood, but she did not waste time to reach the dagger. The man proved himself to be a manly person of war, never failed easily; he gripped her by the hair and dragged her to her knees before she could reach the dagger. He grasped the blade and put it on her throat.

Mithra's heart hammering in her chest, she was listening to the man's heavy breathing.

"I should fuck you bloody and ripped your heart out before you buck more wildly." He made a queer sound, and it took her a moment to realize he was laughing. "I guess you'll have to beg for death, bitch!"

Mithra's left hand had gotten a hold of his wrist and tried to push him back, but he was over her with his all-huge weight that did not give her the chance to move. Suddenly, Black jumped on the man, his lips curled up as he bared his teeth. The man threw his leg at the dog to ward off his attack. It sailed through the air; landed in a step further and attacked again. Mithra tried to shake her head, but the pressure of the dagger dissuaded her.

"Damn you bitch!" The man roared.

Mithra felt the cold blade under her chin more firmly. Crows caw loudly, violently.

"Stop!"

Mithra heard a man's voice, then the man said something in a language that Mithra did not know. Mithra raised her eyes; the man slowly came toward them, three soldiers followed. He was on horseback, sword in hand, dressed as a warrior. His helmet was decorated with rhino horn and covered the half of his face.

It was evident that he was their commander.

The giant man said something to his commander in the same language, easing the pressure on the dagger blade.

"Stop!" The commander yelled again, this time angrily.

"Lucky bitch!" The man said quietly as he sheathed his dagger. Mithra fell on her knees, let out a big heavy sigh. Black went closer and nuzzled at Mithra's face, but he kept a wary eye on the man.

The commander stood in front of them.

"Are your men all dead?" Asked the commander with a strange accent. "Why those goosey guys have sent a woman for shepherding?" He had a smirk little smile.

Mithra said nothing; blood was running from her forehead, but she weighed them long and carefully with her eyes, seeking a way to escape.

"Are you deaf or just stupid?" The commander said, watching her honey-colored eyes, which he had never seen anything like them before. "Say, what are you doing here? Do you know here is the Assyrian authority?"

"Assyrian authority?" She said, in a dangerous mockery voice. "This is my fathers' lands that you have chewed it for a while, and now we are asking for the restoration of our properties and titles!"

The commander stared down at her, with his intense look. He slid slowly from his saddle and came forward. "On your feet!" The commander yelled.

Regardless of his command, she was on her knees, staring at him. He ground his teeth together; put his jeweled dagger handle under her chin, raised her face with pressure and forced her to stand. Mithra had to look at the commander's red eyes now.

"Mannaean people had forgotten who they are; let me remind you, we've conquered your fathers' land. We won, and you are losers!"

"You've won a battle, but you will never win this war!" Mithra said, staring at the commander's face.

The commander lowered his dagger back violently, hesitated and looked at her with disgust. "Go! Go before I change my mind," he said as he turned to his horse. "Tell your people, Adora, the Assyrian warrior, who offered hundreds of enemies' eyes to great Ashurbanipal, heard a little girl's ranting, but he didn't tear her tongue. They must understand and be appreciated my kindness and be obeyed before Adora come back again!"

He backed in the saddle. "Be careful, because if I see you again, your head will be my first present to the king of Assyria!" Said the commander; he swung his horse around and turned back across the hill.

"I will remember your name, Adora!" Mithra yelled behind the commander.

Adora brought up the rear and turned his head. Mithra went to Morvarid. The giant man was staring at her, said something in his language to his commander as he was rubbing his injured leg. The commander shouted to him angrily, and the man walked into the hillside. Mithra gave a low whistle, and the dogs rushed to gather their flocks; she sat on the saddle, an arrogant look on her face beneath her glossy chestnut red hair, galloped down beside her flock.

The commander's eyes were fixing on her furiously.

*****

The thick- gray clouds had torn to pieces, but the sun did not find enough time to warm this cold land, and now the day was closing in with a fiery sunset. All the family had gathered in the garden of the White Mansion. Sheedvash was rubbing poultice on Mithra's forehead.

"It is your fault. You must take the flock to meadow today!" Ashvan growled to Mahbod.

"If he had gone, he was killed!" Mithra said.

"Have a care how you speak about me!" Mahbod said, threatening.

"I'm not mocking you, I just told the truth," Mithra said so frankly.

Mahbod's pale skin grew red with fury. "It is your foolishness that troubled you. I'm old enough to behave like the highborn adult that I was supposed to be, what you never did," he said.

Mithra looked at him with disgust. "Why do not you understand? It does not matter why I've been wounded, it is important to know the Assyrians have come in our land." She turned to her grandfather: "You told me we should pay tribute to them, but they have come to spy on our land! We should attack them before they attack us!"

Zarvan gave a sudden snort of laughter, loud enough so that all turned their head toward him.

"Perhaps you hope that Adora will frighten off your attack, eh?" Zarvan mocked; glanced at Mahbod who was laughing too, then turned to Mithra. "You don't know anything about war, little lady!" His face grew serious. "I've fought with them; they know war better than any of us. We must learn patience because we have no hope of victory."

Mithra looked at Zarvan. He was a fat man, in the last ten years he put on a barrel of weight.

"I don't know how you fight," Mithra said, her voice hardened by sarcasm. ", but fighting is much better than being a servant to commands."

"Mithra!" Ashvan shouted angrily.

Mithra looked at her aunt questioningly. "What?"

"Choose your words carefully; you are so rude," Ashvan said reproachfully. "In additional, you should know that they prevail over us, but we are not their servants."

Mithra shrugged. "They take more than half of our products as a tribute; SO we're working, and they eat; SO we're their servants even if you have found another name for it!"

"We offer a part of our product, but we live in a safe city," Zarvan said.

"Safe for you." Mithra stared at him coldly. "You are rich, but ordinary people are at risk of poverty if…"

"I don't want to lose my life for a bunch of farmers," Zarvan interrupted her, "and I don't need a little girl's advice!"

"I'm not a little girl!" Mithra snarled.

"So shut up and let us live in peace!" Zarvan yelled at her.

Mithra's face twisted in a fury. "I…"

"The war between Assyrians and us has been waged since the time they had begun," Taham said, "… and it's not done yet…," the old man stepped forward, "… but if we want to fight, we should know to fight. If we don't know to fight, it's not a good time to fight. If it's not a good time to fight, we have to pay tribute to them before they have a reason to attack."

Sheedvash soaked a clean cloth with some poultice, placed it on Mithra's wound. "May we never have an army that could be like Assyrians, so what?" She glanced at her father. "The people won't survive in the drought if they can survive the war! No matter how we do it," she said.

Mithra looked at Sheedvash, surprised; her aunt had agreed with her for the first time in her life.

"A brave man is worth more than any army!" Mithra said.

"The Assyrians have something better than bravery, little lady." Zarvan teased her, mocking his own style. "They have many trained warriors; I mean many!" He said.

"How many people do we need? How many do we want?" Mithra gave her grandfather a lingering look. "In this vast land; eight different tribes live; our alliance with other tribes is the sword that could break the Assyrians warrior's power!" She said.

"Alliance, huh?" Taham asked frowningly. "Such things seldom come without their price!"

Sheedvash's hand involuntarily pressed tighter on Mithra wounds, with an advantageous marriage, from now on, Sheedvash had to pay for this alliance.

"Ouch!"

Mithra's voice brought Sheedvash to her senses. "We have to pay the price!" She said in a low voice as she put aside the poultice container and clothes.

Her voice made the old man flinch. "I… I have always has sacrificed my beloved but…," Taham said.

"Yeah, we have made enough sacrifices…," Zarvan said. "Why we have to fight the storm when we can't defeat it?"

"Because that was the way of the Mannaean men; a man must fight for living honorable," Mithra said.

Zarvan stood speechless for a moment before he recovered enough to say, "How… how could you say… you, a half-blooded, who is got the wild Assyrian blood in her veins…"

"Enough!" Taham yelled. "You can go to your room!" He said to Mithra.

Mithra's face had twisted in a fury; she opened her mouth to answer, but his grandfather's gaze kept her silent. She pushed aside her aunt's hand angrily, wiped the poultice off her forehead with her sleeve and ran toward the front door, hustling up the stone steps.

"She doesn't seem to understand the meaning of kindness!" Sheedvash murmured angrily.

"Say farmers to keep the herd in the stalls and feed them hay," Taham said to Mahbod dryly. "Stop being lazy; check them every day. We should be more careful, never to let this occur again." He turned to Sheedvash. "Do not allow her to go far!"

"Nobody could keep a watchful eye over her!" Sheedvash said as she rose to gather up her things.

Taham frowned more darkly than ever and darted a furious look at Sheedvash. "Women have their own unique languages; you understand her better," he said.

"I've always found it hard to speak with her." Sheedvash watched her father for some moments. "You let her act like a boy; maybe it is better you talk to her and realize she's odd," she said, ironically.

The old man turned to his daughter and looked at her angrily.

"I'll talk to her." Ashvan calmed her father with a touch. "I'll find out what she thinks about being at home early tomorrow!"

Taham nodded, walked toward his own apartment, which was in the corner of the garden, and at the same time, he looked at Zarvan.

"And you speak with people instead of shouting over girls. Tell them, we want to help everyone pay his tribute if he has problems paying, and…" Taham stood in front of him, stared into his eyes. "My own blood runs through my children's veins; PUT IT IN YOUR HEAD!" His voice was cold as ice.

71

Taham went, and darkness of the garden swallowed him. Zarvan was foaming at the mouth when he heard Taham advice. "I go home," Zarvan said.

Mahbod put his hand on Zarvan's shoulder in propitiation. "Can I come with you?" He asked.

Zarvan nodded and went to the door.

"I come too!" Nahira said, running toward them.

"He always blames others to cover for his own bad behavior!" Sheedvash muttered sullenly.

"Gods be damned." Ashvan gave her sister a long look, wondering. "Sheedvash, why did you make him angry? Sometimes you act like your young niece!"

"I'm just telling the truth!" Sheedvash said calmly.

"You see? You talk even like her!" Ashvan said.

Sheedvash gave her a dismissive shrug and turned, without suffering herself one look at her sister's face. She went with quick steps towards the mansion.

Ashvan sighed and got out.

*****

Her chamber was dark and cold when Mithra entered. She knelt and made a fire in the fireplace, to drive the chill from the room. She went to the window, opened the heavy velvet curtains and unlatching the wooden shutters. The wind came in, strong with the earthy smell after rain. She leaned against the sill for a breath of the cold evening air, her face hot with anger, her heart pumping. She tried to tell herself she did not care. She wanted to make herself feel better by saying it was up to him if he wanted to be a jerk, but a tear rolled down her cheek, ignoring her will.

She laid in her bed, but she did not sleep. The wind crawled into the chamber, and the flames swirled. Mithra pulled a necklace out of her shirt and dangled it from her face. She stared at it, a medallion that engraved a double-headed crow on it. In the dim light the rubies, the crow's eyes glowing like blood on the winged gold disc, precisely like the sign that she had seen on the Assyrians commander armor. She held up the necklace, turning it this way and that so the rubies caught the light.

It's funny, she thought bitterly, looking at it, the only reminder of her mother was the sign on her enemies' symbol, those who had killed her father. The necklace slipped through her fingers, fell on her chest. Her fingers moved slowly over her face, touched the birthmark lightly on her cheek, but suddenly she drew her hand back with a shake as if she had touched fire, "The sign of the evil!" She whispered. The people had named her, evil's goddess when she was six. A name fit for her, a gorgeous girl who has got the wild Assyrian blood in her veins, and was an ominous creature that has killed her mother birthing her, a mighty name for who had the sign of evil, inscribed on her face.

Mithra felt hot tears on her cheeks. There was nothing she could do to prove, she is a normal girl. Mithra wished she could escape this place, go somewhere, where people accepted her as she was!

*****

The sunlight had filled the entire room with a warm sensation, gold but pale. Into the fireplace, there was only ash now, and a few fragments of dead, charred wood. Through the opened window, the north mountain wind was blowing.

Mithra heard a faint hissing sound to her right; a hand touched her arm. She spun away, fast enough to grab her and clasped her hands in one of her. She heard a short gasp beside her and then a burst of loud laughter.

"Good heavens! Are you crazy?" Nahira said laughingly. "How could you sleep on your dirty cloth?"

"God damn you!" Mithra said grinding teeth. "I had told you; don't touch me." With a low groan, she sat up in bed, looking at Nahira with angry eyes. "What are you doing here?" She yawned and rubbed her eyes.

"Having lunch; you're welcome to share," Nahira said.

"You're not serious!" Mithra looked at her, wondering.

"I never thought you'd be able to sleep until noon!" Nahira said. "Aunty Sheedvash was worried about you."

"Worried? That's weird!" Mithra said with a grin.

"Not as weird as you think!" Nahira shrugged her shoulders. "She's your aunt, she loves you!"

Mithra stared at Nahira with her big, beautiful golden honey eyes. Her thick dark red hair tangled mess of curls around her neck. She managed a sad little smile.

Nahira could read the thoughts that hid behind her face. "My sullen friend be a little more optimistic, please!" She said. Nahira raised her hand to touch Mithra's face, but she turned her head to hide the birthmark on her face and covered it with her hair as always; Nahira dropped her hand.

"Your wounds … your wounds are swollen." Nahira gave her a look of reproach. "That was unwise…" She pointed Mithra's forehead. "Wiping the poultice off your forehead; I feared they not to be healing cleanly for your aunt's wedding ceremony!"

"What? Don't be silly; I won't be there," Mithra said, laughing with a mocking style.

"You should not make mock," Warned Nahira. "It's important for everyone in the family to have…"

"… but not for me?" Mithra's voice was icy quiet. "I am not important enough, am I?"

"You are as important as everybody in this family," Ashvan said, standing on the threshold, "How could you say something like that?" She entered and put a pack on the table.

"That's not what I have heard," Mithra said.

"Only fools love to hear that they are important," Ashvan said as she was sitting on the edge of the bed, "Others know that, they are important as long as they want!" She took Mithra's chin between her thumb and forefinger and turned her face towards herself. "For God's sake! Look at your face... Nahira, bring the jar of prepared poultice, wait... and some food; she's very pale," She said to Nahira.

Mithra took her aunt's wrist and brought it down slowly. "I have to go!" For a moment, Nahira hesitated.

"Hurry!" Ashvan said to her daughter, regardless of Mithra. Nahira left the room, and Ashvan continued. "Father has ordered to feed the cattle with hay, and I've also sent Mahbod to inspect the horses, so you have no excuse to go."

"I've imprisoned?" She said her face as still as stone.

"You don't feel your wounds' pain? Or you can't understand that we are worried about you?" Ashvan's voice was thick with coldness. "You have stopped feeling, you have stopped thinking, you have stopped being you, I mean you, not your own made sullen mask. You ran away without informing anyone."

"Who wants me?" Mithra barked. "Those people, who you speak about them, called me the devil's daughter."

"Who knows you? My father has hidden you after the people's words and you escape from them too. You must understand they are afraid and tried to protect themselves from devils, but you're not a devil, show them you are like them!" Ashvan said.

"But I'm not like them...," Mithra said under her breath.

"Why?" Ashvan asked, getting a bit frustrated.

"Because of the dire fate that overhangs me. Its sign was inscribed on my face!" Mithra said, swallowing a lump in her throat.

Ashvan had been overwhelmed by her words. "God! What do you say? No one knows the future!"

A tear rolled on Mithra's cheek, hot, bold and cruel.

Ashvan stared straight into her beautiful eyes. "Stop crying and don't cry from now on," she said. "God didn't create dire fate for anyone, but they make such a fate for themselves." Ashvan's fingers gently tuck her hair behind her ear. "This birthmark shows nothing!"

"I bring you food to break your fast," Nahira said as she returned with a plate of hot food from the kitchen.

Ashvan smiled. "Yes, she needs to eat," She agreed, smoothing her niece's brow. "Listen to me as you eat; you know, we will need to make a great wedding ceremony for your aunt…" Ashvan glanced at Mithra's frowning face and continued before she had a chance to say something. "I think it suits you," Ashvan said as she opened the package that she had brought and held the fabric up for her inspection.

Ashvan turned to Nahira who was sitting behind her. "What do you think, honey?" Ashvan asked.

"Wow, this is beautiful!" Nahira touched it, the soft cloth waved in her hand. "You are right mom! The midnight blue color will bring out the gold color in her eyes," she said.

"What do you want from me?" Mithra said, after a very long pause.

"You need to start trying things out," Ashvan spoke softly and stroked her cheek with the back of her fingers. "Don't hate people back because they may also become like you one day."

There was nothing Mithra could say to that.

CHAPTER FIVE

ASTYAGES

Ancient Land of Mannaeans, 628 BC, Autumn

The great room that had been neglected years looked impressive now. The designs of fruit and flowers were seen everywhere. The huge mahogany table took up most of the vast space the room offered, two tall, silver candelabras commanded attention from the center of the table, holding smooth white candles whose wax never dripped.

Ashvan was waiting in the dining room at the base of the stairs.

"A chapar[1] has come from uncle Zarvan," Mahbod said, "They are on the way home, along with the King Convoy. He says the King seems well pleased with his bride." He looked at his aunt excited. "I do hope the King stay in our mansion."

Ashvan smoothed down the cloth of her skirt nervously. She was dressed in white silk, bordered with pearls of the size of beans. "This wedding ceremony is just a demonstration for King," Ashvan said as she glanced at the second floor. "I have no doubt he stops one night in the tent and then continues his journey."

A servant approached. "The food, my lady," the servant told Ashvan.

---

[1] Is a term in Persian, meaning courier

When she did orders, she took the chance to glance nervously at the stairs again. Mahbod looked at his aunt curiously. "Everything is going to be all great. Just relax," he said.

"I hope so!" Ashvan said as she climbed the steps up.

She went slowly toward Mithra's bedchamber and opened the door. Mithra turned to her suddenly; she looked gorgeous in her ruby red dress! Ashvan stepped backward, throwing her hands up in acquiescence. It was the first time since childhood, Mithra had worn a dress. Taham didn't care about Mithra's boyish look, even he made her feel brave and tough like boys and conversation between Mithra and Sheedvash about it always turn to a fight. Gradually they got used to seeing her in the messy boys' clothing, but now Ashvan was seeing a beautiful princess in front of her.

The dress was floor length with a slightly longer in the back length. The deep blue color of the dress had a mind-blowing effect in combination with Mithra's tanned skin; the golden embroidery on the dress that Nahira had pinned had a beautiful arch on the chest that showed her firm young breasts for the first time. When she turned, her silk gown caught the light and glowed like a candle's flame.

Ashvan smiled in satisfaction. "You're so beautiful and lovely, even more than I thought."

Mithra was looking at her aunt in sullen silence. Ashvan did her best to ignore Mithra's knitted brows with dissatisfaction and went forward, took her silk bandanna but Mithra moved to the window and stared out into the garden. "There is no need for you to trouble yourself," Mithra glanced at her aunt impatiently. "Enjoy the feast. I'll join you when I'm ready," she said.

Ashvan put aside the bandanna slowly, hesitated, then nodded. "Whenever you're ready…," she said uncertainly. "You have no need to worry about it."

Mithra's backward glance caught Ashvan's expectant look, just before the door closed.

Mithra turned her face to the window immediately. "No need to worry!" She whispered, smiled a bitter smile.

Mithra knew there was many people, sat downstairs and she could hear their voice. She felt uncomfortable in her outfit and became more perturbed by the idea of walking into the room full of people. Mithra was just a child when she started to notice that she was different. She noticed the people did a double take to look at her or take a different route. The playground was a horrifying experience for her; always mothers came and kept their kids away from her. Mithra soon learned to lower her head and pushing her hair on her cheek, she got used to hiding herself from the people sight.

"They may also become like you one day." Her aunt's voice echoed in her head. She sighed, got up and grabbed the bandanna. She stood in front of the mirror, a long time, and finally decided. She tied it around her hair, fastening at the back of her neck. It did keep the hair out of her face for the first time.

She heard the sound of a bark of laughter, dared to peek out of the window. A group of girls and boys was gathered together on the corner of the garden, laughing every once in a while. A shiver of fear went through her. *I can't!* Mithra thought. She leaned against the wall and closed her eyes, for her who didn't seem afraid of the cult's tough challenges, worries about the going amongst guests were so extreme that had made her feel sick to her stomach. She put her hands over her mouth, her palms were slick with sweat.

"Are you all right?"

Mithra opened her eyes. Nahira came forward and hugged her, but Mithra wrenched herself out of her arms quickly.

"I don't know seriously why you liked to hug me constantly!" Mithra said as she straightened. "I'm all right, just… just this stupid gown makes me choke." She glanced at Nahira. She looked happy, dressed in sky-blue silk and silver bracelets on her wrists.

Nahira chuckled. "Don't tell this to my mom; I know she will be mad at you," she said.

Mithra nodded, stole a glance at the window.

"They are not fearsome creatures!" Nahira said.

"What?" Mithra made herself smile, pretending she was calm, but her eyes held worry that she could not hide.

"What are you afraid of?" Nahira asked.

"Get off my back!" Mithra growled.

Nahira sat on the edge of the bed. "I'm serious!" She stared at Mithra. "You are so beautiful," She announced with admiration. "If I were as beautiful as you, my life would be so much lovelier. I have always been jealous of your beauty. Your big honey eyes, golden skin, and…"

"And a birthmark like a human skull, you loved it too, huh?" Mithra said coldly.

Nahira's smile faded on her lips.

Mithra sat by the fireplace staring at the cold ashes. "I am sick of hearing about these!"

"Well!" Nahira stood beside the door. "It is not my intent to linger here long. I just wanted to say the people who are outside are human, like you, and you can't expect others to believe it when you don't believe!" She opened the door. "You can come anytime you want; the bride not home yet."

"Where is she?" Mithra raised her head suddenly and asked in a changed voice by wonder.

"Nobody knows." Nahira shrugged her shoulders. "I think you have got your aunt's craziness!" Nahira disappeared out the door before Mithra could say nothing.

Where is Sheedvash? Mithra thought, but the voices from the garden got her attention again. She looked out the window; her mind's storm was more significant than she could be concerned about her aunt. Mithra took a deep breath and went out.

The garden was crowded, the servants came and went, and the guests were talking and laughing loudly. Mithra just needed to pass fifteen steps through the corridor, and then she would go outside of White Mansion. She stood at the top of the stair that led to the garden. She felt a cold breeze on her face. The mansion's garden had worn a beautiful autumn dress. The crisp copper leaves falling off the trees that sway gently in the autumn wind, yet there were still big red roses on the large bushes around the garden, and the lakeside air was pungent with the fragrance of salt and red roses. The clouds overlap each other, making the sky a gloomy gray.

Even at this hour, the garden was ablaze with light. Lanterns swung from iron chains above the tables of flowers and fruits. In different places, the night fires burned on red stones to obtain pleasurable warm glow such as the guests can well enjoy, who had gathered around the flames.

Mithra closed her eyes for a moment. "I must climb down!" She whispered and crept down the stairs.

"I can't believe my eyes, is it you, Mithra?"

Mithra knew the voice. She looked at her brother. He had stood smilingly beside his friends, young boys, and girls who had gathered underneath a beautiful pergola covered with ivy leaves that gave the spectacular autumn color of gold through to deepest orange. She could feel them all watching her, her trembling fingers pushed her hair on her cheek unconsciously.

She swallowed and tried to put a smile on her dry lips. No one said anything; she did not know what should do so grabbed a wine cup from a passing servant with a silver tray, sipped, hoping it might calm her nerves.

"Your sister is here. …very funny, we had forgotten you even had a sibling!" A tall boy, Mahbod's best friend said as he was looking at Mithra.

Mahbod grinned. "Me too!"

A beautiful girl with cinnamon hair, dressed in a gown of white satin with the orange dahlias that made her look like an expensive doll, looked at Mithra, disgusted. "Because she doesn't look like a girl!" Said the girl in a Mannaean aristocracy accent and a fat girl, covered in a fluffy velvet dress laughed.

"Are you joking?! She's a beautiful woman, she looks like a goddess!!" A young man said as he was looking at Mithra with his keen black eyes. His waistcoat has opened in front of his embroidered shirt and showed off his athletic body. His clothes showed he has come from another city. "Hey, Sina what do you think of her, then?" The young man asked his friend.

"She is indeed a beauty, an incomparable beauty. No doubt!" The shorter brown haired boy said.

"If she is a goddess so Mahbod would be a handsome god!!" A thin girl said, almost leaning on Mahbod, looking at him with coquetry.

Mithra knew her; she was from a family of aristocratic and fantastically wealthy merchants.

"A god with some special supernatural abilities!!" Said Mahbod with one of his wicked smiles. His teeth were white, his lips full and dark.

"Prove me now!" The girl whispered in Mahbod's ear, catching his sleeve with the fingers.

The bangles danced on her arm like the hoops of a magician, her gown blew about her feet as she went out the pergola. Mahbod followed her up the gravel path, enchanted with the vibration of her big breasts under her purple silk dress.

Mithra looked around apprehensively, vaguely hoping that Nahira was not around.

"What about you?" The stranger boy said.

His voice drew Mithra's attention to him; his leering eyes were fixed on her.

The stranger boy laughed. "I wonder if you have some special hidden power, Goddess!" The boy said with a silky voice.

Mithra raised her eyebrows, a cold gleam in her eyes. She did not look pleased. "Nothing you like to know," she said dryly.

"I love to know everything about the goddess!" He laughed, and his friend started laughing too.

"Don't mess with her, Kavan," the beautiful cinnamon hair girl said; her eyes lingered on Mithra, and she put a wicked smile on her small and rosy lips. "She might call down demons to devour you!"

Kavan glanced at her. "Stop fooling about!"

"I'm serious!" The cinnamon hair girl looked at her fat friend. "The boys see only what they desire," she said smiling.

The fat girl laughed again, and Mithra's fingers clenched tightly around her wine cup.

"Shima, you're jealous because she is prettier than you. You are beautiful but ... her beauty is beyond yours!" The boy said.

"You're right!" Shima said as she was stepping forward. "That's what makes me so damn jealous,"

Mithra was staring at her with angry eyes.

"She is different!" Shima said, regardless of Mithra's burning eyes. "No girl has her olive bronze skin, beautiful honey eyes and ..." Shima stood beside Mithra. "And the sign of evil on her face!" Shima said as she pulled aside Mithra's hair.

Mithra heard the fat girl laughing, louder than before, saw the boy's haunted face and Shima's jeering smile; for an instant, she felt dizzy. The glass slipped out of her hand falling to the ground and shattering loudly onto the floor, spilling the red wine over the white stone. Then, so faintly, it seemed as if she heard thousands of Ravens' caw. Mithra could not control herself, quickly grasped Shima's neck; her face almost clinging to Shima; a face dark as gathering storm clouds.

"That bastard boy is not the only one who must not test me," Mithra said, through her clenched teeth. "You have only heard your old Nanny's scary stories of the beasts, something that made no sense to you but there's still a chance you feel them free!" Mithra gave a wry laugh. "You'll see I am too scared to hate."

Shima tried to cry out, but Mithra's fingers dug deep into her neck, choking off her protests.

"She kills her!" The fat girl gasped.

The boys were frozen with fear.

She would have the face of a goddess but... her dangerous, sinister eyes... the boy thought.

The fat girl's screams drew everyone's attention.

"Make her stop!" A middle-aged woman, who seemed drowned in silk and Jewelry shouted.

Mithra looked at her, she recognized Shima's mother. Soon after that Ashvan appeared in front of the crowd, her eyes wide, her face contorted with shock. Mithra released Shima's neck and stepped back, trembling with icy cold waves spreading through her body. Shima fell to her knees, gasping and coughing. Her mother ran to hug her. "You devil, go away from us!" Her mother yelled.

"How dare you say something like that about the paramount of the tribe's granddaughter?" Ashvan said, her voice was quiet and cold.

"Are you so blind, or is it that you do not wish to see?" The middle-aged woman roared, hysterical with fear. "She nearly killed my daughter!"

Ashvan's mouth twisted in disgust. "You've completely misjudged her." She looked at Mithra. "She could explain..."

Mithra wanted to speak but her throat was so dry, she could do no more than a grunt. Above a tree, a crow muttered. She glanced at it. She needed to make an escape.

"Mithra…"

She ignored her aunt, turned and ran hurryingly before Ashvan had a chance to oppose her. It took only a few moments to fight her way through the crowd.

"Mithra wait!" Nahira shouted behind her.

The tears came unbidden to Mithra's eyes; she heard the blood pumping in her ears. She ran as fast as she could toward stable, her head spinning, but there was one clear thought in her mind, she just had to go away, the only way to get off that horrible mess.

Mahbod and the thin girl were in a dark corner of the garden, near the large stalls. Mithra saw Mahbod bending over the girl and talking; heard the girl's moaning and Mahbod's soft chuckle. Mithra felt a sudden rage at the girl, her perfect, spotless face, and her normal womanhood. She passed them, paid no attention to the girl's frightened scream and Mahbod's angry eyes and went into the stable. She opened Morvarid's halter and jumped on it without putting the saddle.

She was riding without a destination. Morvarid was galloping at a higher rate of speed than she could race, but Mithra spurred her horse again. The rode bent along the mountain, and the city was lost to sight behind her soon. "I never come back," Mithra swore to herself, sobbing. "I want to be far away from everyone, from their fearful tales and their black hearts. I never come back…," she shouted, into the wind.

All these comings and goings in her mind and she was galloping as fast as she could against the wind, but suddenly a man appeared in front of her, covered in a plain black cloak on a black horse. The horses faced each other head-on, both reared up on their legs, blind with fear.

"Damn…!"

The man's shout faded in the horses' nicker before he fell down.

Mithra bent over and clasped her horse's neck. Her bandanna fell on the ground and her long wavy red-brown hair curtaining her face. She was hearing a lot of uproar around her, seeing from the corner of her eye the men that were rushing toward her but she could not leave her horse neck. She was trying to calm Morvarid down, but the horse was too excited to be calm easily. Mithra clung more tightly to her neck, whispering in her ear.

"Under the command of the king, unmoved!!" A young commander yelled.

"Would if I could!" Mithra said through tight teeth.

She swallowed and then began to sing the song that she had taught from her nanny and always sang for Morvarid. It seemed ridiculous, but she had no other choice. Only a few moments later Morvarid was quiet, standing and sometimes pawing. It appeared the men also had been calm by her voice and she did not hear the shouting anymore. Mithra raised her head up and looked around. A dozen Imperial spearmen had surrounded her, their round shields gleaming in the sun.

"What are you waiting for? Drag her off the horse!" A man who had fallen shouted.

Mithra looked at the man. He was scrawny and short, even seemed smaller beside the stout Imperial soldiers.

"Mithra!" Zarvan's familiar voice rang out. He was looking at her with widening eyes "What're you doing here?"

"Damn!!" Mithra mumbled when she found herself in front of the king, his convey and a group of elders of the city, who had gone to greet the King.

Some of the soldiers rushed up to arrest Mithra.

"Just leave her be!" A voice commanded, and the king came out from his nobility and jeweled chariot. Cyaxares was forty-eight years; he had some gray hairs around the temples, but he still seemed young and handsome. Unlike, as usual, he had worn like his soldiers, a red shirt, red breeches and a cape of tiger skin. He stepped forward.

"She is just a young woman, don't you see?" The king growled.

The soldiers dispersed, hurried to obey the command that the king had given to them.

"You looked so scared Lord Commander," the king said to the fallen man. "Like you've never fallen off the horse!" King smirked.

The man seemed irritated. "I am not here for myself Your Majesty, but to guard the king's life!" He said.

"It's your job... I know...," the king went on, "... but you don't really think that a little lady can kill your king, isn't it?" The king raised both hands. "I have a weakness for the beautiful women, I confess; but they can't kill me!" Said the king, laughing.

Every man fell in laughing but Saber, the fallen man, who had a cold smile on his lips.

The king studied Mithra, carefully with his eyes. "Might I know your name, Lady?"

Mithra was staring at him, frowning. Every conversation about her always made her feel profoundly uneasy.

"Her name is Mithra, Your Majesty." Zarvan knew Mithra well, and he was worried about her reaction so said hastily. "She is Armaz's daughter, our tribe's chief commander in the Assyrian's battle."

That took the king by surprise; the king narrowed his eyes and stared at Mithra "Yes, I remember that brave man," he said, "... and I know he loved your mother with all his heart, the sweetest love story that I've ever heard."

Her dark red, curly hair had framed her face in wild disarray, her bright honey eyes glazed with pride at the king. Mithra even did not bow before the king. *Assyrians arrogance and Mannaean disobedience, an unpleasant mix*, thought the king. Maybe he could bear pride, but he would lose his nerve before disobedience. The king made himself to smile, but he knew that he would not like this girl.

"Young girls are supposed to be eager to attend the wedding ceremonies, especially if they were as beautiful as you, what are you doing here?" The king asked.

"Mithra's nanny lives in the mountains, all alone; Mithra regularly goes to visit her," Zarvan said instead of Mithra, hurryingly.

Imperial guard's golden shield had dazzled Zarvan with reflected sunlight, and he made a great effort to look respectfully at the king. The king looked at him, wondering how the paramount of the tribe's proud family could bear this liar, flattering man.

Mithra saw the smallest hint of a smile playing around the king's lips, but Zarvan did not notice.

"Good," the king nodded and turned to Mithra. "But you should join the throng of girls around the bride; absence of one of the most beautiful girls of Mannea would ruin her fun." He pointed his finger at her. "Maybe the bride could forgive your absence, but I won't!" The king said, and then smiled. "I'm kidding but don't be late!"

The king entered the chariot, motioned for the caravan to move. "Please Lord Commander, lead us and guard us!" The king said laughingly.

"I am yours to command," Saber said with a sullen face as he mounted on a stallion as black as his cloak.

Mithra could see the hard glitter in his eyes as he stared at her. She bent her head slightly to respect to the king but still, her arrogant eyes were bothering the king. The king's chariot, his soldiers, slaves, and entourages passed. Mithra was looking at them, caressing her horse, at the end of the caravan, she saw from the corner of her eye, a figure, riding down the path, on a stout chestnut mare. Mithra raised her head up.

The young man's coal black eyes were fixed on her; Mithra's ice looking eyes melted with his glare on her, like the heat of the blistering sun and showed a slow smile that attractively twisted his lips. The man's lips were pale and thin and his nose slender. He was robust and tall and heavily built like the king's soldiers. She guessed he was a native of Ecbatana[1], undoubtedly one of the courtiers.

He stood in front of her. "It's a good horse...," he said as he was caressing Morvarid's forehead, "... and she has an excellent rider, so strong, so experienced and ... so pretty!!"

Mithra blushed, not sure what to do with his compliment. She felt a heat within herself like a flame that been lit inside her, growing in intensity; a strange feeling, so soft, so warm and too unfamiliar that frightened her. Mithra put spurs to her horse and rushed hastily. She used to escape from whatever was strange for her.

The young man followed Mithra with his eyes, as far as he could see her. He got down from his horse, picked Mithra's silver bandanna off the ground and went slowly toward the convoy.

*****

The king knew the art of oratory.

All men were enamored of his words and listened in fascination. The king was unbeatable in strategic politics, as well as oratory. He had never attended any member of his family's wedding, but this time was different. The king needed a strong army, strong enough for any tribe or nation to watch out.

Atropatene[2] tribes were the wealthiest and most powerful tribes. The southern and northern shores of Chichest Lake were critical economic centers. On the mountain, below the permanent snow line, many vines, fig trees, and pomegranates grew, and long grass in the fields generously feed the herd. The tribes' boys were strong and skilled in the art of riding; they could make the king's armies, to become the men of war. In this way, the people were pleased to provide all the army's needs. The king knew that this trip, this wedding, and this meeting led to valuable results.

---

[1] Was an ancient city in Media in western Iran

[2] Atropatena state was formed in 323 BC. Atropatena lands were within of Ahemenids (Haxamenesi) state borders.

The Great Hall of Taham's mansion was hazy with smoke and heavy with the smell of roasted Kabab and fresh-baked bread. The leaders of Atropatene's eight tribes and their sons were sitting in Taham's colossal guest room. The king was seated as a usual guest, speaking about unity, a strong army and the war tactics and tools, which could make the Median army strong and invincible. All the men were listening to the king eagerly even Taham who believed the former king and his unwise war was liable for the killing of his son and his wife. The king's speech was thick but easy enough to understand. Astyages, an attractive young man, who was always beside the king, conveyed the essence of his remarks, more attractive. He talked about the current situation of the Assyrians.

After many the bread riots in the Assyrians territory, the Assyrian king had to send large numbers of the troops to different parts of his vast country. The Assyrian commanders and warriors were involved in the civil wars, and hence they were not recognized as the greatest army in the world like earlier. On the other hand, after the death of the great king, his youngest son had been proclaimed king of Assyria but Sinshar, the king's eldest son, could not accept his younger brother as a king! After one year, two brothers were still fighting over the throne. Assyria was sleeping on a bed of insecurity and chaos.

Astyages was speaking fluently and eloquently, looking at the tribal elder's face frequently. He knew words were important; his words had been selected with a view to being understood and acceptable to the listeners. He had an attractive face and dark black eyes, shining with intelligence. He was very young, but he spoke very maturely and intelligent so even the elders were also affected by his speech. Unlike the Atropatene men, he had shaved his beard and had long black curly hair, but he wore like them: white silk shirt, high black boots, a black wool cloak, another trick to attract the attention of the eight Atropatene elders.

"The Assyrian government now is very different from previous years," Astyages said. "We can defeat them if we are cautious." He swallowed another gulp of wine, and the sweet, fruity taste of Mannea's vineyards wine filled his mouth. "Even, a prophet who the Assyrians believe him has predicted the Assyrians defeating." He glanced at Saber, who had stared at Silk Carpet underneath his sandals. "Of course, Lord Commander is much more aware of Assyrian's history and books."

Saber was listening to his words with a mocking smile; his plate was full of food, and he did not eat even a bit. He raised his head.

"I am aware of that, Senior Commander..." Saber made his small eyes tighter as he looked at Astyages and his mocking smile showed a slightly of his tiny teeth. "The name of THAT prophet is Saai, a great man." He reminded Astyages with more than a touch of irritation. "The Assyrians are not the only who believe him. I know him too well to believe him!!"

"It's great; so we make your favorite prophet's dream come true!!" Astyages said with a sardonic smile.

"We need strong ethnic unity, more than ever," the king said. "The future will be marked by glory if you join with the Median kingdom," He raised his goblet.

Cheers filled the room. "King Cyaxares!"

The King smiled, and the musicians began to play music for the King. Nobody noticed Saber's going but Astyages, who moved along behind him like a shadow.

*****

The wind was blowing, swirling and gusting and beneath the window. The slender branches of a cherry tree, bare and brown, were shivering violently. Nany was singing to her, stroking her hair, and comforting her.

Mithra loved her more than everything in the world. Unlike others, Nany would not blame her, whatever she did. She might advise but would not require her to do anything. Every time Mithra ran into trouble, Nanny just was hugging her tight, letting her buried her face against her chest and hide her tears.

"You should return!" Nany said. She had a strange accent, in additional, the corners of her burned lips were stuck together and made her talking stranger.

Mithra was feeling much better, and her mind's tempest had subsided. She was grateful for Zarvan's reminding; she had forgotten that she could fly for refuge to her nanny's bosom. She knew she needed to get back home, but with passing every minute, it had become more difficult.

"It's not late, besides I can stay with you tonight!" Mithra said, turning away from the window.

Nanny smiled up at her and kissed her hair, her lips lingered, smelling Mithra's hair. "I have promised. You can't stay with me baby!" She said.

Mithra sighed. She was aware of Nanny's promise to her grandfather: Mithra could never stay with her nanny.

*****

It was past midnight.

The blackness of the night had swallowed everything. The path in the garden was lit with thousands of delicate flames, each no bigger than a fist. These candles had made of beeswax with a cotton wick, an expensive product that lasts for hours. It was windy, and the flames were flickering rapidly. The candles were bright enough to relieve the darkness of the garden, but not bright enough to show the mansion.

Mithra stared up hard. It looked like the ceremony was over, but she was not sure yet. She went further, turned around, hesitated, then started to climb up a walnut tree beneath the dining room's window on the second floor. She could see no sign of anyone having been in there. All she had to do was climb the tree and crept into the room through the open window. *It's a night like every other night when I came home late!* Mithra thought, trying to comfort herself.

She jumped from the tree and grabbed the edge of the sill like every time, but she had forgotten that she had never worn a long skirt ever.

Her dress got stuck on a branch. She was hanging out of the sill with one hand so with the other, grabbed her skirt, trying to make herself free but her dress tucked in between the branches more than before. She was dangling in the air, one fist desperately clinging to the ruffle of her dress.

"Damn this stupid fucking dress," Mithra said, gritting her teeth.

"Who would be believed? Ladies are not expected to be hard-mouthed!" A voice said.

Mithra spun, terrified that somebody of her family had found him. He was the young man who she had seen him along the convoy of the King. He had leaned against the wall, laughing. Mithra felt the soft warmth wave within again, but this feeling faded very soon, gave its place to angry. She did not want to be seen by anyone, getting into such a ridiculous situation.

"What are you doing there?" Astyages said, laughingly.

"What the hell are you doing there?" Mithra asked angrily.

"I'm here because you need help!" Astyages said.

"It's none of your business!! Now go away," Mithra said as she was struggling to make free herself.

"You're right; your family finds you next morning for sure!" Astyages said, going on.

Mithra hesitated. "Wait!!" She said.

Astyages stopped immediately, looked at her carefully.

"Help me!" Mithra said firmly.

"Why? You said I should go!" Astyages asked.

"NOW I say help me!" Mithra replied angrily.

"I am sorry Lady, but I am bound to obey only from the Lord Commander, I have the king stamped ruling!!" Astyages said calmly and turned to go.

"Wait!" Mithra snarled, more than before.

Astyages looked at her, waiting in silence.

"Help me!" Mithra said again.

"Why?" Astyages asked again.

"Please!" Mithra said through gritted teeth.

"It would be my pleasure, my Lady," said Astyages with a triumphant smile. "I enjoy helping LITTLE Ladies!"

Astyages heard the chewed words coming from the top of the tree, but it seemed Mithra's intense anger was entertaining for him. He climbed up on the tree and sat on one of the branches, then he raised his hand, but did not move or release her skirt instead caressed her skirt fabric.

"It's beautiful; so smooth that it seemed to run through fingers like a river!" Astyages said, staring at her eyes. "And the color has brought out your lovable unimpaired spirit in your eyes!!" His eyes locked with hers. She could feel him caressing her body with his mind, but she would not allow her body to be lured by him, so she only stayed there awkwardly not knowing what to do.

"What are you waiting for?" Mithra said firmly, trying to hide her feeling.

He grinned; suddenly he did not look serious anymore. "Nothing," Astyages said. "Just, if you don't like to meet anyone, stay outside because a small crowd of the women had gathered in the small hall to visit the bride."

Mithra looked at him, her face dull with suspicion. "How do you know?" She asked.

Astyages shrugged. "Everyone knows it; of course except the fugitives," he said as he released her skirt, then he raised his hand to help her, glancing at Mithra, who stared at him, her honey eyes looked uncertain, but finally, she put her hand on his. They came down together then Mithra past Astyages, stepped rapidly straight to the garden, without glancing at him.

"Where are you going?" Astyages asked, but Mithra was going too fast! "Would you like to know the name of your savior?" He asked. Mithra kept going to the stables, muttering angrily; she threw out pebbles with the toe. Astyages was following behind her like a tamed bird regardless of her anger. "Hey, I've saved you; you can't leave me alone, it's not fair," he said.

Mithra glanced at him with a sullen face as she opened the old stable's door.

"Come on, It's a beautiful night, stars shine ... oh sorry, no star, by the way, it's very romantic ...," Astyages said.

The stable's door closed heavily against him before Astyages could finish his words. A smile danced across his face, stepped backward without taking his eyes off the door. A cold wind came swirling through; he wrapped himself in his cloak more and went towards the exit door. He had to go to the king's tent. There were many words to say.

*****

Next morning, the sound of the door opening waked up Mithra. She was asleep over a mass of hay; her legs were stiff as wood, and her body twitched.

"Are you crazy girl, what are you doing here?" Nahira said, kneeling beside her. "If one of the king's gourds didn't hear Morvarid's sound inside the old stable I never supposed you are here."

"I came late last night," Mithra said, rubbing her eyes. "The women were in our house, so I had to sleep here."

"Where? You just had a bad dream, honey. No one was in White Mention last night," Nahira said.

"What? No one...," Mithra said, shocked.

"No one... unless you have seen ghosts," Nahira said.

Mithra looked at her in shock. "I'll put you in so much fucking pain that you'll forget joking, stupid damn guy!" She mumbled angrily.

"Ouch!" Nahira's mouth was twisted in disgust. "I don't know whom you meant, but a lady should not talk that way!" She said.

"Don't fuck with me Nahira!" Mithra said, hot fury boiling into her eyes.

"All right," Nahira grumbled. "See my mother; she was worried about you more than words could say."

Mithra moved her fingers through her messy hair, trying to tame it into some semblance of order. It seemed Nahira's words could not turn her attention toward Nahira.

"We were lucky that my father had seen you on the road. Oh! My father said about Saber!" Nahira remembered laughingly. "That proud man falling off horse has been truly funny."

"Where are they?" Mithra said.

"I don't know; they should be in the king's tent! There was a camp for them, but grandpa would give them a source of supply and a secure base so they could teach our boys the war arts…"

"I meant where my family is… my aunt?" Mithra mumbled angrily.

For a long moment, the only sound was Nahira's laughing. "The King's special chef is with him, along with many kitchen servants but the King has preferred to eat Mannea's local food. He is fantastic…"

"Where is my aunt?" Mithra said again, seemed frustrated.

Nahira made a face. "If you allow, I would say that mom is in the kitchen. She keeps an eye on chefs, and of course, she is furious, besides you, aunt Sheedvash escapes for every occasion. My mother is like a bear with a sore head."

Mithra stood up, slapping the dust off her clothes. "Don't tell anyone that you have seen me. I'll change my clothes and go out for a while," she said as she was going to the door.

"It is impossible! Mom kills me; besides, some of the guests are in the garden, and she would know you have returned soon enough," Nahira said angrily.

Mithra opened the door, frustrated and angry. "Got it, don't matter," she said and stepped into the garden.

She had just taken a few steps out of the old stable then she saw Astyages, talking to a group of boys, who were listening to his speech with fascination. Astyages bowed his head as he was smiling insidiously. Mithra's angry eyes meet him only for a moment. She had a strange feeling, something between joy and anger like when you love swimming, but you prefer to put your feet down on something substantial.

She went to her room hurryingly and changed her clothes, but before she could leave, in the doorway she faced with Ashvan and Nahira, who was behind her mother.

"You want to leave out quietly without saying goodbye, how nice!!" Ashvan growled.

Mithra did not see herself as worthy of blame. She stood straight and stared into her aunt's eyes oblivious to her aunt taunting.

Ashvan frowned at her, "I want to know, why you escaped from your house like thieves?" She asked.

"It is better to ask your guests," Mithra said resentfully, with angry looks.

"That would not be necessary, I know them very well." Ashvan was in a sullen mood, angry that had been forced to say her words even when she saw that Mithra's mouth trembled. "You escaped before an unworthy wordy duel, how weak you are!"

"I'm not weak," Mithra yelled furiously. "I would walk over her, but you didn't let me!"

"How did you do that?" Ashvan asked as she shot her a sharp look. "You foolish girl, you almost killed her, one of these people, your people!"

"They're people I hate. I want them to die," Mithra said then she wanted to pass her aunt quickly, but a slap in her face stopped her.

"Mom," Nahira shouted as she rushed to Mithra.

Mithra, her hand on cheek, was looking surprisingly at her aunt; she had never seen her so much anger. Ashvan's white skin had turned red, taking sharp breaths.

"Never again… never again don't say that," Ashvan said in a meek voice, though she was too angry. "Your people are your roots; you can't hate the roots of a tree and not hate the tree!"

Mithra turned to go, but at the last moment, Ashvan took her wrist.

"If you want to be enlightened begin by giving light to someone who has less than you because at that very moment someone else who has more light than you will give you his. This is a law, little lady!" Ashvan said.

Mithra wrenched herself free. Nahira was crying, Ashvan and Mithra shouldered in opposite directions and eyed each other dubiously as Mithra passed, but no one said a word.

Out of her room, everything was normal. Mithra walked toward the exit door through the corridor with firm steps, trying to hide the tears that blurred her vision but unbidden tears in her eyes rush down her face. She speeded up and when she reached out of the massive bronze door found a burst of running. She ran until she felt her lungs would burst. She kneeled down, panting. She heard a crack, on a low branch a crow had sat, its feathers ruffled up against the cold. Mithra's fingers forcing themselves between stones, she grabbed one, "Go to heeeeell!" She yelled as she threw it at the crow.

The bird flew a little farther off, and she burst into tears. "Damn you and my fate!" She said between sobs.

She did not know where to go; she just wanted to be alone, so she walked to the river. The river passed through the jungle. The gentle murmur of the water was the only sound that could be heard. The water was so clear that you could see the smoothness of the rocks underneath. She cupped her hands, took a draft of the water. She found it icy cold but her flushed and swollen from crying face needed it.

On the edge of the river was an old tree. Its leafless branches were bent on water built a couch on top of the water. Mithra went, sat on the branches and took her head between her hands.

"I didn't know here is a possible refuge for you... like me!"

Mithra had no need to turn; she knew Sheedvash's voice so well.

"Go home; everyone is looking for the bride!" Mithra said dryly, staring into the water.

Sheedvash stepped forward slowly and sat beside her. "This wedding ceremony doesn't need a bride!" She said.

Mithra realized that her aunt's voice scratched by heavy crying, but the last thing in the world she wanted was to talk with her aunt, so she preferred to keep silent. Unlike her, Sheedvash seemed to prefer to spend her time in Mithra's company.

"Today I couldn't stop thinking about you; I'd like to speak to you alone!" Sheedvash said. "It is interesting that you came to me."

Mithra did not know why Sheedvash was thinking about her or why she wanted to see her alone, it was impossible she could feel interested in such a conversation.

"I've come here for nothing, don't take yourself so seriously!" Mithra was irritated.

"I had not been kind to you, I know you didn't come to me consciously." Sheedvash smiled a sad smile. "I know that, very well," she said as if she muttered to herself. "This river has a special name; do you know?"

Mithra knew where she was but said nothing.

"The River of Love," Sheedvash said softly, no wait for Mithra's answer. "Many lovers come here to meet each other, secretly," she grinned. "Here is very romantic, quiet and beautiful, just lovers' kind of place," she hesitated for a few moments, "... but for seventeen years this has been the River of Sorrow for me."

Sheedvash's speech interrupted with flowing tears on her cheeks. Mithra did not know what to do or say. She had not ever been able to love Sheedvash; her aunt has a too bitter tongue, and Mithra was too headstrong. She had no words to comfort her aunt.

"Do you come here often?" Sheedvash asked with a shivering voice.

"No," Mithra answered shortly.

"I've always loved the tranquility of this place and enjoyed the sound of water. The leaves of this tree built a cool and beautiful shade in summers," Sheedvash said as she was caressing kindly the tree's trunk. "I felt in love here when I was your age." She seemed lost in thoughts. "He was one of my father's workers; a simple and poor man. Sometimes I asked myself, why do I love Behbood, and each time I saw him when I found him so much kind, honest and loyal, I noticed he is the only one that I could love forever.

My father had only one condition for our marriage; he said Behbood didn't need to have properties, he didn't need to give me expensive gifts, but if Behbood loves me, he must have the courage to love. My father said Behbood should love me more than himself, as much as he can able to sacrifice himself. Behbood peeked over at me shyly and said, 'I love her more than anything else in this world, my Lord, and I am ready to sacrifice my life for the good of Sheedvash,' he said to my father.

We got married... only one month later the war went on, everywhere. You know this part of the story; the Assyrians attacked Mannea. We had to leave Diheh and took refuge on the mountain. Everyone was frightened but your mother much more than the others. She could barely walk; her big and heavy belly didn't let her move quickly. We were ready to leave, but suddenly we saw a few Assyrian soldiers who were coming toward our mansion. We had hidden beneath the bushes; your mother couldn't stay moveless. The soldiers had taken everything which they thought was worthy; it seemed they wanted to go, but at the last moment one of them turned to us.

I never knew he saw us or not but your mother was so much frightened, her eyes grew wide. Everything happened in just a few minutes. She stood, said something in a language that we did not know; her voice was trembling but her attitude was like a queen who commands to her soldiers, that was her foolish, arrogant behavior.

I grabbed her wrist, but I couldn't stop her. 'Wait, wait,' she said to me. I caught her arm, following Behbood who was running to our cart and dragging her after me. 'Hold on, they won't do anything to us!' She cried. The soldiers were coming to us, and we had no more time. We began to run. They were following us, so close. We reached our cart. Behbood helped Amitira to climb the horse up and then put me on the saddle. He looked at me. 'Don't stop before get to a safe place,' he said.

I read his decision from his eyes. I screamed. I begged. He slapped the horse hard, and the horse galloped quickly away. I saw my husband, fighting, very clumsy but so bravely. I didn't cry. I just looked at him until the last moment that I could. I wanted this picture to never disappear from my mind."

Mithra had put her head down. She did not want to see the grief on her aunt's face. She felt ashamed without fault. Sheedvash wiped her tears with the back of her hand and stood up.

"Your mother killed my husband and took my chance to live a normal life," Sheedvash said with an icy cold voice. She took a long sigh. "Forgive me! I know that I was not a good aunt to you but… you look like your mother so much. Every time you look at me I remember Amitira and her beautiful, proud eyes; even if I had another chance, I could not behave better than that." Sheedvash strolled toward Diheh.

"Don't marry the person you think you can't love with!" Mithra shouted behind Sheedvash.

Sheedvash looked at her; smiled a sad and colorless smile.

"We need this marriage to be united and established a strong government: Government of Ecbatana. This wedding ceremony is not because of me; it's for this land and people," Sheedvash said.

CHAPTER SIX

BETRAYAL

Ancient Land of Mannaeans, 628 BC, Winter

More than one month had passed since Sheedvash had gone. Sometimes Mithra found herself surprisingly missing her aunt but at least in some ways, she had more freedom now. Grandpa was always in his own apartment at the end of the garden and Mahbod was in the house rarely. If aunt Ashvan and her family did not come to visit them, they did not see each other for weeks.

After the words that had passed between them and the king at their last meeting, Zarvan always was talking about why they need to build up a strong army to war. Mithra was surprised how he had forgotten that he became angry when Mithra was talking about war. Mahbod would have welcomed to this conversation every time, but others preferred to be far from them and their loud conversation.

The sunshine cascaded through the naked branches of the winter trees, dancing on the forest ground and made a brilliant, glossy rug.

Nearby a bird sang, the sweet tumble of notes. The winter wind howled through the woods and bit at her flushed skin. Her breath rose in visible puffs to join the thick fog surrounding.

Mithra lifted her ax high over her head to cut the woods. There was a frosty chill in the air, but she had worn nothing but a white silk blouse. Her body was wet with sweat, and her shirt had stuck on her body, showing her firm breasts. A droplet of sweat ran down her elegant neck, and she brought the ax down hard.

She raised her ax again, but she heard a sound, Morvarid also was sniffing and pawing. She held the ax with both hands firmly, ready to attack. She held her breath and lifted her head, sharpening her hearing… another sound, nearer and behind her. She immediately raised the ax on the head, turned and lunged towards him but suddenly noticed Astyages in front of her.

Astyages took a few steps back in horror. "Hey, hey, look out!" He said.

Mithra threw the ax down. "God damn you! What are you doing here? I was nearly killing you!" She shouted angrily.

Astyages laughed hard. "It's not easy to kill me baby; although your beauty truly is a killer!" Astyages said.

She noticed his gaze fell to her breast; she turned to her leather satchel and grabbed her coat. She threw it over her shoulder and sauntered to the pile of woods. "What do you want?" Mithra asked as she threw him an angry looking.

"Nothing, I saw you over here, and I just wanted to say hello to my friend," Astyages said, bending to collect firewood.

Mithra grinned. "Friend?! Do you honestly think you're my friend?"

"Yes, I helped you. Do you remember? You were hanging out of the window," Astyages said, laughing. He caught Mithra's angry eyes and smiled. "Sorry but it was so funny, by the way, I kindly helped you."

"Yes, and then you mocked me and told me lies to put me down in front of others!" Mithra growled.

"Yeah, that night was awful," Astyages said thoughtfully, "You ruined the night, made me feel so bad!" He was staring at Mithra with a serious face.

"Me? You can't be serious!" Mithra said, frowning.

Astyages put on a reasonable face. "I am! I was not in the mood of the wedding feast, just like you; I told a lie only because I didn't want to be alone." He wrapped the rope around the firewood and tied a knot at the back. "I didn't know you wanted to go to the stable like a wild horse…" He glanced at Mithra's angry face, "I mean like a wild lady, and locked the door on you!"

"Get off my back!" Mithra said, as she wanted to snatch the firewood out of his hands.

Astyages held the firewood tight. "You shouldn't talk that way to your friend!"

Their eyes were locked together, her heated blood rushing through her veins. "You picked on the wrong guy, find another friend!" Mithra said as she took the firewood from his hands violently. She went to her horse.

"I can't!" Astyages said behind her.

"Why?" Mithra asked without looking at him.

"Because I've saved you, not others," Astyages said calmly.

Mithra closed the woods on the horse saddlebag hurryingly and begun to walk.

"Hey wait! I come with you," Astyages said as he ran toward her.

Mithra stood against him. "Why should you stay in Mannea?" She asked.

Astyages was wondering about the question. "I should learn the war art to your men!"

"So go and do your job!" Mithra said dryly. "You were far too kind, but I don't need your kindness anymore!"

"Don't worry you can repay my kindness somehow…," Astyages said.

Mithra's head cocked slightly on the side, stared suspiciously at him. "How?" She asked.

"You can tell me about the Assyrian soldiers who attacked you!" Astyages said.

"How do you know that?" Mithra asked angrily.

Astyages put his head down, trying to pretend that he wanted to close the ropes more tightly. "Everyone knows!" Astyages said.

"Everyone means Zarvan, who can't stop his chatter but him!" Mithra snarled. "Well! Ask; I'll get rid of you easily enough."

Astyages banged his hands together several times to clean wood chips from it. "No! Now isn't a good time to talk; as you said, I should do my job," Astyages said. "I'll come back soon to talk together, as friends."

Mithra gazed at him for a few moments and went without saying a word.

"See you soon!" Astyages said behind her.

"I don't think so," Mithra said without looking back.

*****

Nanny's hut sat like a timid ibex beneath a big rock into the heart of the Mountain. If someone dared to see her ugly face, he found her small hut at the end of the forest, where the mountain and dense forest meet together. However, no one able to find the courage to see her. She had hidden in the hill, isolated and alone for years.

Mithra did not know how old her nanny was; her look was destroyed by fire. Mithra remembered her face like that since childhood, burned with horrified white patches on her chocolate brown skin, stuck lips in left, one empty eye socket and almost bald.

The sun was covered by the great thick sailing clouds and the bright morning air seemed blacker suddenly. The frozen puddles crack under Mithra's wolf-skin winter boots. The mountain was dark and icy, even the dark green of the pines is mostly coated in the crystalline ice. The world seemed to lie barren and lifeless before her as if God had put it to sleep.

Soon Mithra saw the hut at some little distance ahead of her. The stony gray walls were furry with moss that sparkled silvery with dew in the winter light. Its roof was thickly thatched with coarse straw, and a gray stone chimney stuck up like a solitary, erect ear listening for the rustle of the coming strangers. Mithra smelled warm, fresh bread. *Nanny is waiting for me,* Mithra thought and went faster.

"I knew you would come this morning, my dear beautiful doll. My hut was filled with your lovely smell." Nanny was coming to greet her. "Have you brought the firewood? Oh, baby, you should not, it's a frigid day. Come on my darling!" Nanny said while she had her arms open for a hug. "You should have a warm bowl Aash[1] to make you feel better…"

Mithra was accustomed to her behavior. She never answered to Nany's nagging, just enjoyed of her kindness. Mithra knew well she was the only reason for Nany's life.

"Hi, can I join you?" A voice said.

Mithra looked back quickly; Astyages was a few steps behind her, smiling.

"What are you doing here?" Mithra shouted.

He raised both hands high as if he tried to defend himself. "Don't bite my head off, hear me first…," Astyages said, anxiously.

"Are you chasing me?" Mithra asked.

"Don't get the wrong idea, I just remembered we still don't have a base for soldiers that I could train them there, so I come to see you and ask my questions," Astyages said with an innocent face. "Do you remember? You told me I can ask any question because you want to get rid of me!"

---

[1] An ancient food like soup

"Not here," Mithra barked; then she glanced at her nanny who had covered her face with the scarf. "Not now!"

Astyages looked up at the sky. "There is a blizzard," he said.

"Go to the hell that you have been!" Mithra said, but when she turned her head, saw a smile on Nanny's deformed face.

"Come in son. It's too cold to be outside!" Nanny said.

"You are most kind, grandma," Astyages said.

"Please speak loudly, son, I can't hear well!" Said Nanny as she was looking at Mithra with joy and led them to the cottage.

Mithra looked at Nanny's happy face. "Damn you! She has supposed we are lovers!" Mithra said quiet enough to draw Nanny's attention.

"Yes, and she is happy about that!" Astyages said quietly too, blinking.

Mithra chewed her lip; her eyes flare in anger but had no choice but to be silent.

Inside was cozy and warm; there was not so much furniture, but everything was arranged by the cleanliness and taste. The sound of crackling fire and the smell of baked bread, mixed with the scent of a freshly burned pine stick gave them a good feeling instantly.

Astyages did not seem to feel like a stranger at all. He put aside his coat. "Wow, what a beautiful hut!" Astyages said, looking around.

"My house is small and simple," Nanny said with a wry smile on her stuck lips. She put a large tray of foods in front of them. "How you meet together?" She asked.

"Up the tree." Astyages looked at Nanny's shocked face, smiled and added. "Honestly, I saved her," he said, helping Nanny. "Then we became friends."

"He's not really my friend, we're just acquaintances." Mithra turned to Astyages. "If you tell that story one more time, I'll break your neck!"

She said with a low voice, which Nanny's heavy ears could not hear it, pretended to smile.

Nanny seemed fazed, but when she saw Astyages' smile, she smiled too. "Don't be embarrassed dear, falling in love is the most beautiful thing that every woman should experience," she said to Mithra. Mithra wanted to resist, but Nanny added. "It is a breathtaking moment when you feel heat within yourself, and you realize that you love someone."

Mithra bit her lip when she recalled that familiar sense.

"Mithra gives herself all a hard time about everything, doesn't she?" Astyages said smiling.

Nanny sighed. She put her hand on Astyages' hand but immediately remembered that people do not like she touch them, so she pulled her hand back hurryingly. "Take care of her son!" Nanny said.

Astyages smiled, but his face was serious unlike a few moments ago; he took Nanny's hand. "Be sure. I will take care of her," he said.

"I don't need your help!" Mithra muttered.

"Every woman needs a man and every man needs a woman, baby!" Nanny said as she was leaving them to bring some bread. Her voice was hoarse with grief.

"I'd never seen her like this before!" Mithra whispered, turned to Astyages and she saw the dread on his face too.

Astyages noticed her looking, his eyes found hers, "I recalled my mother, she was as kind as your Nanny." He paused a moment and then staring into the fire, his face reflective. "In the imperial court, it is a tradition to grow up boys with the nannies for five years. They say mothers tend to spoil children so boys won't be brave in the future, if they stay with their mothers. My mother never accepted them. Growing up with my mother showed me she was different from all the women of the court, she was unique. I learned from her sword fighting, horseback riding, as well as love!" Astyages said.

"This is great," Mithra said. "I've never seen my mother and others don't like to talk about her. That's why I can't recall her with pride like you." She had remembered Sheedvash's words with bitterness.

Astyages closed his eyes, his mother's cry echoed in his ears off once again. "She was killed; when I was ten years old, in the courtyard of our house," he said turning away from the fire.

The thought made Mithra shudder.

A few hours later, they were sitting beside the fireplace, hearing Nanny's story. The story of the most crucial day in her life, when she had found Mithra in her arms, a miracle, as she said but at the end of the story Nanny had gone to sleep.

"You have to listen to this story over a hundred times, I'm sure," Mithra said quietly, trying to hide her embarrassed of the story of her rejection.

"It doesn't matter. It's a story that shows the beauty of true love." Astyages looked at Nanny. "She is a wonderful woman!" He said.

"Everyone is afraid of her, because of her face!" Mithra said.

"I'm afraid of people who have an ugly heart, not face!" Astyages said; he hesitated. "How can you trust others?"

"I don't trust others!" Mithra said, frankly.

"Never?" Astyages said laughing.

Mithra nodded seriously.

"Oh, God have mercy!" Astyages said but then his face got serious, and he looked straight at Mithra. "I follow my heart!" He said quietly, "I can trust you."

Mithra blushed, put her head down and stared at her hands; looking into his burning eyes was not easy. Astyages clasped her chin and raised her head up. Mithra's heart was pounding. She could feel the energy, filling the space between them. He was sitting so close to her, his dark smoky eyes were staring at her. He leaned forward, slowly stroked her cheek. Mithra's breathing was shallow; she could not move, watching him hypnotized as his hand stepped on her skin.

"You have such fine, delicate face...," Astyages said, his voice was soft and melodious.

Mithra closed her eyes, let go of his hand and leaned forward a little, unconsciously. She was feeling his hot breath against her skin. His fingers were running on her face and accidentally over on her cheek, where a sign of skull was showing itself.

"No!" Mithra suddenly turned away.

Astyages was shocked; he took a deep breath. "Actually... actually, I have to go! I need to do some things, nothing is left to sunset," he said.

Outside, the rain was stopped. Mithra wished vehemently it was rainy even ice storm. She did not want him to go. "How do you reach to Diheh?" Mithra asked.

Astyages give her a small smile and then put two fingers on his lips and ran a whistle; a few moments later, a beautiful brown mare came from the mountain slope toward them. The horse stood beside her owner.

"Why didn't you bring her to the stable?" Mithra said as she was looking at the horse with admire.

"She is a warhorse. She knows how to take care of herself," Astyages said stroking the horse lovingly, then looked at Mithra. "And, if you yet want to get rid of me..."

"Yet I want more!" Mithra said pretending to be indifferent.

"Yeah." He couldn't tell her that he did not believe her. "So be ready tomorrow morning, I'll meet you just outside the village, at the pond by the village bridge; you shall lead me to Assyrians fort."

"Diheh is not a village...," Mithra said frowning.

Astyages grinned. "Well, I'll meet you outside of Diheh..."

"And you cannot command me!" Mithra said.

Astyages was finding pleasure even in her naggings. "Lead me there, please!" He said.

"I'll meet you, tomorrow morning!" Mithra said.

"Do not be late and don't tell anyone!" Astyages said.

"I never tell anyone where I would go, so don't bother yourself to ask!" Mithra said dryly.

"And… Thank you so much for this lovely evening, Mithra; being with you was the best thing," he said softly.

Mithra's cheeks blushed hotly; she glanced up into his captivating dark eyes. Astyages leaned down, resting his forehead against hers. Mithra watched breathlessly as his eyes studied hers with silent intensity. His warm breath ghosted across her face. She stifled a surprised gasp as his soft lips captured hers, causing her body fired by his heat. The heat travels through her veins, warming her. Just as she felt a rush of euphoric bliss envelop her, making her heart sing with pure joy, Astyages drew away.

Mithra opened her eyes, slowly. She found him gazing down at her.

"Then you trust me?" Astyages breathed.

Mithra nodded, wide-eyed.

"Tomorrow morning, just before sunup!" Astyages whispered in her ear.

Mithra's eyes looked at him until she could. She could not believe that she fell in love so easily.

*****

The sun shone down upon Mithra full and strong from out of the white mist. She was waiting for almost one hour. She sat on a rock, picked up a pebble, span a bit in her hand and then threw it out. Astyages' words echoed in her ears, "Do not be late and don't tell anyone!" She was worried, but she did not find a reason for it. She got up, stared impatiently into the east, where Saber and his men were camped at a riverbed, no one coming. She sat on the rock again; she had no choice but to wait. Mithra heard the sound of galloping from the opposite side, from Diheh. She turned back. Astyages appeared from the far, on his brown horse.

"Come on! We must get there; before him," Astyages shouted before reaching to her.

"Who?!" Mithra asked as she was jumping onto her horse, but Astyages had moved away so fast, riding into the woods.

Her stomach did a lurch, and she slammed her spurs into her horse, galloping across the outer road, beneath an arched stone bridge, into the woods. Just a few moments later, she reappeared beside him.

"You go a little ahead of me but wait for me a few miles before," Astyages said without having to slow down.

The sun was streaming through a break in the murky clouds, but despite its struggle, the air was freezing, and every breath they took, gave their heat to the visible white puffs. Mithra drew rein and, dismounting, came on the frozen solid mud toward Astyages. She pointed with her head. "Here; behind the hill," she said.

Astyages climbed down off his horse; stood beside her and looked around carefully. "Are you shivering?" Mithra said, her voice dripping with sarcasm.

"Of course I am. The Mannea's winter air is wicking my heat away faster than my body can replace it!" Astyages said frowning.

"This season is my season, I love it!" Mithra said with a certain pride.

Astyages did his best to ignore her. He pointed out, where the cypress trees stood mute in the icy cold winter air. "We can hide the horses there," he said.

"Why would we be hiding?" Mithra asked with surprise.

Astyages went up to the trees. "We'll have to wait and see… hurry!" He urged.

Mithra hesitated, looked into his serious face and followed him. They tied the horses to the trees. Astyages reviewed their position carefully.

"That's Diheh over there…," Astyages said. "So we climb up another way. No one sees us."

"Who are you waiting for?" Mithra said, looked at him with suspicion.

"I'm not sure…," Astyages gave the cautious answer, looking at the piles of thick bushes that were grown on the slopes of the hill. He turned to Mithra. "Can you crawl over the rocks?"

"Of course, I do!" Mithra said irritated.

"But all the way is full of thorny bushes…" Astyages could not finish his words.

"Go ahead," Mithra said.

Astyages smiled for the first time today. "Follow me!" He said.

Mannea's weak autumn sun was not enough to keep warm the Assyrian soldiers who were not used to the cold weather and they were warming themselves by the fire that they had kindled. The giant soldier, who had attacked Mithra, was grilling a chicken skewed over the flames. A little further away from him, his commander, Adora, was sitting on a rock, staring into the fire.

"You would know them, I bet," Astyages said very quietly.

Mithra nodded. The soldiers were talking to each other. The giant man, who was eating a big piece of chicken, said something to their commander and the commander replied to him.

"Good," Astyages said. "I had guessed right; they are waiting for someone."

"And how would you be knowing?" Mithra asked surprised.

"That man said, their commander!" Astyages said.

"Do you understand what they are saying?" Mithra said, widen eyes.

Astyages nodded. "Don't tell anyone!" He said.

Mithra stared at Astyages. She was seeing a man who was different from the witty and funny boy that she knew before. Astyages now seemed like an experienced commander; a seasoned spy, who had specific skills at arms that no one must know. Mithra had found that she has really underestimated this boy.

"What are we waiting for?" Mithra asked.

"You'll see!" Astyages said, looking carefully at the road.

The Assyrian commander stood; he looked down the slope through the trees, where a waterfall filled a broad pool beneath it, was seen a human figure, riding toward them, dressed in a black cloak cape that he had pulled down its hat close to his eyes.

It was apparent that the Assyrian soldiers were not surprised by a man that loomed before them. The man slid down the horse, stepped forward and took off his hat.

Mithra gave a little gasp; she could not believe her eyes. Saber passed the Assyrian soldiers and stood in front of the commander. She saw with horror that Saber had wrapped his arms around the commander, but Astyages did not seem surprised, he had stared at them carefully.

The Commander said something in a language that Mithra didn't understand, and two soldiers went ahead to leave them alone Saber, and the commander sat on rocks and began to speak in Assyrian, a language that seemed so strange and terrible to Mithra. She glanced at Astyages; he was calm, listening to what they were saying, with full attention. She was scared, even had seen a kind of grim in his calmness.

Almost an hour later, Saber stood up hugged the commander again and left.

"We can go back but be careful!" Astyages said very quietly.

They descended the hill, crossed the cypress trees, and stopped when they reached where their horses were standing. Mithra stood beside Astyages, panting. There was absolute stillness; the silence was hung so thickly in the frigid air. No air stirred the grass or leaves. Not a sound could be heard either close at hand or in the far off distance. Even her own breath seemed to die as soon as it left her mouth. The stillness of such a place made it hard to believe what had happened a few minutes before.

Astyages stood beside his horse with a wry smile on his face, watching and enjoying the view. "There is nothing I love more than hot summer days, but this is a breathtaking view, even in winter!"

"This is a terrible nightmare of betrayal!" Mithra whispered.

"Don't worry; we'll work it out somehow!" Astyages said, smiling. "I want to get some food in your belly." Astyages pointed to the bags that he had tied to his horse. "I have some things for eating." He pointed to the bag.

The median's army chief commander betrayal did not seem to have enraged Astyages as much as Mithra would have expected. "Are you here simply to enjoy the view or eating foods?"

Astyages looked up calmly. "You have taken him more serious than he really is," he said.

"What did he say?" Mithra asked curiosity.

Astyages' mouth grew tight, and he gave her a lingering look.

"Don't you trust me?"

Astyages took a deep breath. "The less you know of him, the better for you!" He said.

Mithra stared at him in silence until Astyages cleared his throat. He raised her head and looked at Mithra.

"Don't be afraid," Astyages told her and turned to his horse. "And there are far better things to talk about than that nasty man," he said in a calm and sweet tone; his voice was changed. He peeled his gloves off.

"I love to feel your warm, soothing breath, caressing my face one more time…" He pulled some stuffed bread with cheese, and walnuts out of the bag. "But best have some food and drink, then …" Astyages was laughing.

His face once more was a carefree and witty mask, but Mithra was not in the mood for jokes. She disentangled her horse from the tree, but Astyages rushed forward, catching her horse by the bridle.

"Hold on, you can't let go now," Astyages said.

"You can't give me orders!" Mithra retorted.

"You have to wait; we could not turn back the way we'd come!" Astyages said.

"YOU have to wait." Mithra pulled the rope out from his hand. "Not me!" She said.

Astyages grabbed her wrist before she could go. "Saber should see us together!" He said with a serious face. "He must assume I am in love and I don't have any attention to him. He should consider himself abandon of any suspicion or otherwise everything will be ruined."

He must assume I am in love. The words echoed in her head like a hammer, painful and harsh. Mithra looked at him as if for the first time. Astyages stood before her, dressed in a fur suit of the yellow tiger. He was too well-dressed for a spy. Unbidden and unwelcome tears pooled in her eyes. She stared at the ground, angry with herself for this reaction. *Why am I crying?* She thought, *for the loss of something I never had.* Mithra wrenched herself free.

"Listen to me…"

Mithra interrupted him. "Everything was planned, yes? This was not a real love from the very beginning…," she said, with tears of despair in her voice. "You did something that I thought you're different from the others. You were kind with Nanny, unlike others. You… you pretend that you love me!"

"You are wrong…"

Mithra didn't want to hear his voice, didn't want let him see her tears, she gave him a stiff shove and tried to pass beside him, but Astyages firmly stopped her, staring into her honey eyes that shone by anger!

"You are important to me, but you should understand; we are dealing with a national crisis!" Astyages said.

"I don't mind. I'm not important to you and these people; why should I worry about you, your plans and this country!" Mithra cried angrily.

Astyages' strong hands wrapped her slim west and drew her to his side before she completed her words.

"You're wrong! You're very important to me… important and very dear…"

Mithra's heart madly smashed into her chest. Astyages' head turned his wary gaze to her, his eyes burning coal. She tried to release herself, but he pressed her more. His fingers tighten in her hair, pulling her head back. She had to look at his face. "Dear than anyone…," Astyages whispered.

Mithra did not struggle anymore; she rested in his arms, hypnotized by his eyes. His fingers slid over her face; ran his thumb down her cheek and across her lower lip. He leaned against her face, inhale her shallow breathe deeply. "It's a great deal of pleasure, breathing in your breath…" Astyages' hand fell on the silkiness of Mithra's hair. He leaned some of his weight against her, "Smelling your smell!" Mithra felt the heating on her face, leaned her head slightly into his fingers, and closed her eyes. "Kissing your lips!" He told her, before pressing an open-mouthed kiss to her lower lips.

Mithra hardly had a moment to react before he kissed her. It was a very sloppy kiss with the strong scent of old wine. She timidly reached up along his sides, pressing softly. Astyages gasped in delight. He leaned down, moaned into her mouth and sucked at her lower lip. A weird soothing wave traveled through her body. Her body felt drained of all its tension. *I'm light as a feather as if I've drunk one large glass of Ephedra sap,* Mithra thought before she drew back her lips, remembered how she hated everything that could make her infatuated.

"The same trick doesn't work twice!" Mithra pushed aside him violently. "I know people like you; whatsoever they desire of world, they must grant," she said, turning to her horse to go.

"All that I desire is you, but I have learned to put the needs of my country before my own desires," Astyages said behind her.

"And I have learned I cannot trust you," she said, rising lump in her throat.

"I didn't lie to you… Look!" Astyages said.

Mithra was going oblivious to him.

"Look… I loved you since the first day I saw you."

Mithra turned her gold-flecked eyes on him, wavering, her silver bandanna was in Astyages' hand.

"It's not a desire; no man could ever look on you and not desire you but when I saw you, I knew, I'll love you until the end of my last breath. From that day, this bandanna is always with me, right here on my heart but…," Astyages said in gloomy tones "We have to pay tribute to Assyria from our people efforts result, we pledged, but they are poor. We are living under foreigners' yoke. Our people have looted, raped, killed on each attack of the enemy. My people, our people, are bleeding." It was hard to hide his emotion. "Some were chosen for a big purpose, for a goal that is much bigger of their desires, dreams even their love," Astyages sighed, to control his harsh breathing. "Unfortunately, I am one of them."

Astyages' image shook in front of her eyes and rolled out with tears on her cheek. She turned her head away, to hide her tears.

"Why does everyone want me to sacrifice for the people who don't like me?" She murmured.

"This can be very dangerous for our country, more than you imagine," Astyages said and took a step toward her.

"I'll stay with you, just… just don't talk to me." That was the only thing Mithra could say in a loud voice, between her silent sobs, after her lost belief, which she had planted just one day before.

An hour later, in the Median troop's camp, Saber saw them not long after they arrived. He was in front of his tent, looking at his soldiers who were struggling to build a place for military training. Astyages slid gracefully from his saddle. He was playing his role very well. He took Mithra's fingers and smiled. It seemed they have had a lovely romantic day.

"I'll see you soon!" Astyages said, pressed her fingers firmly.

Mithra said nothing, managed a beautiful but pale smile on her face then put spurs and left him quickly. Astyages stared at Mithra; his back was towards Saber, locking eyes with her until she reached a point behind the rocks.

*****

Mithra was galloping toward Diheh. The cold wind that was whipping on her hot face could not reduce the flame of anger in her inside. She had almost reached Diheh, but she brought up the rear, looked at the adobe houses. The golden light of the sun was struggling to find a way through the leaden clouds for warming this cold small city. A crow landed on a boulder on the side of the road. His round eyes stared at Mithra, cawed loud.

She looked at crow with hatred. "I can't get rid of you, isn't it? Neither you nor the ominous destiny that was determined for me." She cried. Once again, a huge lump formed in her throat. She closed her eyes; remembered the hot in Astyages' embrace, with joy and sorrow.

"You have come to remember me that I'm not like others," Mithra whispered, her voice shaking with the emotion she barely managed to hold in her chest. "That I can't love or be loved." She swallowed past the lump in her throat. "You won; I'll go the same way, as before."

Mithra looked at the last view of the sun, before hiding behind clouds.

*****

It was too late!

The twisting path passed through the mountain, so steep. Mithra had to climb up, hauling herself along a narrow line inch by bloody inch. Out of the corner of her eye, she saw slide pebbles, falling beneath her feet in every step. In this hard climbing, only a man could be safe who has had climbed in Dark Mountain and knows how to slip past dangers, wisely and unmolested.

She traced this narrow path with a beating heart. The way was so familiar to her by moonlight, so she was climbing up the boulders, quickly, losing in her thoughts. She wished she knew what Saber had said to the Assyrian commander. It was better if she could tell everything to Holy Pater to find an appropriate solution to this problem. She remembered with bitterness that Astyages did not trust her to say anything.

"Maybe it could help us to solve this conundrum!" Mithra murmured angrily, but she knew very well what really made her upset. Her subconscious mind turned toward Astyages. She remembered his hot breath on her cheek, his fingers moving on her spine and the enjoyable pressure of his lips on her. She closed her eyes unconsciously with pleasure; suddenly a frightened fox ran out of its stone shelter and fled headlong.

Mithra startled, whirled, shell and fine gravel rolled on beneath her feet and pulled her down. Her hands grabbed every stone through her way to the end of this broad valley, but the rocks removed and fell along her. She thought for a moment, there is no way to save her, but her fingers unconsciously grabbed a thin branch of a plant, and she nailed to the trunk of the sharp slope. She dragged herself up; sat on a firm place and looked at the bottom of the valley, where was far away from her and a river which was crawling forward like a thin snake. She drew a breath of relief.

*****

It was too late!

It was the past midnight and Mithra was the last one on the cave, masking. The cave was all too full of the men, lion mask, most of them. Everything was the same but seemed different. The men were more passionate and enthusiastic, more than ever. They were drinking wine mixed with Ephedra sap and shaking their heads along with exciting rhythms of the Dafs[1]. Mithra had never seen men drinking Ephedra sap at their monthly general meeting; she went ahead among men who seemed obviously senseless even behind the mask.

Half-naked young boys were entertaining with a mask of crow. Mithra pushed aside a cup of Ephedra that was offered to her with behind the hand. The smoke of burning torches and recurrences has filled the cave, and she could not see the seats of the paters clearly.

The platforms of the members were on the concentric circles, and the paters sat in the middle of them, beneath the altar that was decorated with a statue of Mithra, God of Love. In front of them, there was a large bowl fill of the blood of a sanctified cow mixed with wine and Ephedra sap, a special drink for welcomed guests. Mithra kneeled in front of Holy Pater.

"You're late, my son!" Holy Pater said with a smile.

Obviously, Holy Pater had a good mood today; he turned to a man who was beside him. "This young man is one of my best disciples," he said to him.

The man turned to her and Mithra's eyes met the tiny cold eyes of Saber who stared at her too carefully. *I knew those honey-colored eyes, but where and how!* Saber thought. Mithra felt slipping off a drop of cold sweat on her spine. She could not take her eyes from Saber's face for a few moments but after Saber's curious look, she put her head down, pretended showing her respect to him.

"So, is this lean young boy your best disciple?" Saber said as he still tried to recall how he knew those eyes.

---

[1] Daf is a large Middle Eastern frame drum used in popular and classical music

Holy Pater put his hand on Mithra's shoulder. "Yes, lean and young but very brave and eager for a fight," the old man said proudly.

Saber put a cold smile on his face and nodded. "Courage is a debt that we pay to secure the future," he said. "Although it seems your young student's courage and intelligence hasn't helped him in his way to the cult meeting," he added, looking at Mithra's bloody hands.

Holy Pater ignored his taunt. "He'll show you how his courage helps him, but surely he should refresh himself first," he said. "On your feet son, go and sit; Holy Master has brought important news with him that everyone should hear," Holy Pater said.

Mithra said nothing, feared her voice might betray her. She bowed again and went backward with respect. Saber stared at her with accusing eyes until she lost herself in the crowd. He always believed in what he was feeling, and he felt this young man, with his alert eyes unlike others in the cave could not be trusted.

Mithra walked away from the podium as much as possible. She sank down to the bench, her whole body shaking grotesquely. The Daf's sound seemed to echo in her ears. Too loudly, leaving her head feeling like it had been hit by a sledgehammer. The air was heavy with the lantern's smoke and the men's poisoned breath.

What on earth should I do now?! Mithra thought, feeling light-headed, none of this seemed quite real. One moment it felt like some nightmare, like a bad dream. Her palms were slick with sweat. She wiped them on her legs. She wished that she could make runway from here but recalled Holy Pater's words, 'Holy Master has brought important news with him that everyone should hear.'

Astyages was right, she thought. Saber was obviously much more dangerous than she had initially thought. She had to stay; she had to find out what is going on in the cult.

Dancing and singing hymns lasted more than an hour, but finally, Holy Pater stood up, raised his hand and the music turned off immediately. Mithra could see the men's red eyes staring up at him. Holy Pater went to the statue of Mithra, stood up against it and raised his hands towards the statue. "We worship God Mithra; on this glorious day, two of God's disciples proposed to challenge their biggest enemy: themselves! They will suffer to take their bodies and minds far away from sins and be closer to the light. Whoever suffers for Mithra God, She will guide his heart."

Holy Pater turned to the men and pointed by his cane to Mithra and then a young man who was sitting near the altar; two Persia men came to them. Mithra stood up and went with them to the altar, kneeled in front of the Paters, trying to stay calm, but being calm was not so simple under Saber's cold eyes.

"On this holy night, the sign of the Mithra will be imprinted on your arm," Holy Pater said to his disciples. "You will experience pain, but if you can learn to endure pain, you can survive anything!"

A Parsi man came, bringing in his hand a tray containing a mixture of soot and fat of a sanctified cow and a dagger.

Suffering from dignity or faith, on such a night... It will be more difficult than ever! Mithra thought, but she did not want to show weakness, so before the Parsi man came closer, she stepped forward, ripped up her shirtsleeve with a quick movement and stood, trying to pretend that she was not frightened.

Holy Pater smiled a satisfied smile. He pointed to the Parsi man to begin his work. The man came forward.

"Wait!" Saber's loud voice drew every attention to him. He went to the altar, where Mithra was kneeling. She stole her eyes from him and stared at the ground. Saber slid out a small bottle, containing green liquid from his robe.

"I've been in many cult ceremonies, I've never seen in any ceremony, a simple test like this!" Saber said as he glanced at Mithra. "If you imbued your knife with parsnip[1], although the wound will be swelled, the sign will always remain on their skin and will bless them." He held the bottle in front of the Parsi man's face.

---

[1] A plant's sap that can break down skin cells and tissues

124

The man looked at Holy Pater, reassuring himself that he agreed with Saber. Holy Pater hesitated for a few moments and then gave a weary nod. The man took the bottle, slowly poured the thick green liquid on the tip of the daggers' scrapes and began to tattoo on Mithra's arm…

"Hang tight!!" Mithra repeated to herself, for the hundredth time.

The dagger grazed her right arm that time and left a blaze of pain in its wake. The burning pain was unbearable; much more than she could imagine. Something cold and wet pervaded into her wound, made it hot, burning and itchy immediately, worse than before. She heard her chattering teeth's sound, and the pain blinded her for an instant. She had to bite her lip to make sure she did not cry out in pain.

"Hang tight!!" Mithra clenched her fists tightly, nails digging into her palms. She grew dizzy. *If I fell faint, my secret undoubtedly will be revealed,* she thought.

The Parsi man looked at Mithra's bloody arm and the sign of Mithra cult that was tattooed on it now; he smiled with satisfaction. Daf's sound filled the cave; men cheered and drank wine again to celebrate her success. She raised her head. Holy Pater was looking at her with pride. Saber was sitting next to him, staring at Mithra, smiling. Saber was taking a wicked pleasure in Mithra's helpless pain, but she did not intend to let him have that pleasure.

She stood as if she stood atop a giant hill. "The Mithra God is amongst us," Mithra yelled, a shivering hot scream that made a man's bones seem to thrum within him. Her cry lingered in the damp cave air. "YEEEEEEAH."

All eyes were fastened upon her. "Yeeeeeeah," a cry of admiration burst from every mouth. Mithra glanced at Saber from the corner of her eye; his smile curled up and died. Mithra had won. She knelt, tried to ease the pain with a deep, long breath. Holy Pater stood up, raised his cane and the men became silent immediately. "God Mithra will surely reward your efforts; she is most merciful…"

"And the only reward for rising up against Mithra God and his messengers…" Saber stood beside Holy Pater, his voice threw every attention to him, "… will be that they will be killed, or will be expelled out of the land. It will be their degradation in the world, and in the Hereafter, theirs will be an awful doom." He stared at the men with his tiny eyes, silent for a few moments. "Brothers, the king of the Medes, Cyaxares has betrayed us by serving Ahura Mazda[1]. He has failed in his promise to Mithra, and he has backed God. The king obeys Magus. His first minister is a Magi and the king dominated by him in all his commands," Saber said as he was looking at men with a blushed face with anger. His neck veins were swollen, his voice trembled with excitement and became louder every moment more than before. "We have an enemy who is more dangerous than the Assyrians, the king of the Medes, who has stood against us, it means he is against Mithra and must be destroyed…"

Saber's words disappeared among men's angry shouting.

*****

On that moonless night, even the silhouettes are gone. The usual friendly smattering of stars is obscured utterly by dense cloud. Mithra wrapped herself in her cloak tightly and walked with agonizing slowness down the slippery path, this time with more caution. The cold wind was spinning all around her, stirring the snow but her face was hot, and large drops of sweat had covered her forehead. The mountain path seemed too tough and endless. She could hardly walk a few steps without interruption; her knees were bending involuntarily, and she had to rely on the boulders to take a few steps forward.

Mithra took a deep breath and drew the cold mountain air into her lungs. She was dizzy and wamble. She knew she had to go home soon or she will collapse in the mountains. Mithra stopped, heavy panting, looked around. She could hear the sound of the river. She was up close to the ruins, where she had changed her clothes, but even that distance seemed too much.

She sat on a boulder; weakness was gradually overcoming; her body was hot, but she was trembling violently. She wrapped the cloak on

---

[1] Avestan name for the creator and sole God of Zoroastrianism

herself more, put two fingers in the mouth and drew a short whistle. Just a few moments later, Morvarid was galloping to her.

Morvarid caressed her head with its snout. Mithra looked up. Morvarid was sniffing anxiously. "Help me!" She said weakly.

It was as if Morvarid could understand the words; she lowered her neck. Mithra took the horse's neck and stood. She cannot draw herself on the saddle, so she walked to the ruins, and when she reached there as soon as she left her horse's neck, fell down on the ground.

She didn't know what excuse she would have for her family for her fever and bloody arm but knew she should change her clothes as soon as possible and return home. *I didn't want to die here,* Mithra thought. She dragged herself to the whereabouts of her clothes; bent down to pick them but hearing a voice made her freeze.

"I saw you from the distance, I knew this is you, but I didn't believe my eyes! What're you doing here?"

Mithra heard Astyages, hastily hid the mask in her sweater's collar. She did not dare to look back. Astyages came forward; stood beside Mithra and stared at her. Mithra leaned against the broken mud wall, closed her eyes and sighed. "I don't know, what my sin is that wherever I go I have to see you," she said through her clenched teeth.

"Honestly, I don't know what your sin is, but I'd like really to know," Astyages said dryly.

Mithra's knees bent unintentionally; she slipped on the mud wall and sat down on the ground. Astyages was looking at her with a sullen look, unlike always. "Get up and say what are you doing here?" Astyages said.

Mithra could not get up, even if she wished.

"Leave me alone! Please get out of here," Mithra said as she hid her mask in her cloak. She was trying to keep her eyes open.

Astyages grinned. "Really?!" He knelt in front of Mithra. "You're bullshitting me! What did you hide?" He asked.

Mithra closed her eyes and leaned her head against the rotten wall. Astyages was frustrated, he took Mithra's head and turned toward himself. "I'm talking to you as the king's officer; this is quietly serious. I have an order if I found someone dangerous for the kingdom of the Medes, kill him, do you understand? What I need to know is: what you are doing here?" Mithra hardly was seeing his face. Everything seemed blurry and vague. She heard his voice from a far, far away. Her hands loosened and fell on both sides, and the mask revealed from her collar.

"What the hell were you thinking?" Astyages could not turn his astonished eyes from the mask. "Do you know they will kill you instantly if they know you are a woman?" He runs his hand through his hair. "Idiots! How didn't they recognize that you are a woman? How … how could you pass those challenges? O' God, it was impossible even imagine such a thing to me!" He said as he threw the mask on the ground nervously.

Astyages grabbed Mithra's arms with both hands firmly. "Did you tell them that I was chasing Saber?" He barked. His hands had made hard pressure on the wounds; Mithra screamed painfully and fainted.

Astyages quickly drew back his hands. He felt his fingers wet, in the faint glimmer of sunlight rising, he looked at them; his hands were soaked with blood.

"What they've done to you?" Astyages roared. He pushed aside Mithra's cloak, seeing the wound on her arm. He frowned; the big blisters could be seen on the wounds. He looked at Mithra again; her pale face was covered in sweat droplets. Astyages touched the wounds with a fingertip, smelling his fingers. He knew well the smell of Parsnip. This venom was not lethal poisoning but if he left Mithra… *she will die in the cold mountain of bleeding and fever before somebody found her,* he thought, and my secret stays safe. He detested his own thoughts, immediately. He stared at Mithra's face that still seemed very beautiful. He was in love with this woman… but on the other hand, he had an important task. He took a deep breath. Morvarid was behind him, she knew Astyages, so she was calm, but she was sniffing and pawing, wittingly. He looked up at the horse and then lifted her onto the horse. He climbed up behind her, putting his arms around her to grab on to the bridle.

Astyages tapped his heels to encourage the horse to go and took a short whistle. His brown horse came out from the trees and followed Morvarid obediently.

He knew what to do!

CHAPTER SEVEN

AN UNEXPECTED LOVE

She opened her eyes slowly; the light hurt her eyes. Mithra did not know where she is. She did not remember anything but vague figures that came and went, but she could not recognize them. The only image that she could remember clearly was Saber's face that had stared at her and enjoyed seeing her suffering.

Mithra blinked several times, but she saw everything blurry still.

"Do not be afraid! It takes a few days till you can easily see."

She recognized Astyages' voice.

"Blurred vision is a common complication of poison Parsnip," Astyages said as he picked up the wet cloth on Mithra's forehead. "Finally, the fever came down. Do you want something to eat?" Astyages asked.

"Where am I?" Mithra asked.

"In your nanny's hut!" Astyages said and sat beside her bed.

"What are you doing here?" Mithra asked.

"I'm taking care of you, like always!" Astyages said, smiling.

"Why?" Mithra asked dryly.

Astyages grinned. "Why? Because taking care of you is the best entertainment that I know."

Mithra recalled what happened to her; she knew her secret was revealed. "How long have I am here?" She asked.

"Three days, with a high fever; you were saying pure deliriums. I don't know how I've endured your bullshits every day. I guessed you are stronger than that," Astyages said. "Mithra's disciples are powerful!" He added with a sardonic tone.

"Well, who else knows about this?" Mithra asked impatiently.

"Wait! Let your nanny knows you're wake up. The poor woman has cried without stopping for three days," Astyages said. "I told her, a bad thing never dies, but she didn't believe me."

He ran to the yard and yelled, Nanny's heavy ears needed to hear him. "Come on, Nanny! Your daughter is awake; I'd told you she would be treated!"

Nanny was beside Mithra caressing her face, almost immediately. Tears welled from her only eye. "You scared me, baby. Astyages had said that snake bite doesn't end up dying, but I could not believe him." She put a kiss on Mithra's hair. "I went to the Temple of the Mithra for pray but it was full of the people, I hid behind the door prayed to god to let me die before you," Nanny said, and then wiped her tears hastily. "What am I doing? I would not upset you, baby. My daughter is hungry, right? Do you want to eat?"

Mithra nodded to satisfy her.

"This won't take long baby; I'll prepare your favorite food, bulgur soup, and roast chicken!" Nanny said as she rushed out.

"You are right. A serpent stung me; a python called Saber!" Mithra whispered.

"I knew," Astyages said. "He always takes Parsnip with him; before each battle, he imbued his sword with it to make his kick swords more painful." He stared at Mithra curiously. "Why did he do with you?"

Mithra shrugged. "I do not know!" She said. "I suppose he enjoys others hassle..." She closed her eyes, saw Saber's face, staring at her with pleasure. "His eyes were full of wickedness. When he talked about Cyaxares, hate resonated in his voice..." Mithra recalled Saber's words about the king, becoming wide-eyed with fear.

Astyages noticed her mood change.

"What did he say?" Astyages asked.

"He said Cyaxares has forgotten his pledge with Mithra and he must be destroyed. This man is more dangerous than we thought," Mithra said trembling.

Astyages did not seem shocked. "What else? Did he say anything about his plan to destroy Cyaxares?" He said.

"Nothing, I suppose if he wishes to express his plan, he will in a more private meeting," Mithra said.

Astyages stared at her. "Will you be attending that meeting?" He asked.

"I don't know... Maybe! Holy Pater likes me," Mithra said hesitantly.

"Oh, so that's why he let you receive Saber's grace?" Astyages said with a mockery voice.

"It's clear that he loves and trusts me because I could pass these painful tests?" Mithra said frowning.

Astyages was staring at her with a solemn face. "What about you? I want to know how much you trust him!" Astyages' suspicions had awakened. "Do you trust him enough to tell him about me?"

"If I had found Holy Pater alone, I told him but with seeing Saber everything changed," Mithra said.

Astyages looked as if something did not please him.

Mithra gazed at him with eyes like molten gold and said, "What do you think, I might be spying for Saber?"

Astyages shrugged. "I don't know; I only know that the Mithra's cult is a place, where the men lost their way and identity; became addicted by Ephedra sap, and forced to believe that suffering is the only way to holiness for unholy people." His mouth had hardened. "They forced men to give up their freedom and just obey orders without thinking," he added dryly, "Moreover, they don't believe in the ability of women. Maybe you don't know that, but no woman can be entered into this cult. If a member brings a woman to their ceremonies, his punishment would be death."

Mithra had put her head down. "I've never drink Ephedra sap," she added angrily, "And I have not killed anyone."

"So what are you doing there?" Astyages asked.

Mithra closed her eyes; it was clear that she did not like to talk, but Astyages did not want to leave her alone.

"Tell me! Truly what are you doing in a cult that has nothing but pain?" Astyages crossed his arms over the chest. "Don't ask me to believe that you want to reach light through suffering, to the God who loves to see your pain! I can't believe that you are believed in those bullshits!" He snarled.

Mithra seemed as frustrated as she was angry. "No," she shouted. "But... But I needed them."

"Why?" Astyages asked stubbornly. "Aha! I had forgotten Holy Pater likes you, who's been so kind to you," he nodded slowly. "As I see!"

Mithra did her best to ignore his taunt. "Because there is the only place, where I feel I'm accepted," Mithra shouted as she was crying. "The only place that my face is covered and I'm not ashamed of the sign on my face. Where no one knows me or my mother and the people do not know me as a sinister. Do you understand?"

It was Astyages' turn to shout. "No, I don't; you got me beat!" His mouth twisted. "They don't even know you're a woman, it is not important for them what your name is, who your father is and where your mother come from, for them it's just important that you bear the pain for no reason and obey without question, it does not deserve to be there." He stood in front of her. "I'd prefer to stand in front of the others with my strange sign on my face; stand enough to show them that I'm so proud of my mother. She left her country for her love. I'd prefer to stand enough to show them that the demons seal the sign on their hearts not on the faces, stand enough to show them who I am."

Astyages finished his speech, panting. Mithra said nothing, tears slipped down from her eyes on her beautiful face. Astyages looked at her, he was sorry about his angry words, and he did not know what he should do now.

"Would you like a glass of milk?" He said the only thing that came to his mind.

Mithra wanted to be alone, nodded.

Astyages got up. "Forget the milk." He sat down once again. "I said something silly. I always do, you know," Astyages said. "Look at me!" He took Mithra's face with both hands.

Mithra opened her eyes. She could not see him clearly, but she stared at his face. Astyages stared at her beautiful eyes. Suffering, loneliness, fear, her eyes held all those deep-seated emotions that danced like fire into her eyes but nothing was important for him, he just knew he was so much in love with her, knew it from deep down in his heart. *Sometimes a man must be bold enough to follow his heart,* Astyages thought. He took a deep breath to calm himself and began to stroke her face with his fingers.

"I love you," Astyages said. "I want you to know this; while I breathe I am yours in mind, body, and soul. I love you because I know your true identity… Mithra, someone who doesn't know you would never love you."

Mithra was crying, and her hot tears wetted Astyages' fingers. "You don't know…" Crying did not let her speak easily.

"I don't know what?" Astyages asked as he was looking at her patiently.

"People are right…," Mithra said. "I'm really a bad omen!"

"Bullshits!" Astyages said.

"They're not." Certainty was waving into her voice. "I know better than others that I'm not like them. I cannot live like a normal woman. I cannot love. I cannot be loved. This is my destiny…"

Mithra gasped with shock when Astyages' lips touched hers. It was a sweet, tender kiss. She could smell him, tasting him and could feel hot of his body so close to hers. Astyages drew back and spent a moment studying her face. "Even if this is your destiny… I will change it!" He said. Astyages held her gently, cupping her face with one hand. "Do you trust me?" He asked.

Mithra nodded.

"I love you," Astyages said. "I love you, and no one, not evils, not angels, not even God able to stop me." He put a kiss on her lips. "I will love you until the last moment of my life."

Mithra gave an approving nod, closed her eyes, and sighing in pleasure.

Astyages heard a dialogue outside the house. Suddenly the door opened sharply, and Taham rushed to Mithra and crushed her in a bone-crunching hug. The old man was taking her delicate shoulders with his large and clumsy hands, and his stout body was shaking. Mithra could not believe her grandfather was crying.

"I know baby, I know you had a lot of pain; I know how hard it was," Taham whispered in Mithra's ear. "I won't let them get hurt you again, I swear!"

Astyages went out to let Taham cry freely. Taham drew back and stared at Mithra's face. "How have you gotten away with this for so long? All this time, you've had a hard time!" He said as he was crying like a child.

Mithra did not know what she should say or do. She was unused to being asked so directly, to react emotionally but Taham did not look waiting for her response, he was staring at her, but he seemed oblivious, lost in thoughts. Taham hesitated for a few moments. He had hidden his past for many years; he did not like to think about that, and it was not easy for him to confess, but he wanted Mithra to know that he could feel her pain.

"Believe me; I know exactly how you feel…," Taham said and lifted up his sleeve.

Mithra stared at her grandfather in wonder; Mithra's sign on his arm was so clear that even her blurry vision able to recognize it. She could not believe her eyes.

"Grandpa…" She had no other word to say.

"Yes, baby! It's like a waking nightmare," Taham said, his voice still trembling. "I've passed this fucking challenge, just like you!"

His words frightened Mithra. "And now…," She asked.

"No, No, it's been years that I left that fucking mystic cult!" Taham stared at her, sighed. "I don't blame you. I know why you had taken refuge in there. I know, and I blame myself, but I swear you I never leave you alone again, never!"

Astyages entered, and Mithra looked at her grandfather curiously. The old man nodded. "Yes, he knows everything. Astyages is a reliable man, and he needed to know everything to help us," he said. Astyages came forward and sat beside Taham. The old man looked at him with affection. "He has already saved your life," he added.

Astyages smiled. "I'm not really sure it's appropriate time but…," he sounded weird, "… but there's something you should know." He paused, and it made Mithra more worried. "You know, Saber got news from several people in Diheh… Mahbod is one of them…"

"Who does he fucking think he is!" Taham grumbled with disgust.

"Since he shouldn't find out about our absence…" Astyages paused.

There was this long pause. Taham finally stands up, overwhelmed. "You're as slow as molasses in January!" Taham said to Astyages and turned to Mithra. "We're supposed to find you, right? Our delay has aroused that motherfucker suspicions. We did what we had to do, cooking a story for the whole people." He cleared his throat. "So we've said you escaped at night together! The king sent a special messenger that allows you to get married; this confirmed our story and Saber believed it too," Taham said hastily but then hesitated for a moment. "Your engagement ceremony is tomorrow night," he added merely.

Mithra was staring at Taham uncomprehending, beneath that gaze, the old man wilted.

"Your life was in danger; I must come up with a plan soon...," Taham said grumbling as he was going to the door to get out of the house, his voice murmured behind the door. Astyages came to her, slowly, looked at Mithra. She stared down at her hands. No one could know what was inside her mind. "It was your grandfather plan..."

Mithra raised her head slowly and looked into his face with a sweet, dim smile. She grabbed his shirt, drew him down and kissed his lips, firmly and passionately.

*****

The bride and groom should not see each other during the ceremony; it was an old Mannaean tradition.

The room was warm and airless of women's breathing, despite the chilly winter weather.

Golden filigrees were dancing on her forehead, Mithra pushed aside them, so tense. She crossed her arms and let out a deep sigh. *Too many peoples for too many hours,* Mithra thought. No one had seen her smile that since she grew bored with the women's gabbling about herself and she was looking at others with a serious face.

"Look up and smile."

Mithra raised her head and saw her aunt. The filigrees trembled on her forehead. "Must I look ridiculous?"

"Yes, unless you'd not really want to marry with Astyages!" Ashvan said as she put a fake smile on her lips to hide her irritation.

"Those things." Mithra pointed to her forehead. "I can't tell you how much these things itched," she said with a sullen face.

Ashvan threw an angry look at her. "Don't have to say it, I know how you feel, I was a bride myself once!" then she smiled a sweet smile when she saw one of the influential nobles' women from the corner of her eye. "Smile!" Ashvan said to Mithra as she was leaving her.

Mithra's lips twitched in what might have been a smile. She was feeling a very chill weakness crawling up her spine, surrounding her. She had taught to show no pain, but she has turned weak and lost her power.

"When they will get off from here?" Mithra whispered against Nahira's ear.

"Huh?! They? Who's they?" Nahira said as she was watching the girls' dance with joy.

"They: women, men, guests," Mithra said. "Everybody who dropped anchor in here."

"Well, whenever the ceremony ends!" Nahira said.

"When does the ceremony end?" Mithra asked impatiently.

"When the groom comes to see the bride and take her bandanna," Nahira said.

"So, Why Astyages doesn't come to get this damn bandanna?" Mithra asked.

Nahira was staring at her, surprised. "You're kidding me, or you don't really know that the groom doesn't come until the middle of the night," she said.

"Why?" Mithra growled.

"It's the custom, everyone does it!" Nahira said as she was laughing.

Mithra turned her face, her eyes met Ashvan's fat maid, she watched her smile that turned up the corners of her firm mouth, she could recognize her derisively laughing even with her blurred vision.

"So when the groom takes the bride's bandanna, the party will be over and all go, right?" Mithra asked quietly.

Nahira looked at her and smiled. "Yes!" She said.

Mithra got up immediately.

"Where are you going?" Nahira sounded shocked.

"The groom is too late!" Mithra said as she went to the door.

"Mithra Wait!" Nahira rushed to her. "Please don't, please!"

All the women stared at Mithra. She went with firm steps to the main chamber, where the men had gathered. She opened the door suddenly. The sound of the door drew the men's attention to her. She entered as she was taking off her bandanna. Mithra looked for Astyages, her blurred eyes saw him seated among the men.

"Take it!" Mithra shouted.

Astyages caught the bandanna before it hit the ground, laughing. The guests were staring at this strange scene; no one said a word. Ashvan came there in a hurry, but nothing could be done. She looked at the people who stared at them and begun cheering with joy; almost immediately after her, the room burst into loud applause.

Ashvan put Mithra's hand in Nahira's hand. "Take her to the upper room before I kill her," Ashvan said.

There was no need to force, Mithra went upstairs hurryingly, and Nahira followed her. Mithra sat at the corner of the room, next to the fireplace and closed her burning eyes.

"Okay," Nahira said. "Now tell me everything!"

"What do you want to know?" Mithra asked without opening her eyes.

"You must tell me what happened?" Nahira was looking at her with great interest. "How did you fall in love with a guy and ran away with him in a few days? Tell me everything!" She said.

"Why do you ask, when you know I say nothing?" Mithra said dryly.

Nahira shrugged. "I don't know! I thought, now that you can fall in love, you must be a natural human," she said.

"Don't ever expect such things from me! Now tell me." Mithra opened her eyes and stared at Nahira curiously. "Since when did the people know about Astyages and me?"

"Two or… three days!" Nahira said.

Mithra grinned. "That means since the first day!" She said.

"You can't hide the news from the people," Nahira said.

"Yes, especially if you have someone like Zarvan!" Mithra taunted.

"Don't say anything about my father behind his back!" Nahira said, threatening.

"I'm right; you knew." Mithra turned her face to the fire. "Always remain true to yourself!"

Nahira hesitated. "Sorry, I cannot be you… besides nothing's changed, they'd find out sooner or later!" She said irritated.

Mithra glanced at her. "Well; don't overdo it," she said.

Nahira had sulked, although not for too long. "You are the object of girl's envy, they hate you!" She said, laughing.

"I got nothing new!" Mithra said calmly.

"Well, I think he's very handsome that makes perfect sense!" Nahira looked at Mithra frowning. "What would Grandpa have against Astyages?" She asked as if she figured out the something new.

Mithra did not want to hurt her feeling again. "Because Astyages is poor… I suppose." She had no better answer.

"Please, don't bullshit me!" Nahira said, looking sullenly. "The king's nephew can't be poor!"

Funny thing was; she even did not know who her husband's father was.

"Quit leering at me!" Mithra said. "I had said not to mention that again!"

"You'll never change, will you?" Nahira said and turned her face to the window. "The guests are almost gone."

Mithra had a fever, and she was feeling chilled with cold sweat. "Good, I'm dying to find a quite a place to sleep," she said.

Nahira grinned. "It was idiotic," she said.

Mithra moved, trying to prevent of rubbing her silk shirt onto the wound. "What are you smirking at?" She said.

"I've never seen so much indifference bride in my entire life." Nahira glanced at the people through the window again. "It's only the beginning when all others leave, we should go to the guestroom."

"Why the guestroom again?" Mithra moaned, wondering.

"It's a custom!" Nahira said calmly.

"May not you run the customs to me with all the details?" Mithra growled.

"It's not our fault," Nahira answered irritated. "Grandpa has personally ordered us to run everything well and with all the details."

"Quite good," Mithra said bored. "Why would we go there?"

"The groom and his family come to visit the bride to wish her a happy life!" Nahira said with frustration. "You really don't know those customs?"

Mithra ignored her taunt. "The groom doesn't have a family!" She said impatiently.

Nahira looked out. White Mansion's huge garden gradually became empty of guests. The cold wind was sweeping around some remaining, made them walk faster; even the women who were carefully holding up, so their expensive dress's long skirt did not touch the ground.

"I've heard he'll come with Lord Saber," Nahira said.

"Lord Saber?" Mithra was looking right at her. "Who would see him as a Lord?" She asked angrily.

Nahira was shocked by Mithra's sharp tone.

"I don't know… Well, Mahbod was calling him like that," Nahira said.

"Yeah, Mahbod should call him LORD!" Mithra said sharply. "That son of a bitch is his master!"

Nahira's mouth twisted in disgust. "You hate him, but that doesn't mean he's a bad guy."

"Listen to me." Mithra got up and moved closer to Nahira. "You do love Mahbod, don't you?" Nahira was staring at her with no word. "If you were, put as much distance between Mahbod and these filthy vermin as possible!"

Nahira noticed tonight for once, Mithra's eyes were too red and watery. "You scared me!" She said.

"You should be!"

Mithra's dry voice echoed in Nahira's head many times.

*****

Saber entered the room. The way he looked, precisely the same, dressed in a coarse black woolen cloak and a sullen face. He kissed Taham's shoulder as is customary in Mannea and sat down beside him.

Mithra was hiding her eyes from Saber. A few moments passed with silence.

"I think your daughter can't live without trouble. Isn't it?" Saber said as he put a cold smile on his lips.

"No, actually the trouble is looking for her," Taham replied, his voice was trembling a little.

Saber laughed. "If you're speaking about my young commander, I have to say he has been a diffident young before; I don't know why he has shifted in Mannea," he said.

Zarvan glanced at Taham's angry face. "Love comes softly," he said hastily, hoping to change the moods. He looked at their faces with fear to see the result of his words. For Zarvan, this marriage could be a big advantage; he was sure he will be the next the paramount of the tribe with the support of the king.

"Yes, Love comes softly!" Taham said thoughtfully as he stared at Mithra.

The pain was more than Mithra could endure it easily; she could not smile and hide her irritation.

"Tonight I had one of the best nights I've ever had," Zarvan said, trying to get things straight.

Saber looked at him out of the corner of his eye; obviously did not like him. "But our bride doesn't seem very happy; it is better we leave her," he said as he stood up; others followed him. He went to the Mithra, looked at her eyes and took her arms with both hands.

"God bless this marriage and make this woman happy, abiding and fertile," Saber said loudly, sticking his hand in the exact same place of her wounds. He was monitoring Mithra's face carefully. The pain was unbearable, and she was breathless from the sharp pain, but she looked at Saber with a calm face. *Old fox, you know well that disciples of Mithra have learned how to endure the pain without words,* Mithra thought.

Saber grinned, left her hands and sauntered to the door.

"I'll see you in the camp, Lord Commander!" Astyages said.

Saber turned to him. "Yes, it's the groom turn to break the traditions!" He said with an archly smile and went off. Zarvan followed him quickly.

Taham looked at Ashvan and Nahira. "Why are you standing here?" He Shouted.

Nahira and Ashvan exchanged looks, stunned. "Where else would we be?" Ashvan said.

"I don't know, wherever you want; your home!" Taham shouted again.

Ashvan and Nahira went out of the room surprisingly, and Taham rushed to Mithra. "Let me see, take off your shirt!" He said. "That fucking bastard knows everything. There is not a thing he doesn't know."

Mithra was standing motionless, and Astyages was beside her.

"I told you to take off your shirt; right now," Taham shouted angrily.

Mithra pulled her sweater off shyly as she was trying to wrap herself in her thin underwear more. There was some bloodstained piece of the white bandage around her arm. The old man turned to the Astyages.

"Close windows panels and bring my bag from the closet," Taham roared.

Astyages obeyed his commands quickly, and Taham began to change Mithra's bandage.

The wounds were almost being restored, but the poison was still working; at least once every day Taham was cleaning the blisters on the scars but new blisters apparent which burst easily and made her skin injury and filthy.

Astyages sat beside Taham. "Saber knows nothing. He could not be sure...," Astyages said.

Taham interrupted him. "You can go. Your commander is waiting for you," Taham said as he was rubbing prepared poultice on Mithra's wounds.

Astyages hesitated. "You are upset; you should be, but please help me to take the right steps. We need Mithra's help to get out of this dangerous situation," he said.

"Help? Mithra is a young woman, just a young woman not a warrior or spy; could you understand?!" Taham growled.

Mithra wanted to say something, but Taham's angry and heavy look kept her silent.

"The cult's last meeting before spring will be a few weeks later," Astyages said discreetly. "It will be our last chance to know what Saber's plan is."

Taham threw the bowl of poultice aside angrily. "Damn the cult! I don't let my daughter goes to that dangerous place, I don't." Taham kept his voice low, but they could hear the fury in his tone.

Astyages did not know what he should do. "I suppose it is better to talk later!" He said finally.

The old man was trying to calm his anger by tearing the dressing cloth. "No! There is no word. Mithra won't go to this meeting, you can also tell your commander you regretted of marrying, and everything ends easily," he said.

"But...," Astyages said.

Taham did not let him speak. "Your king has taken my son from me; I don't let him do the same thing again." Taham stared at Astyages. "If you want, you can take your life in danger, but my daughter should not be sacrificed for your king," Taham said.

Astyages grinned. "What? You suppose I want to finish this mission for the king; because I am the king's nephew?" He said. He went to the window to hide his emotion. "You are wrong my Lord; you're wrong," Astyages said as he was staring out through the panel gaps. "Cyaxares has killed my father by a conspiracy to don't have an heir to his throne, and you think I want to sacrifice my life or your daughter's for my king. My parents have sacrificed their lives for this country, and I'd learned to do that."

Taham peeked at Astyages and then put his head down; trying to pretend that he had done the bandage.

Astyages turned to them. He had overcome his feelings. "Cyaxares is a selfish and cruel man, but he knows politic well. He knows what is good for carrying forward his plans. He has plans that will give strength to our country. If he wins, this land won't be a place where every ethnic occasionally attack it, massacre the people, burn our young boys and girls and looted their assets. Median won't be a nation longer; it will be a country, a strong country. The Persian land!" Astyages said breathlessly.

Taham was wrapping the cloth around Mithra's arm. "We had believed in the words of Phraortes[1] once, the former king and your grandfather. He had spoken nicely too. We decided to attack the Assyrians. The only thing we have earned is ignominy, disgrace, and more tribute," Taham said without looking at Astyages.

Astyages came forward and knelt beside him. "This time is different. As I said, Cyaxares is the man of war and politics. He is currently preparing an army that will be more powerful than Assyrian, but we should help him. It's not because of the king, but because of our people, our country, for what your son fought valiantly, with honor and dignity," he said then paused to see the impact of his words on the old man's face.

Taham seemed to be a bit calmer.

"Also, if Mithra won't be in that meeting, Saber's suspicion changed to certainty and..." Astyages did not finish his words.

---

[1]Son of Deioces, was the second king of the Median Empire

"He kills me!" Mithra completed Astyages' words. Her arm dressing was finished. "I'll go but not for my life. I want to change the future of this land as well as I!" Mithra said as she wearing her shirt.

*****

It was night, the dark night as evil's heart, with no end. A heavy curtain of silence seemed to have fallen around the world, and the coldness had crept into the flame of fire. It was the end of the world. Suddenly, in the mountains, into a cave of Marble, a sharp light that glowered in the East took shape! She was born into the fire, dressed in red silk, of flames; long wavy hair as black as smoke and big beautiful eyes, which shone like an ember.

She stepped out of the cave, shining on the earth. Mithra stood on the mountain, and looked over the world, which was cold and lifeless! It was time to flow the life on Earth. Mithra glanced at her golden dagger on her waist scarf, took her bow, and walked; she must found Holy Red Bull.

Holy Red Bull was pawing with the forefeet, deep in the meadow, sending dirt flying behind. His long horns seize up the sky, and his thick muscles showed the extraordinary power of life blown by Ahura Mazda in his body. Mithra stared at him behind the trees, wondering why life should be started from death!

Evil trembled, imagined how difficult it will be for him when life spread over the world.

He hated the light, the growth and the birth of love. He did not grow in love so had to remain in death. *This never should've happened,* the evil thought angrily. He looked around, saw a scorpion crawling in the mud and a satisfied smile sat on his black and ugly lips. If life was going to born, he should have his part in it.

Mithra was on the back of the Holy Red Bull, breathlessly. The bull that had no more power slept under her thighs obediently. Mithra pulled the dagger out from her waist scarf and put on the bull's neck. She turned her face Involuntary; the death was painful for her, although it was a sign of life. Suddenly she saw the scorpions on the ground beneath the bull's foot, insidiously.

The sound of the evil laughter echoed in the deepest hole in the ground and filled the sky.

The scorpion that had made poisonous the holy bull's seeds of life fled to seek refuge in the darkness with all the speed it could. The evil's cold voice was heard from the underneath, from the heart of the earth, "All living will desire the darkness in their hearts on this earth, from now on."

Mithra stared at the outburst blood. This blood was her share of life on earth, but the god of love cannot live alone; she let the land be stained with the blood of Holy Bull. The plants began to grow, and life flowed in the veins of the earth!

Mothers in Mannea, in the darkest and longest night of the year, the last night of autumn, whispered the story of the birth of love to their children's ears. When the children gazed at their mother's face, sorrowful, the mothers were saying, "but one day Mithra will come; in a golden chariot, pulled by a white horse that the ground caught fire below its hooves."

*****

Icicles dangled from the shadowy skeletons of trees, each one like an ominous crystal spear from the gods. Sometimes a terrible sound of cracking ice on the frozen river was heard through the night.

Astyages had grown his hair out and has a full beard like Mannaean men. He was wearing a sheepskin coat under his fur cloak, but still felt the coldness even through his bone marrow. Mithra was going by on her horse, wearing a wolf fur cloak, through down the snowy slope, watching the snowfall. Astyages slipped his hand down; taking a bottle of wine from his saddlebag, drink deep. *I disobeyed a direct order and drink wine during my essential mission,* he thought. However, he was feeling the fear like a cold blade on his heart. He was not commanded to be brave, but they ordered to hide his fears. He gulped. *I couldn't find a better way,* he thought. He shook the bottle; there was not much left.

"Mithra!" Astyages said.

She seemed oblivious, lost in thoughts. "Hum?"

"What are you thinking about?" Astyages asked.

"Nothing!" Mithra answered simply.

That answer broke his hope for a conversation with her. He retook a sip of wine. A deeply colored wine of purples and reds, full-bodied from vineyards on the Shore of Chichest Lake, that was sweet, aromatic and a rich earthy flavor; the wine that was heavy enough that made his head spin. Astyages was riding slowly, a few steps behind Mithra. He looked at her; she was sitting straight on her mare. Her hair was blowing wildly in the wind. Unlike him, she was not wearing too many clothes, only a wolf fur shawl over her shoulder. She was blind to everything and stared into the distance, riding slowly with a slow, mesmerizing rhythm that swiveled her hips.

Astyages swallowed. "Slow down, we have at least one hour before the ceremony starts," he said.

"Could I riding slower?" Mithra said, grinning. "We'll be in the remnants a few minutes then you can get some rest." She hesitated then added, "You insisted come with me, isn't it?"

"Goddamn your mouth," Astyages growled. "Your mouth gives me bad feeling all the time!"

Mithra seemed not to hear him. Astyages swallowed the rest of the wine with a gulp, slammed the empty bottle down, on the thick layer of snow, and wiped his mouth with the back of his hand. He noticed a crow sitting on a rock watching them.

"That crow, see it? It may seem corny, but it's chasing us!" Astyages said.

"It's okay. That's with me!" Mithra said calmly.

"Are you making fun of me?" Astyages said irritated.

"No," Mithra said. "Come on. Under here."

"I know it's here!" Astyages said with a gloomy face.

Astyages was sitting on a rotten bench in the remnants, wondering why the wine could not help him or at least warm him.

Mithra tied her horse to a nearby tree with loose reins so the mare could walk around.

"Stay here, I'll back soon!" Mithra said.

Astyages' mind caught fire with these words. He recalled his mother's voice. 'Stay here. I'll be right back.' However, she was never returned; her body was found in the backyard of their home as Astyages was hidden beneath the rose bushes, which his mother so loved them. "I'm sure you know what's going to happen to you, if Saber had just recognized you, right?" His voice was hoarse with remembered grief.

"It didn't seem he had recognized me." Mithra pulled her mask out of the saddlebag. "I have to go," she said. "I still have a long way to go!"

"Why are you going there?" Astyages asked.

Mithra heard his voice right behind her ears, turned and saw him, staring at her with worried eyes. She smiled. "Someone told me to do." Then she added with a serious face. "We need to know what's going on in tonight's ceremony." She turned to go. "And I shouldn't be late for it!"

"Forget about what I said that day," Astyages said. "You don't have to go up there if you don't want to!"

Mithra could smell wine on his breath. "Are you drunk?" She asked, surprised.

"Yes, I am so drunk!" Astyages said as he was staring right into her eyes. "I'm shitty ass drunk!"

"You've lost your mind?" Mithra said angrily "You got drunk on a night like that?"

"Yes," Astyages yelled. "I got drunk because I'm afraid." His voice was trembling. "I had never been so afraid."

He turned to hide his emotions.

"I'm afraid too," Mithra muttered, low under her breath. "The brave man is not who does not feel afraid, but he who conquers that fear."

"I don't want to be brave!" Astyages struck his fist against the rotten wall; turned and stared at her. "I want to spend my life with you."

Mithra looked at him. He looked like a little boy, asking for his mother; Astyages needed her most, even more than what she needed him. She smiled. Her hands raised, slowly, her fingers curled around her shirt collar and gave a hard yank. The silk came tearing away, baring her to the waist. Astyages was staring at her; widen eyes. In the lantern's glow, her skin shone smooth, her face serene. The wind was ripping around her, and her curly red-brown hair was dancing in front of her face. Her breasts were high and firm, round with large brown nipples; the snowflakes kissing her tender skin and melted immediately.

He had faded into her, could not keep his eyes from her, half-open mouth, that showed a little of her white teeth. Her eyes were lakes of melted gold turbulent with passion. Mithra was breathing heavily; her warm breath was turning into puffs of smoke in the chilly air. She opened her scarf belt from her waist and stepped forward as her black pants fell down to the ground. She was naked, wearing only tight leather boots.

Astyages tried to control his breathing; it's probably one of the only things he can control. Mithra came closer; her burning eyes were fixed on him. She stretched forth her hand towards him, removed the cloak from his shoulders and threw onto the ground. He could not imagine himself bare into the snow, but he desired to seize her above all things.

She pushed him down on his cloak, wrapping her fingers around him, raised his hand above his head. She sat back on her knees and pulled herself over him, her tongue stroking along his bottom lip and into his mouth.

Astyages could not move as Mithra's powerful hands grabbed his hands and tied him to the ground. If she did not break her kisses, he could not breathe too. Soon, he understood Mithra going to seize him. She was making love in her own way, breathtaking and somehow violent. He felt he had never made love before, she was different from others, she struck pleasure in his heart, mind and every part of his body which was in contact with her; the way Mithra had made love to him he didn't want it to end.

Her hands moved slowly along him and grabbed his hair, turn his head to one side, and her full lips slid on his skin towards his ear and start to sucking his earlobe. Her fingers began to slowly push through his hair up towards the top of his head, curl her fingers slightly and gently bring them down in the opposite direction, lightly scratching his head. Astyages moaned, feeling the inevitable quickening of his pulse.

She pinned him on his back by sitting on his chest; she stared at his half-opened eye and smiled a wicked smile. A tentative smile quirked at the corner of his mouth. He watched her fingers work the first unopened button of his shirt…

"How would you be able to endure the chilly cold at that stormy night?" Astyages asked.

"Are you cold?" Mithra asked, flirtatious.

"It's fucking cold here!" Astyages said as the icicles fell over his face.

"So I was not hot enough!" Mithra asked.

"No, no, no, I didn't mean…" He could not finish his words; she took a handful of snow and rubbed it on his bare chest. "OH!" Astyages whispered.

Her lips curled into a smile before they closed around his nipple. Snowflakes started melting between her hot lips and a desirable heat spread throughout Astyages' body. A small moan emanated from his throat; at his sound, she looked up at him, nipple still between her lips, and grinned. Astyages could watch his roll the point between her teeth and felt her tongue flickering. Slowly and torturously, Mithra began moving her fingers between his thighs.

Mithra looked up at him, her flushed face was dotted with beads of sweat, her beautiful eyes shining. She moved down, hesitated for a moment and then walked down fast and heaviness. Astyages pushed out his breath, closed his eyes and Mithra's fingers clenched against the sensation, digging into the snow, and her body froze for a few moments, then she started to move up and down. Astyages opened his eyes and stared at her.

Mithra's movement was something like a dance, a magical, fantastic dance. She was swaying, fingers plowing through her hair and rolling her belly's muscle. The wind was howling, and the snowdrops seemed dancing around her, motivated by her beautiful movements. Astyages arched his back as he cried out with delight, feeling those intense waves of pleasure…

Astyages lied down on the ground, shivering, but he was not cold; he did not feel the coldness anymore. He took a deep breath, trying to calm his pounding heart. "How could you do that so fucking fantastic?" He asked.

Mithra stood up, slowly; Astyages looked up and noticed multiple thin streams of blood trickling down her inner thighs. "You're… You had not had sex before?" Astyages said; half raised.

Mithra went to her saddlebag. "A Mannaean girl loses her virginity only when she has chosen a man that is worthy of her love!" She said quietly.

Astyages stared at her; she looked a bit peaky; he felt ashamed of himself.

She glanced at him as she was pulling a handkerchief out of the saddlebag. "Don't look at me!" She said.

Astyages turned, immediately. "A…re you sore?" He asked as he poured himself into his clothes.

There was a long pause. "No!" Mithra finally said.

Astyages stood up, dressed in the clothes that were a bit wet. "It was not my first time to…" He had to confess. "Can I turn?"

"Yes!"

When he turned, saw Mithra, dressed in Mithra's cult burnouse. "Where are you going?" He asked, surprised.

"Where I'm supposed to be!" Mithra said.

"Why? I thought you didn't like the people!" Astyages said.

"Sometimes the heart sees what is invisible to the eye," Mithra answered.

*****

Many men had gathered in the behind the altar to pray. The altar, in turn, led into the entrance hall, there were twelve similar pairs of pillars, which made the antechamber, two long, narrow chambers branched off from either end, and two huge statues of Mithra were on the dark passages. Mithra entered, trying to make sure that she did not attract any unwanted attention.

There was coming a great Daf's sound, and men in black were humming weird spells. The paters, including Saber, were sitting on the platform, talking to each other with the most serious faces. There seemed to be a severe problem with no agreement.

Mithra looked at Holy Pater, neither of them seemed happy, but the old man seemed distinctly upset, even angry. Mithra could see the tightness around his mouth and barely suppressed anger in his eyes. Holy Pater was talking quietly, but suddenly Saber sat up straight, raised his hand to stop Holy Pater's words regardless of his angry eyes and went to the men.

He made a hand signal, and the Dafs fell silent. Saber stepped forward slowly but firmly. He stood in the middle of the altar, in his long white robe and a halo of burners smoke, he seemed taller, broader, more imposing than he really was.

"Brothers," Saber glanced at the men.

Mithra moved closer and listened, expecting to hear something essential but her movement dragged Saber's eyes to her, and he stopped talking at once. Mithra put her head down and hid behind the men who were crowding forward to hear Saber's words. He paused uncertainty but then continued. "Brothers, Mannea's long, tough winter has begun. During the winter we don't have our usual meetings, we get together again when the long, cold winter nights fade into spring, so I want to inform you of some my news. All you are trusted members; I trusted you and shared all my worries with you. You have faced tough challenges, and you are always bringing victory tough. All these challenges have made you brave and strong because you should fight at war with darkness and win to reach real light," he said, looked at the men carefully. "But not here, not into the caves… your king seeks immortality on Earth, a false paradise. This is heresy. He leads you towards vanity, away from the spirit. You must get out of the dark caves and fight in the battlefield."

The uproar that followed was all Saber could have hoped for that.

"Cyaxares, the king of the land of Medes has broken the oath that he swore with blood, and the government, which was designed for pleased Mithra, has got into the hands of the Maggie's who worship Ahura and don't believe Mithra." Angrier voices were raised in the hall. "The king needs his permission to make decisions for our land!" Saber said with a swift, bitter chuckle. "We can't just sit here and do nothing," he shouted, and everyone fell in silent. "If we do not act quickly, our faith in God will be lost forever!"

Men began to yell, showing their anger to the king. Saber waited until the uproar had died away then he said, "I won't endure the darkness, we are going to fight against it, against the king or any enemy." The anger had crept back into his voice, and his tone rose steadily. "If our God just gives us his command, we fight to destroy the king."

His voice faded in the men's rough roar.

"I want to feel the full hate in your voice…," Saber shouted, above all and the men screamed again somehow with their whole body. The eyes wide, the fists clenched with blanched knuckles, it sounded like a scream of wild panic.

The voices were shrieking in Mithra's head, she wished to be as far away from them as possible. She was not the only one who could not wait until the meeting finish, the horns played before the appointed time. The session was ended, but the men did not seem to want to get out very fast. They founded their faith endangered, and they were wrathful. They were talking loudly, mouth foaming, a mad glitter in their bloodshot eyes, seemed as though they stood threatening heaven, and earth, and hell. Saber stood in the middle of the hall, raised his both hands and stimulated the men with reading spells with dirge-like voice, and they went out gradually when some of the paters left the room with the rage.

Saber had stood still in the middle of the hall, whispering spells with a sort of hissing voice. Many of the men were kissing his hand as they passed and the other held his shawl before their face to bless themselves and he caresses them with his hand on the head. Mithra hid away in a shady nook then tried to slip away unseen whilst Saber and Holy Pater had their attention elsewhere.

"Our favorite disciple!" Saber took her by the arm. "Where are you going in such a hurry?" He said.

Mithra looked up; Saber's cold eyes were staring at her and his fingers squeezing her arm so hard that they hurt. She watched him, tempted to wrench herself free and run away but she had not been as foolish as want to fight with those men.

"He's your disciple, isn't he?" Saber said as he was walking to the platform where Holy Pater was talking seriously with the paters. "I haunted him escaping out of the temple secretly!"

Holy Pater turned, stared at him with sullen eyes and walked to them.

"Just how well do you know him?" Saber asked.

"Very well, he has been my disciple for two years; he is brave with a big desire to God," Holy Pater said, frowning.

"Yes, he is brave…" Saber glanced at Mithra. "I would see this brave young man's face for myself," he said.

His word sent a chill through her, the room felt colder than it should. Saber raised his hand, wanting to take her mask off. Mithra tried to wet her dry lips with an equally dry tongue and breathe normally.

"Enough!" Holy Pater's loud voice stopped him. "I am unable to deal with this humiliation any longer."

Saber rushed into the silence he left. "My apologies if I have given offense," he said. "I'm clearly suspicious of him, and I must be sure of his identity."

"This is against our rules, and I see no reason for it." Holy Pater kept his voice low, but Mithra could hear the fury in his tone.

"He knows our secret; what reason can be better than that?" Saber said calmly.

Holy Pater put his hand on Mithra's shoulder. "I think you're going too far," he said. "You started to speak without my permission, about something that I haven't entirely agreed with it and now, you dare to accuse my disciple of being a spy, I can no longer turn a blind eye to this situation."

"I feel certain that SHE is a spy!" Saber said, looking at the men who stared at them, grinned and added. "Yes, SHE is!"

Others who had gathered around them seemed curious. Holy Pater glanced at them. "I see no reason for it, because...," he looked at Mithra's widen eyes and added, "... because I have seen him without a mask." Mithra felt his fingers trembled on her shoulder.

A silence fell.

Saber looked Shocked "But..."

"Enough!" Holy Pater almost shouted.

"Everyone knows Holy Pater have never lied," one of the paters said with a sullen face.

Saber gave him a puzzled face. "Yes," he said. "I know Holy Pater does not lie!"

"Go home!" Holy Pater said to Mithra.

She glanced around herself nervously, Saber was frozen in his place, but no one else seemed surprised. She rushed out, looked back before she got into the corridor, the old man was looking at her with worried eyes. Her heart filled with gratitude, she knew how it had been hard to tell a lie to him.

A rush of wind came whispering through the rocks as if scary music by the devil ghosts. Mithra did not believe that she was outside of the temple… in no danger. "It's over! It's done!" She whispered, looking at the temple's dark corridor. She began to run, crouching as she scrambled crab-legged down the hill. She stumbled and fell, rose, then fell again but did not stop until she found herself far away from them.

*****

It was only hours later, they were sitting in Nanny's hunt kitchen, watching as the gray light of morning bled through the mountain.

"Why don't you just arrest him in Mannea?" Mithra asked, lying in Astyages' arms. "I don't see what on earth keeps you to ignore him and his dangerous ways! That bastard is building an army; our chance of stopping him will get slim if he succeeds."

Mithra was so close, Astyages could smell her pleasant scent, feel hot of her body. He closed his eyes for a moment, feeling her was so good and he preferred to think about something better than Saber, but Mithra was anxious.

"It's not easy," Astyages said briefly, caressing her tender skin.

Mithra was not satisfied with this answer. "What do you mean?" She asked.

Astyages sighed. "Saber has hidden behind the god's name to gain power and wealth, many people in Mannea still believe in Mithra so if we catch him we had only provoked the people to fresh outrage when we need to be united at times like this!"

"You're absolutely right!" Mithra said thoughtfully. "Then what do you say we do?" Astyages kissed her lightly on the nose

"Make love!" He whispered softly in her ear.

"I'm serious!" Mithra said, frowning.

"So am I!" Astyages said laughingly. "There are two important things to know. First, Saber is colluding with the Assyrians, and it will mean trouble for him because the people of Mannea strongly hate the Assyrians more than they hate any other tribe because all the Assyrian attacks have ended in death, disaster, and disgrace for Mannea. Second, as you say it is clear that not all the paters are agreed with him. You will see; both of these reasons are enough to settle down him."

"I don't quite see what the hell's that got to do with making love?" Mithra said.

"When he sees us busy loving each other maybe he would make things run a little more smoothly around him and make a big mistake." His thumb caressed her jaw as he gazed down into her face. "Make love is a pretty delicious opportunity to defeat him," Astyages said.

Mithra kissed his thumb. "Are you ready?" She said.

Astyages raised his brows. "Ready for what?" He asked.

She laughed. "For defeating Saber!"

"I want to defeat him more than anything in the whole world!" Astyages said.

CHAPTER EIGHT

THE GOLDEN CUP

Ancient Land of Mannaeans, 627 BC, Spring

Quite softly, one day following another, bleak winter has passed into spring. New buds have appeared on the apple trees, the promise of spring blossom and leave to come, the grass was green and the flowers all the colors of the rainbow! The air now positively vibrated with birdsong as the nesting parents called to one another in the fresh air and gentle breeze. The sunlight flooded the farms, with its golden glow, giving its heat to the rich sandy soil that had been like ice only weeks before.

In Mannea, spring was the king of seasons, a time to be born again, a time to build, a time to love and a time to heal, when love was waving in the air, an opportunity for hand-in-hand strolling. Love was born in spring, tapped into the soul with a glance but remained into the heart for a lifetime.

A little sapling that sixteen years ago had seen on Chista's grave was now a tree above the grave, already in blossom, its branches spread over the grave.

A gentle breeze passed through the tree and hundreds of delicate cherry blossom petals, fluttering through the air, like a soft flurry of pink snow scattered across the mountain slopes, landing in her headstone. Taham always liked hanging out with the one he loved her more than everyone, like all lovers in the world, he rode hours to visit his wife's grave, sit beside her, confess his feelings for her, his sadness, his loneliness, his missing for her.

Taham's fingers brushing across the rough stone as gently as if it was Chista's face. He began to go over in his mind, the dark rock brought back the memory of years ago, the last time he had seen his wife's face. He even did not notice that she has grown thin; her cheeks have sunken, making her black eyes too large for her face. The vanquishing of his enemies was Taham's only concern. The victory seemed easy, but he had expected the result to be so essentially serviceable to him, more reputation, and money. *I considered no one but myself,* he thought, *but Chista never forgot her man.* She had picked up her husband luggage with high precision, made new footwear for him, and escorted him as her anguished, tearless eyes, burning in her white face.

There is nothing in the world like the devotion of a married woman; her husband is her world's hero. She believes in him, even if the whole world stands against him. *It is a thing no married man knows anything about but it doesn't make any difference because she is a woman in love,* Taham thought and burst into tears. A shadow devoured him and the tomb of Chista suddenly. Taham returned to the world. He hastily wiped his face with the back of his hands as he turned back.

"Lord Commander?" He said with an unwelcome tone.

Saber was standing there, staring at him. "I had come to check the old castle, it needs repair," he said. "I saw you in the distance, and I headed in that direction, I don't bother you, isn't it?"

"No," Taham said as he grudgingly rose to his feet. "I should return."

"Great; which means we both have the same way?" Saber said.

Taham chuckled. "We can't go together," he said. "You have the stronger horse!"

Saber laughed. "Don't be afraid! We go as slow as your old horse likes," he said oblivious to his taunting, and he mounted his horse.

They started back the way they had come. Taham was sitting quietly in his saddle, watching the road. They ride in silence for a while.

"I saw you, crying at the grave of your wife," Saber said.

The mention of his crying made Taham furious, but he only nodded slowly.

"Hard to believe," Saber looked at him with his sharp jeering look. "It's a little funny, you're still in love after years," he said as he stared at the road with his cold eyes again. "Strong men start looking for a new mate fairly soon…"

Taham rushed into the silence he left. "She was my world, my rock, my best friend, and my wife! I owe my life to her," he said, his mouth tightened into a hard line. "I learned so many things from her."

Saber gazed up at him with wonder. "You have learned from a woman? Are you kidding me? They have nothing to teach but getting pregnant and gabbling!" He shook his head. "I'm assuming that you were blinded by love!" He said.

"And I'm assuming that you are blinded by pride," Taham said dryly. "I've seen a lot of women that were more intelligent, honest and loyal than men!"

Saber laughed hardly. "Surely they were pretty! Before the fucking, her every word is so beautiful but after that…" He laughed again. "Bullshits."

Taham stared at him. "Have you ever been in love? A wife? A mistress?" He asked.

"Never!" Saber answered proudly. "I have a different important goal to achieve; much more valuable than love." He smiled at Taham. "I never let a woman stopped me at achieving my goal," he said, with a straight back and an arrogant smile on his face.

"Sounds good, what's your goal?" Taham asked with a grin.

"That can reach to gods' pure light!" Saber stared at him, expecting to admiration.

"I'm afraid that's a difficult and miserable way of life that never works out!" Taham said, calmly. He could see the flush creeping up Saber's cheeks.

"How do you know? Do you know me? Did you know my austerity?" Saber said without pause.

Taham looked at him as if he was nuts. "No need to know you, this chain has a missing ring, so it doesn't work," he replied coolly.

"What ring?" Saber asked staring at Taham, waiting for an answer impatiently.

"Love!" Taham looked at him carefully. "You can learn the truth of love only through the love!" He said.

Saber laughed. "Aha, so if I want to find the light, the true love, I have to get married, fuck my wife and put damn babies in her belly, isn't it?" He said, his quizzical look and half-smile were telling Taham that he meant nothing to him. "How can you believe I'll find a love that's so pure and true by doing shit, isn't it foolish?"

"Dating a woman, making love, having a baby… if all sprinkled with love, you will know how to be a man, how to give love and how to receive it," Taham said. "You learn the rules of love so you can love people, love yourself and reach the true love without austerity."

Saber shrugged. "Love begins with God and has no meaning for whoever doesn't believe him, at this time, when infidels are everywhere you can just go forward with the sword, love comes to nothing," he said with hatred.

"Darkness cannot drive out darkness," Taham said. "If you don't love others, you can never love yourself. If you don't love yourself, you won't be able to love God who is true love!"

Saber grinned. "How can you love someone who wants to destroy you?" He said, shaking his head. "No, this idea is only a dream. It might be a sweet dream, but it's not true." He climbed down off his horse and grabbed the reins of Taham's horse, and pulled it to a stop. "Do you really believe what you said?" He asked.

Taham followed him and climbed down. "This belief has changed my life how I can I deny it?" He said.

Saber sat down on a rock close to the ground, and in the stony slope. "Now, you and I are alone in the mountain, nobody knows I'm with you... If I tell you, I hate your granddaughter, dear Mithra, and in the future, I will disappear her from the scene of life, no doubt... don't you try to kill me?" He said, smiling in that disgusting way he had.

A big drop of sweat slipped on Taham's spine. He tried to remain calm. "She is still very young, inexperienced, rash... I know, she has hard times trying to curb her fiery spirit which is continually getting her into trouble, but she is only a young woman, why do you hate her so much?"

Saber shook his head impatiently. "This is not a negotiation, Oldman. My nose is sharp, very sharp! It feels the smell of trouble very soon. I understand such things that others could understand much later. Your granddaughter seemed a young woman, but she is actually a small and gorgeous snake." He chuckled. "If I ignore her, I'll be regretted in the future. You can be sure that I'll kill this girl, but you have the chance to kill me before or... you can stay committed to bullshits that you preached for me, which one?"

Taham's hand touched the hilt of his sword unconsciously. Saber was staring at him with a look of scorn. *God, this man speaks from the hell,* Taham thought. He drew back his hand; wiped the sweat from his forehead with his sleeve and went toward his horse without saying a word.

"What happened?" Saber said behind him. "You are afraid of my bravery, or you know you told me bullshit, and now you have to run away?"

Taham did not turn; he went to his horse as he was shaking his head with pity, but suddenly Saber's painful scream attracted his attention.

Saber had taken his ankle in his fist, his face had shrunk from pain, looking at a big black snake that crawled along the boulder down and went away. Taham ran to him with all speed, knelt beside him and pulled out a dagger. Saber pulled back in fear but Taham who knew he should not lose even a moment, he ripped his shirtsleeves with haste; tied it tight above his ankle. He took Saber's ankle firmly, tore the skin on the top of the snakebite with his dagger and began immediately to suck the wound. He was filling his mouth with toxins and blood and spitting it on the ground. A few minutes later, Saber's ankle terrible swelling had reduced. Taham opened the fabric and wrapped it around the wound to stop the bleeding. He knew that Saber's life would not be in danger anymore but some of the poison will penetrate his body and will make him sick.

Taham looked at Saber, beads of sweat pouring down his face and ... he was staring at the tattooed sign on Taham's arm, the sign of the Mithra cult.

*****

It was sunset.

A fiery red orb of light slowly sank beneath the horizon and threads of light lingered in the sky, mingling with the rolling clouds, dyeing the sky orange. The paramount of the tribe's huge stone stalls stood up against the purple sky.

Mithra was surrounded by many sheep, grazing inside the fence. Astyages was looking at her, her arms wrapping around a cute little lamb, holding tight and caressing its soft and tender hair. It was a joy to watch the sheep peacefully grazing, while the lambs raced around, leaped and cavorted until they grew tired and laid down for a nap.

Taham's family treated Astyages like a member of their family now, and he and Mithra were together much of the time. Astyages was leaning against the fence, enjoying the beautiful spring shone around him and watching Mithra. He could spend hours sitting on it on the farm, watching her and dreaming of living with her but only a few moments later he heard the sound of horses' hooves and laughter. Nahira with Mahbod came towards them, horseback. Mahbod was talking about his skill in archery. "My first shot of arrow will hit the smallest apple set on the top of the stick at the end of the garden." Nahira was fascinated by him like always.

Golden Cup ceremony was coming up very soon, and many young men from across the Median land gathered in Mannea for this competition. Archery, horse racing, and wrestling, those were challenges, which gave the players more chance to show their skills. In spring, everyone in Mannea was talking about who would win and who failed.

"Some say there are no worthy competitors for Astyages in horse riding…," Mahbod said, "… but how can anyone look at my young stallion and take Astyages seriously." His voice was loud enough to get Astyages attention. Mahbod wanted to jump off his horse, but he stumbled and almost fell.

"I would never win," Astyages said laughingly.

Mahbod frowned. "Are you trying to be funny?" He came closer and glanced at Astyages. "You can quite be sure about yourself till the game ends when I'll look back and laugh," he said.

Mithra put the lamb upon the ground gently. "It's a pity that the women cannot be a part of the game," she said. "I could trounce both of you."

Nahira jumped over the fence hard. "She's right, her skills in horse riding is far better than others," she said.

"Everyone can be a winner if he had a horse like Morvarid!" Mahbod said.

"Really?" Mithra said. "Ok, fine! I don't need that golden cup; let's just play, right now."

She went to her brother and stared at him. "You can choose any horse you want!"

Mithra, Astyages, and Nahira stared at Mahbod, waiting for his answer.

"What are you staring at?" Mahbod said, frowning.

"You had your chance, why did you hesitate?" Astyages said, smiling.

"It's not a competition," Mahbod said, coldly.

Mithra shrugged. "Most men can't imagine losing to a woman!" She said.

"I never lose! I surely won't, but…" Mahbod did not finish his words and stared into the distance.

Mithra was looking at him with her mocking smile. "What happened to you?" She said.

Everyone looked up at him and then at where he was staring. Nahira's short scream drew Mithra's attention to the road!

Taham was walking right up to them; his shirt was torn in his arm, spotted with blood. Mithra jumped over the fence and ran to her grandfather quickly. Astyages, then Nahira and Mahbod followed her. The fear of Mithra's face made Taham want to open his arms for her. "Don't worry about me, baby, I'm fine," he said.

"Then what is this blood on your shirt?" Mithra asked.

"A snake bit Saber, I have his blood on my hands as well as my shirt," Taham said.

"Lord Saber?" Mahbod shouted at the top of his voice.

"Yes, Lord Saber!" Taham said with a mocking tone. "We were having a conversation in the mountain that a viper had stung him."

"How is he now?" Mahbod asked anxiously.

"Easy, easy!" Taham said; his voice was thick and angry. "He's not going to die. I took him to the army station. He must rest in bed for a few days, but he will be fine."

"I must see him personally," Mahbod said as he ran toward his horse.

Taham waved an angry hand. "Go, go," he said.

Nahira ran. "Let me come with you," she shouted at him.

"It's weird that a viper could bite another viper!" Mithra said, looking at her brother scornfully. "I wished you left him for dead!"

"I'm a healer, not a murderer!" Taham said; irritation in his voice.

"This isn't murder, it is punishment," Mithra said. "Crushing a scorpion!"

Taham gave her a scolding look. "You shouldn't talk about killing a man in such a way!"

"He is a deadly and dangerous creature," Mithra growled.

Taham interrupted her. "He is one of my people," he said. "As long as we stand alone on the battlefield." He sighed. "Who knows the future but God?" Taham was stroking Mithra's red-brown hair.

Astyages was walking along with them. He pointed to Taham's bare arm. "Did he see that?" Astyages asked.

The old man just took a peek at him. "He wasn't very well... yeah, well, l guess he saw the sign," Taham said.

Mithra looked at Astyages, worried. "I hope Saber has faith in humanity, like you!" She said.

*****

The hillside was crowded with dozens of tents and pavilions. The April wind was continually blowing from Binar Mountain, and the flaming red flags with their long tails were waving in the wind.

Nahira and Mithra were running through the camp. It was all just the same as Mannaean camp, the large mass of cook fires was made in front of the tents which weaved from the black hair of goats, at which neighbors cooked in common, the busy women with colorful costumes and children wandering freely. Mithra was rushing headlong to the arena, the match was about to begin in a few minutes. The competitions were held in a broad valley. The people could sit around, on the rocks and follow the games.

They rushing down through the valley. Mithra swiveled the eye and searched amongst the stone benches, she had already chosen her sit, where Astyages could see her face at the end of the race. She dragged Nahira along through the seats.

"What are you doing Mithra? Are we racing?" Nahira complained. She was not used to running on the rocks, making her feel she was about to be thrown off.

Mithra had no time to answer. She seemed to be in a great hurry and wanted to reach to her chosen placed before everyone, but she suddenly stopped and Nahira who was running immediately behind, hit hard her on the back. Saber sat a little further forward, among his commanders. He was among the crowd after a long absence, since he got bitten by a snake. He still looked pale and haggard; despite the nice weather, he has wrapped himself in a thick cloak, watching the competition field with a stern face.

"Mithra, you have no idea where you're going!" Nahira said irritated.

Saber turned when he heard Mithra's name; their eyes met for a moment, disgust and hatred were waving in his eyes.

"I'll go someplace far from here…," Mithra said as she went to the opposite direction, "… where I don't see this man's grim face."

There were many anxious riders ready to get racing. The horses were facing the rope that was stretched before them, restless, pawing. The young men looking prepared to fight.

Mithra sat and stared at Astyages with her concern eyes. Nahira drew her sleeve. "Look! Mahbod is there!" She said enthusiastically. Mithra looked from Astyages to where Nahira had pointed reluctantly. Mahbod was on a tall black stallion that seemed could not tolerate waiting in the back of the rope. The horse was pawing and shaking her head with impatience.

"He will fall off his horse in a few minutes!" Mithra said as she was staring at Mahbod.

Nahira looked at Mithra angrily. "How can you be so cruel?!" She said.

Mithra shrugged. "That has nothing to do with me; his horse has never been in the race court, so he's too excited. Mahbod should shorten the reins, lean back in the saddle, push his feet forward and give his horse a big kick to get his moving forward but look at him!" She pointed at him. "He has hunched, it is obvious that he is afraid. The horse feels his rider's fear and could not trust him. I hope he won't put us in big trouble!"

Nahira was almost going to cry. "You should be ashamed of yourself!" She snarled. "I wish Mahbod wins to piss you off!"

Mithra grinned; shook her head and turned her attention back to Astyages. The valley filled with trump sound and the horses flew. Some of the riders were marching ahead, but Mithra knew just because they were first, did not necessarily mean that they will be the winner. Mithra clenched her hands into a fist. She stared down at Astyages, excited, her breathing became ragged and fast as if she was racing. She was monitoring Astyages every move, guessing his next before he does.

In the final round of competition, Astyages was ahead, and Mahbod was behind several other riders, but Mahbod's mare suddenly began to wince and in a blink threw him to the ground. Nahira screamed, but Mahbod dragged himself on the ground and took him away from the horses who went forward speedy.

Astyages crossed the finish line first and Mahbod's black horse after him, riderless.

"I must go to Mahbod!" Nahira said. "No injuries I hope." Then she ran to the arena hastily, without thinking about falling on the stony mountain.

Mithra wanted to go with Nahira, but she turned with a sort of joy to Saber first, hoping to see the effect of Astyages winning on his face but Saber was not in his place. Other commanders were talking with a passion, looking excited and betting but there was no sign of Saber.

Mithra smiled. *Probably Astyages' winning has been so unpleasant for Saber that he was no longer willing to stay there,* she thought. She decided to follow Nahira to know what has happened for Mahbod, but she saw a shadow that passed quietly behind her. A man dressed in black with a mask of crow. She turned quickly toward the shadow, but there was no one there. The people were talking, loudly and excited. It seemed no one has seen that strange man. A crow cawing drew her attention. The crow sat on a rock, a little further. It was as the crow was watching around with its black and round eyes.

Mithra looked around; she knew her crow. A message from the cult, here and so untimely. *It's weird, I've never seen that before,* she thought, moved forward and opened the letter from the crow's feet. The crow flew without any delay. Mithra ran down the valley where the bushes were grown on the mountain and had a safe place to hide. She opened the paper and scanned the message: Old crypt. As you put the crown on the head. Immediately and promptly.

The message was clear for Mithra. She should go to the old nearby crypt, where Holy Pater put the crown on her head. The blobs of sealing wax, the ribbon, and the signature... there could be no doubt. There must have been something powerful troubling, and Mithra must find out what had happened. She rushed to the camp. She should find Astyages as soon as possible.

In the paramount of the tribe's huge tent, Mahbod was lying on the bed, and Ashvan scrutinized him.

"Has anyone seen Astyages? I've been looking for him everywhere." Mithra said as she rushed into the tent.

In response to her question, Ashvan shook head as a negation sign and Nahira who was crying looked at her angrily.

Mahbod cried out in pain. "Damn horse! It was like a wild animal," he said through clenched teeth.

"Don't curse the poor animal for your fault," Mithra said.

"Don't talk nonsense! If I didn't move at that exact time, my body was crushed under the horses' hooves," Mahbod barked.

"Yes, you did a really great escape!" Mithra said as she was catching her saddlebag on the corner of the tent.

Mahbod looked at Mithra with fury. "You are damn lucky. I can't get up!" He shouted.

"You're really stupid." Mithra looked surprised. "For the first time in my life, I've admired you," she said as she was staring at Mahbod.

"Enough!" Ashvan shouted impatiently. Then she looked at Nahira angrily. "Stop crying! He's alive as you see!"

"I might lose my leg aunt!" Mahbod said irritated.

Nahira's crying voice got louder.

Ashvan frowned. "Stop screaming so pathetically. You're a man, aren't you?" Mahbod got quiet, sobbed like a girl. "Your leg doesn't seem to be broken," Ashvan said then turned to Nahira and added. "Took a piece of raw meat to put on his leg, it helps to prevent swelling."

Nahira ran out of the tent, still pouring tears.

Ashvan turned to Mahbod again. "I wish, Father was here to give a good look at you!" She murmured.

"Do not worry, his leg only has banged, I saw how he fell," Mithra said.

"Where are you going?" Ashvan asked.

"I have to go!" Mithra said. "Tell Astyages I couldn't wait for him!"

"You haven't answered my question," Ashvan said behind her, but Mithra was steps away from the tent.

*****

Mithra blinked a few times to adjust her eyes to the darkness and stepped forward.

The old crypt stairs seemed inexhaustible. It was as if the winter did not end in this damp and cold place. She could feel the wet coldness sliding downward, penetrating her thin shirt. Mithra realized she was shaking, and it was not because of the cold. *Everything is normal, as always,* Mithra thought, trying to make herself feel better but she did not know why she could not believe in her own seductive words. It was as if she walked through a cloudy haze. She took a deep breath and tried to unclenched fears icy fingers, around her heart. She finally stepped into the rotten old crypt.

A number of the paters were sitting on the cracked stony platform, and more than twenty members of the cult were standing around them. Suddenly Mithra saw Saber, sitting on a stony bench, wrapping in the lion skin.

Mithra stepped forward; the men seemed to be lying in wait for her, sitting silently. Holy Pater was resting his chin against his palm, quietly speaking with his vicar; he looked very bored.

"AHA, your smart and favorite disciple is here finally!" Saber roared.

Mithra bent her knee, bowed her head in front of the paters. Holy Pater cleared his throat, looking uncomfortable. A few moments passed by silence until Saber gave Holy Pater a sullen glance, shifted his feet, and grabbed one of the disciples' hand to rise. He stood in front of the paters.

"My dear brothers, only some of our members were invited to this meeting…," Saber said.

"Get to the point Holy Master," said Holy Pater in a bored tone. "I hope you have a good reason for this untimely meeting, in the middle of the day and in a very unsafe place."

Saber had been furious at being blamed by Holy Pater. He threw a sidelong glance at Holy Pater. "We have an important meeting here, and I have an excellent reason for it!" He said dryly as he took a half step back and gave a brief shake of his head toward the door.

Two of those men who were standing behind him rushed to exit and dragged a man from outside with both hands tied behind his back and a bag pulled over his head. They blew behind his knees, threw him off his feet, in front of Saber. Saber glanced at him and continued his speech. "We are here to visit an old friend!" He said as he was picking up the bag from the man's head in front of the paters' stunned eyes.

Mithra was struggling to breathe, her heart pounding, her throat thickening, so shocked she could only stare. Her grandfather was falling on his knees, just one-step further. Mithra was not alone; Holy Pater was staring at Taham with eyes that widened in surprise too. Holy Pater got up and stepped forward. For some minutes, he stood watching intently. Taham's nose looked broken and dried blood caking the back of his head. He raised his head and smiled. "My old friend! I knew one day Javid will be a Holy Pater!" Taham said. "You thought you'd killed me, isn't it? But I'm still alive; you can finish your unfinished job now!"

Javid would just look at him, sort of puzzled like and shake his head.

Saber was looking at them with pleasure. "I have a better idea, it would be better if your favorite student kills him, a great honor for him; also he can prove his loyalty to God!" He said.

Everyone looked at Mithra, except Holy Pater. She was breathing quickly and painfully, wishing that to take the damned mask off and could breathe freely. She closed her eyes for a moment, it is a nightmare, some part of her whispered, refusing to believe, only a nightmare, but when she opened her eyes, saw Saber's scornful face.

Taham turned to the young man that everyone was staring at him. He recognized those frightened eyes, staring at him without blinking, instantly. Taham trembled. He was not trembling for fear of death, he had lived long enough, preferred his spirit to find its way to reach Chista, but he could not bear his granddaughter suffering.

"Come! Kill me without a pause. You'll do it for my well … Come on!" Taham said, wishing such miracle happen and Mithra listen to him.

Mithra felt the burning tears run down her face beneath the mask.

"What madness is this?!" Javid shouted. "Why did you bring this man here?"

"Because this man is a traitor!" Saber shouted back.

Javid went toward Saber. "That all happened a very long time ago." His words were accompanied by little quivering of the lips, in a voice trembling with anger. "Do you really think that I'm dumb enough that I don't know who the paramount of the tribe is? This man has carved out a quiet life for himself. I have no excuse to kill him?" He said. "Why is it so important to kill him? He has nothing to do with us, and serves our people?" He was staring at Saber with terrible anger, waiting for an answer.

Saber moved to him, stared into his eyes with anger, a lot more significant than him. "Because this man has betrayed God. He has broken the oath, he swore with blood. He has turned his back on all we have learned it from the grit and torture. These are the best reasons to kill this traitor, and if you had known this secret and haven't killed him, you are guilty as an accomplice," he shouted angrily.

Mithra's hand went down to her boot and pulled out her dagger, trying to find the right moment and while Saber was staring at Holy Pater, attacked. She jumped forward, swiping with her blade. Saber turned just slightly to the side but held no combat posture. He seemed confident, unconcerned as if he were strolling up to a harmless little girl, not entering a fight. He dodged the knife and easily grabbing her hand with an effortless motion. His fingers were fearsomely strong; he twisted her arm until her hand opened.

Saber knocked Mithra down. He looked down at her, eyes dark, unconcerned, unworried. "You're not the brave warrior Holy Pater think you are, at least not today, not here," he said, "... because you're scared of me, don't you?" He laughed evilly. "It's not a challenge little lady, this is a war."

"Enough!" Javid shouted. "You are going the wrong way. We want to suffer, and by suffering we shall be purified, humble, submissive, patient, full of love... your beliefs tend to divide us, but the worship of the true God has the power to unite people," he added in a lower voice as he walked with firm steps toward Saber.

Saber grinned. "You think I'm wrong, really? That's not true, believe me, you're wrong because you have broken the rules, Holy Pater!" He said and took Mithra's mask face off.

Mithra's face was pale, and large drops of sweat stood upon her brow, as she threw herself forward, trying to wrench free of the man's iron grip behind her. The paters got up, shocked to see her. There was silence, apart from the sound of water dripping slowly onto the floor. Javid looked at Mithra, there was no touch of confusion in his manner, but a mixture of fear and regret has seen into his eyes.

Saber turned to Javid. "This woman has been your disciple for more than two years!" He grinned. "Your most beloved disciple," he said in a mockery tone then went to Javid with slow firm steps, stopped in front of him and stared into his eyes. "You lied and betrayed what we believed in, to protect an unworthy woman!" He said, staring at into Holy Pater's eyes.

Javid looked at Saber for a while. "I just wish you have been half as honorable as she!" He said finally and smashed his stick tied into Saber's face with incredible speed. Saber fell, his face was covered with blood.

"Kill him!" Saber cried, furious.

Saber's men rushed Javid's side, but some of the paters and disciples, who were loyal to Holy Pater, rose up to fight. The men were walking straight towards each other, with dagger uplifted. Mithra took the opportunity, knocked the man holding her on the ground, grabbed his blade, and ran to her grandfather. She helped him to get up.

Mithra glanced at Javid who was fighting on the half-dark corner of the crypt. It was no accident that he had been the senior of the many brave men. He moved like a panther, and his stick seemed a part of his arm. Every man of Javid's men was fighting against two men, but there was too many of them; obviously, they could not hold them for very long. Mithra grabbed her grandfather's arm and ran toward the stairs, but Taham's steps were hesitant. He glanced behind.

"Open my hands!" Taham said.

Mithra read her grandfather's mind. "Let's get out of here," she said. "We don't have enough time."

Taham stopped near the stairs, at the end of the hall, staring at Mithra. "Open my hands!" He shouted.

She cut the rope with one hand but held Taham's wrist with her other hand. "They'll kill us all," Mithra said. "We must go!"

Taham took the dagger. "You must go! Hurry up!" He said as he ran to Javid.

Mithra stared at her grandfather; he did not look young, but he was never an easy man to defeat. She ran to him. She reached right when Taham was attacked from behind by an armed man. Mithra lifted a foot and drove it forward, catching the man in the belly; he fell on the ground. Taham glanced at her, smiling for gratitude.

A tall man with long black hair stopped to face her. The man hesitated as he looked at her, struck by both the beauty of her honey-colored eyes staring intensely at him, and the sudden realization that she is a girl. These thoughts caused him to lower his sword as though he could reach out and grab her. Mithra sensing the confusion in the man's mind seized her chance and planted the dagger deep in the man's chest. He staggered back, realizing his mistake but too late.

The crypt was full of shouts and screams and heavy with the scent of blood; their unequal war seemed very disappointing. A man's body landed beside Mithra, opened throat with a golden dagger. She glanced at him. *Pretty soon, there'll be more of us dead than alive*, Mithra thought, but she suddenly heard the sound of voices and footsteps coming down and then the crypt space was flooded with light and the king's guard soldiers with naked swords. After a little time, the soldiers defeated Saber's men, tied their hands.

Mithra looked at them all in wonder. She saw Astyages with a sudden start of relief, rushed toward him and threw herself into his arms like a child. She buried her face against his solid and broad chest, allowing herself to wholly lean on him, take some of the strength he readily offered and made herself loosen her fear with her hidden tears.

The men's shouting was off. Saber was the only one who was trying to make himself free from the men who were holding him by the arm, blood was pouring on his face. He stared at Astyages. "You fucking traitor!" He shouted.

Astyages did not respond to this insult, but a voice was heard from down the stairs.

"It's ridiculous to hear such a terrible curse, come out of a traitor's mouths!"

All looked back toward the sound. The king Cyaxares came out of the shadow, and all knelt in respect.

*****

Astyages did not participate in the final race, but it did not matter, what was so important that he had made a wise decision and saved the paramount of the tribe's life and arrested a subversive and traitor.

The king gave the cups to winners personally, but in fact, the king was the real winner, who had saved Holy Pater's life, the highest level of the Mithra's cult, and the popular Mannaean paramount of the tribe, at the same time. He gained the trust of people, those who believed Mithra and those who followed Ahura Mazda and now he could hear the cheers for honor the king. Cyaxares admired his old Lord Minister, Great Magi, in his heart for chosen Astyages. He could attract Holy Pater's trust, and Javid informed them timely to march to the golden cup camp. In fact, if it were not for Astyages, the king would have never made such success in Mannea.

CHAPTER NINE

DREAMS & NIGHTMARES

Ancient Land of Mannaeans, 627 BC, Summer

Summer was approaching its end. The wheat farms had turned to golden color, and weighty wheat clusters were thrown upright. Cranes had come back to Chichest Lake. Their beautiful and magnificent birds mating dance was a familiar sight for people of the Mannea.

Summer was the season of grapes harvest. The large grapes cluster with dewdrops shining on them were waiting for Diheh's young girls' hands. They put the wicker baskets on their backs, picking up the ruby red grapes for preparing the best wine in that area.

These days were beautiful days for young women. They were chatting as they were picking up the grapes for hours. They were talking about a teenage dream, a passionate love, a handsome husband and many healthy kids… a beautiful image for all the young women who were waiting for Mithra now, so talking about her seemed to have no end.

Mithra and Astyages had set the date of their marriage, the time that they first met each other. This summer was different from all the summers of Mithra's life. It seems that destiny has taken a hand. Nobody remembered that who her mother was, nobody remembered Mithra was the ominous creature, even it was like no one could see her strange birthmark on her face, all because a handsome young man, Astyages, the king's nephew, was in love with her. Astyages had saved Mithra in a fantastic adventure, and now he wanted to marry him. It was just like the stories that they had heard from their nannies. What could be better than that? Who could say she brought bad luck?

At midsummer days, the paramount of the tribe's home often was about a mess. Mithra's wedding ceremony was not like others girls, the king, the officials, and even royal family were participating in the ceremony, so the women came to White Mansion after work, struggling to prepare a wedding ceremony befitting of the noble royal family.

The men, who realized that the imperial family was behind the paramount of the tribe, care more about this family than before. Almost every night, the tribal elders came together at the paramount of the tribe's house for chatting, and every night Zarvan was talking for so long about that he correctly guessed Saber's evil spirit, just by looking at his face.

In this mess, Mithra and Astyages preferred to spend their leisure time in Nanny's home, away from everyone and everything.

*****

The weather was the kind that felt like a kiss of summer without the fiery heat of noontime in August. The grass was a soft green that almost had a hint of blue and in the sky was enough pristine white cloud to show how beautiful the sky was.

Mithra was feeling the earth under her body, warm and safe, and the blossoms of the bitter orange tree exhibited a powerful, spicy scent, which was caressing her nose and made her sleepy. She closed her eyes, but a surge of joy heated her skin as she remembered last night …

She could hear his harsh, ragged breath.

"Oh, you're a goddess!" Astyages said, breathless. "Otherwise, how can you be the damned love guru while you never been in a relationship."

Mithra blushed, pulled the blanket over her naked body but there was a hint of a smile on her lips. "All right, just try to breathe!" She said.

Astyages lightly touched her soft, smooth skin. He put his head to her chest and felt her heart fast beating. "I can breathe only when I'm with you," he said as he touched her breasts, caressed their contours, and traced the rise of her nipple. "I'd almost forgotten this feeling; all my senses had sharpened for my missions. It's like I've been living underwater, holding my breath, and now I can finally breathe."

"My life is changing rapidly! In fact, I do think my life is too good to be true," Mithra said, stroking the side of his face with the soft blade of her finger. "This scares me! I'll die if I have to lose you."

Astyages glanced at her. "You can't afford to lose me!" He bit her fingers softly. "Listen to me. I'm not letting go of you. Not ever," he said.

Mithra laughed, tipped her head back, offering her throat to him. Her soft, smooth skin welcomed his lips.

"You are a goddess, I'm certain!" Astyages whispered.

*****

Something blue in the shadow of the trees caught her attention. Astyages was going to be coming today, but it was too early to his coming. Mithra looked up and saw Astyages, riding all the way across the slope to join her. She guessed something big has happened.

"Come with me!" Astyages said, reaching for her.

"Where?" Mithra asked hurriedly as she got up.

Astyages stretched forth his hand towards her; she snapped his hand up and jumped onto the horse.

"Come, I want to show you something," Astyages said.

*****

Everything in the abandoned camp showed that the Assyrians soldiers had been there for several days.

"I saw them early morning," Astyages said. "They were preparing to leave, didn't talk so much. I only found out they come back."

"For what?" Mithra said as she was looking around.

Astyages shrugged. Those signs had filled him with concern, a concern that made him angry. "I do not know!" He said.

"The harvest is passing, and the summer will end, may they come for the tribute," Mithra said thoughtfully.

"I don't think so!" Astyages said. "They don't receive the tribute directly from people."

"We never know what conspiracy they'll be plotting." Mithra stared at Astyages.

Astyages nodded. "You never know things will change, we have to be ready," he said thoughtfully. "I smell trouble, something will happen, and I don't like it surprise me."

"Perhaps be better you put some guards here," Mithra said. "Choose someone who you trust him deeply, ordered him to tell no one, even a word." She looked at him seriously. "It's better to stay hidden. Don't let people be afraid, it won't be in our favor."

Astyages was staring at Mithra with fascination and admiring her in his heart; she was speaking like a commander.

"Yes my lord commander!" Astyages said.

Mithra was accustomed to Astyages' witticism. "Do you mock me?" Mithra said, laughingly.

"No," Astyages said. "You know, it's nice talking to you, you get it."

Mithra took his hands. "It's good to have a man with feelings."

Astyages laughed. "What I've come to realize is that you really love me, Mithra," he said. "You need to be ready for the wedding ceremony, and I brought you here to talk about the Assyrians." He put an arm around her shoulders and walked along with her to the horse. "I think you should only think of your wedding ceremony."

Mithra gave him a great big hug. "Don't bother yourself, my aunt was struggling enough before you, but she has not been succeeded," she said.

Astyages laughed hardly. "You're not like other girls; you are unique and special, and that's why I love you madly!" He said.

*****

A young soldier was waiting outside of the mansion. The soldier stood and bowed his head respectfully. "Lord Commander, I'm sorry to break in your day!" He said.

"What happened?" Astyages asked.

The soldier pulled a scroll from his saddlebag and handed it to Astyages. "It is a letter from Ecbatana. They have said it is critical," he said.

Astyages took the letter and let him free. After a quick glance and examined the wax seal he unrolled it. His frown deepened, and the lines on his face became more and more pronounced the longer he read through the information.

"What does it say?!" Mithra asked curiously.

Astyages rose his head and looked at her with a frown face. "News has come from Hegmataneh; Saber has escaped while being transferred to a dungeon," he said. "They said that some signs were showing he might have come here, to Mannea!"

*****

Ashvan looked at her angrily. "If you move again, I'll stick a needle in your feet!" She said to Mithra.

Mithra stood, like a statue in the middle of the room, wore a white wedding gown and Ashvan was trying to stitch a lace shawl from one section of her skirt to the next.

"I'm standing for too long, I'm tired," Mithra muttered.

Ashvan grabbed her shoulders. "Hold, right there," she said. "We are here for your wedding dress, and this will be the most important cloth in your life so it should be nice." The pictures getting life in front of her eyes, others gazing eyes, cinnamon hair girl's words, her running away from home and facing with Saber. She moved again unconsciously.

"Why do you make me wear this fucking uncomfortable thing?" Mithra growled.

Ashvan was frustrated. "Stop! The king and the royal family will come from Ecbatana to attend your wedding ceremony next week; even if I want to cancel your wedding, I cannot. It's not just an ordinary wedding ceremony; this is a great ceremony for Mannea!" She took a deep breath trying to calm herself down. "We have to do this, so stop nagging Mithra; it's getting on my nerves."

Mithra had a big frown. "What difference does it make that…?"

Ashvan interrupted her speech with a threatening tone. "Be quiet! I don't want to hear even one another word," she said then took Mithra hands and fixed her. "Just stop and do not move!" She turned to Nahira who was sewing reluctantly. "Are you finished?"

"Finally! My hand is now quite lame from knitting." Nahira complained and raised a beaded silk bandanna. "But you might want to try it in another time!" She added hesitantly when she saw their angry faces.

"No, we don't have much time! Just bring it," Ashvan said with a sullen face.

Mithra glanced impatiently at her aunt, but Ashvan was paying her no attention. She tied the bandanna over Mithra's head and took a step back. She glanced at her, a satisfied smile playing about her lips. The dress looked as perfect on her as she had expected it would be. Mithra looked more elegant and charming in a slim sheath dress that closely had followed the line of her body, creating a form-fitting look.

"You're the most beautiful bride that I have ever seen," Ashvan said.

"No use trying!" Mithra said sternly. "There's no way I'm going to put on this thing." Then she squatted in the corner of the room near the window like a spoiled brat.

Ashvan sat down, relied on the cushions, tired. "I don't know what to tell you Mithra. Nahira, you talk to her, she may understand your words," Ashvan said.

Nahira had no chance to say a word. Mithra straightened herself when she heard Astyages' voice. She looked at the garden through the window and saw Taham greeted Astyages briefly and guided him to the guesthouse. Astyages was coming to the hall.

"Astyages is coming! I don't know what to do!" Mithra said, her throat tight and her eyes wide as if she saw a snake before Ashvan had a chance to find an answer; Astyages knocked on the door and came in.

"Mithra...!"

Astyages forgot what he wanted to say; he could only stare at Mithra, amaze. Mithra was looking anxiously into him as he stepped forward.

"Wow... I mean Wow! You are incredible!" Astyages said and stroked Mithra's beautiful face that was more attractive with bright beads of silk bandanna that were poured on her forehead with his fingertips. He could not take his eyes off her. "I should have guessed you will be the most beautiful bride that I've ever seen!"

Ashvan stood up angrily. "For God's sake, why aren't you like others?" She took Astyages' hand. "The groom should not see the bride in her wedding gown before the wedding ceremony, it gives presage!" She said as she was dragging him out.

"Mithra, I have important news," Astyages said before Ashvan shoved him out of the hall.

Mithra was shaking with joy. "Wait, I'll come! Just I change my wedding gown!" She said.

"My wedding Gown? I thought you hated it!"

Mithra heard Nahira's irony voice from behind and laughed.

"How much do you love him?" Nahira asked suddenly.

"What did you say?" Mithra said, she looked distracted and yet beautiful.

"I asked how much you love Astyages," Nahira asked again.

"You know well that I don't like to talk about these issues with anyone," Mithra said with a frown.

"Please, it is imperative to me to know," Nahira said.

Mithra looked at her with surprise. Nahira was staring at her, waiting for a reply. Mithra had never seen her so serious like now.

"I love him so much," Mithra answered.

Nahira did not give up. "How much?" She asked.

"I gave your answer; so much!" Mithra said, punctuated by a nervous giggle.

"So enough that you do something for him," Nahira said. "Even if you are not willing to do."

"Yes, I am willing to sacrifice everything for him," Mithra said without pause and then added. "Now help me to take off this uncomfortable dress."

"I have to go," Nahira said as she went to the door quietly.

"Where are you going?" Mithra asked, surprised.

"I have an important job to do!" Nahira muttered, low under her breath.

"What's wrong with you these days?" Mithra asked. She listened for a response but heard nothing but the door bang. *I wish I were able to comprehend her changed behavior*, Mithra thought. Sullen, withdrawn, Nahira just did not seem the same for these past weeks. Mithra had met her only a few times, on special occasions and it was so weird. She was not excited about the wedding ceremony, unlike the past. If Mithra did not know Nahira's feeling about Mahbod, maybe she thought Nahira was jealous of her. Mithra sighed. There was no time for such thoughts. As far as she could, took off her wedding gown cautiously and put it on cushions.

*****

Mithra ran toward the corner of the garden, where Astyages was sitting on the stairs, waiting for her.

Astyages looked at her with pleasure. "My bride, my amazing bride!" He said, and Mithra smiled timidly.

"Come on! You know that I don't like you to talk to me like this!" Mithra said, but her charming smile and shining eyes were telling him how much she had enjoyed his words.

They had stared at each other and Astyages had forgotten that he came for a purpose.

"Please take a few days away from the adventure. We have much work to do before the wedding ceremony!" Ashvan said as she was coming out of the kitchen along with her fat maid.

Astyages just remembered. "Oh, we have to go," he said hastily.

"Where?" Mithra asked, surprised.

"The Assyrians fort!" Astyages said as he went to his horse that was tied outside the garden.

A few minutes later, they were on the way.

"I have no news from the guards; they should come back yesterday," Astyages said.

"Do you trust them?" Mithra said. "Maybe they have left there for going somewhere else?"

Astyages shook his head. "It's impossible that they leave their guarding place. I don't know what happened to them," he said.

Mithra heard a crow caw, saw a leaf tremble on the tree behind it and felt invisible icy fingers touched her heart.

*****

It was a gray day. The weak rays of a sallow sun were barely finding a way through the dense jungle foliage, and they moved forward cautiously in a thick, sticky shadow. On the last days of summer, crisp golden leaves laid like a blanket on the forest floor. They were all ears but there was no sound but the sound of scuffing leaves behind them and the gentle wind howling.

Mithra had been in this forest before, but this day it seemed so gruesome and scary. She preferred to be out of there as soon as possible, but Astyages was going forward slowly and in every step looking around cautiously. Mithra wanted to go faster so was one-step ahead when Astyages took her arm suddenly.

"Look at that!" Astyages said, dropped his voice to a whisper, pointing toward a tree a few steps further. There were bloody fingerprints on a trunk of a white poplar tree. Mithra looked around. It seemed nothing out of the ordinary at first, but a little further, she saw a red ribbon in the mud, which the Median soldiers tied on their forehead.

Mithra looked at Astyages without any word. They went to the red tape, the footprints were fresh and swift, and it led to the density of trees. A voice from behind a rock drew their attention suddenly. Astyages quickly pulled his sword out of the sheath. He moved forward cautiously. Mithra followed him. The body of a young soldier was behind the boulder and two hyenas were chewing on his fingers.

Mithra trembled involuntarily. Astyages waved his sword in the air. "Hey ...!" He shouted.

The hyenas fled as they were skirling and looking at them with their round red eyes. They walked to the body; a sword had ripped the soldier from groin to nipple. His thick army clothes were already black with blood, and the smell of the wound was hideous. Mithra's stomach turned.

"The wounded soldier had tried to escape. The branches were broken in the direction of his body. The wet soil held several footprints," Astyages said as he knelt in front of the body. The soldier had died a few hours before but his face was bruised and swollen and his lips dry and cracked.

Astyages pushed his finger into the wound, then smelt the blood. He looked at Mithra.

"The smell of parsnip…," Astyages said.

The invisible icy fingers pressed Mithra's heart harder. "That means…" She did not want to finish her words.

"Saber had been here," Astyages said instead of her. He stood up, looked around; there was no sign of the other soldier. "We should get them from the back of the fort; the space in front of the fort has nothing to hide us," he said.

My bride, my amazing bride! Astyages' voice echoed in Mithra's ears, *only a few weeks … and then we could live together*, Mithra thought. She did not want to be in danger for the first time in her life.

Mithra swallowed. "We should get help. We can come back later, right?" She said hesitantly.

"What if there's no future?" Astyages looked at her with worried eyes. "We must find out what's going on." He took her hand. "Follow me!" Astyages said as ran up the hill fast.

They climbed the hill overlooking the Assyrians camp, positioned themselves behind the boulders, and dragged themselves forward as they lay at full length with arms on the cracked rocks so they could look and see what was on the other side. They looked at the plain, and for a moment Mithra dared not breathe.

The plain was covered with the Assyrian soldiers wearing combat armor. The young guard was tied to a wooden beam among the soldiers on a rock, naked.

Adora, the Assyrians soldiers' commander, climb the rock, flinging back the edge of his sheepskin, stood beside the captured guard and began to speak. His face was hidden behind a rough steel helmet so Mithra could not see the expression of his face and his speech was unintelligible for her. Saber was at a little further wearing armor like the Assyrians. He had taken his helmet in his hand he was looking at the soldiers, with a stern face. None of the Assyrian soldiers' faces was visible; their helmets that were adorned with animal horns had covered their face and had given them a horrific look. They were wearing armors with a lot of oval metal sheet, showing them more robust and more massive than they really were. They listened quietly, their face still.

Mithra did not even blink. The Assyrians would kill them within moments if they were found hiding there. The commander was speaking Assyrian, which seemed so scary for Mithra at that time, but Astyages was listening carefully to his words.

The commander ended his speech finally then turned to the young guard, grabbed handfuls of his shoulder-length hair close to his scalp, beheaded him with a swipe of his sword. The commander tore his gaze from the guard's head, locked eyes with the soldiers and threw the head to the ground, his terrible roar echoed among the rocks and cavities. The soldiers followed him and the mountain filled with their wild shouts. They were cheering with a sound like wild animals. Mithra's eyes were fixed in a daze on the severed head. The young man's face going pale and turning blue, his eyes becoming a thick black at incredible speed, she was feeling sick.

Astyages took Mithra by the shoulders; she looked up at him with a blank look poisoned by shock.

"We should go, hurry up!" He whispered.

Mithra was staring at him, seemed not to hear him.

"We have to hurry! We have so little time, and we can't lose it. The Assyrians are going to attack us." Astyages kept his voice low.

Mithra could not move as if she was paralyzed. She did not want to die, at least not today, when she had felt lucky for the first time. She heard a crow plunked and raised her head. A group of crow flew over their heads. *Does Astyages see them too?* Mithra thought.

Astyages cupped her face in his hands and prompted her to look into his eyes. "Do not worry baby, trust me!" He said. "We found our safe way. We just need to hurry; we'll go to Orin Mountains and take shelter, yes? Let's go!"

Mithra slowly nodded. Astyages kissed her lips hurriedly, took her hand and ran down the hill.

We found our safe way ... We found our safe way ... Mithra constantly mumbled this sentence.

*****

Astyages galloped into camp with shrill cries. Only fifty or sixty soldiers had gathered around him. He looked at the curious faces of them.

"Hurry up! The Assyrians will be here in a few hours. Gather the people, we should go to the old castle," Astyages said as he leaned forward a bit and stroked his excited horse's neck, gently cooling to him. "Remember; we have not enough time to gather food or livestock, only the people," he added.

"But people will die of hunger!" One of the soldiers, a youth of Diheh shouted.

"They won't stay for long; they're trying to frighten us," Astyages said. "There is no time to delay, hurry!"

*****

Taham and Zarvan were talking on the porch, they heard Mithra's voice calling to them, and they looked. Mithra jumped down from the horse and ran to the garden.

"The Assyrians are coming!" Mithra shouted. "Let's hurry!"

They were staring at her, shocked.

"You must hurry," she shouted again.

Zarvan's fat body froze for a moment, then he turned and ran to prepare the carts. Taham was staring at her; Mithra could see pity in his eyes. The old man smiled a sad smile.

"We'll leave this behind too, well?" Taham said.

Mithra tried to smile. "The people need you!" She said.

Taham nodded. "I'll get my things… we'll need medicine," he said, going to his apartment with trembling steps.

Mithra did not waste time and ran to the guest room. Ashvan still was sewing Mithra's wedding dress. Mithra rush to her.

"Hurry up! The Assyrian soldiers are coming, we should go!" Mithra said.

Ashvan was staring at her; she looked perplexed.

"We should help people to flee," Mithra said.

Ashvan nodded slowly and got up. Mithra's wedding dress landed on the ground from her knees. Ashvan looked at Mithra, confused.

Mithra tried to swallow the tie in her throat. "Do not bring anything even food, just hurry up."

*****

Mithra was against Taham's large barn and stable. She looked up the hill. The people were gathering outside Diheh on the old road. The men had been equipped with the axes and knives and even forks, the children and women were weeping, and the soldiers were searching all over Diheh to find the seniors, children and those tried to bring their assets as well to lead them to the caravan. A chain of soldiers came up round about the people, guiding the people to the top of the next hill.

Mithra opened the big door, encouraged the flock to go out with loud sounds and screams that the herd knew it well. The dogs were running and led the sheep to the meadow. Only Black, Mithra's special dog had stood and stared up at her, waiting for her. Mithra bent and hold his head in her hands. "Go and take care of them. I can't come with you," she said. The dog did not move. His black and gentle eyes were staring at her with concern. Mithra stood up. "Go, I can't come with you," she said again.

Black moved slowly toward her, bit Mithra's sleeve and pulled, howling. A massive choking lump formed in Mithra's throat. She picked a stone up and hit it on the ground next to the dog.

"Go!" She shouted.

The dog jumped back a bit, but he still waited for her. Mithra rushed to the dog and hugged him. "Go, if I can, I'll come back and look for you, but now please go!" She said in his ear.

The dog looked at her and then ran to the herd. Mithra stared at her flock from behind the tears that had covered her eyes. She did not have more much time; she mounted her horse and marched to the top of the hill.

*****

Ashvan was walking among the people. She was shouting; intuiting, calming those were moaning with calming words or threatening. She was placing the seniors in the carts, putting the children in their mothers' arms and taking care of everybody and at the same time her worried eyes glimpsing around, looking for Nahira. She had searched all over for her, but she could not find her.

"Oh, God. Come on, Ashvan. Do something, they are coming!" Zarvan said angrily and loudly.

Ashvan glanced at him. Zarvan was sitting on the cart, waiting for her. He was more scared than Ashvan could expect him to look for his daughter, her father as the paramount of the tribe had a responsibility to lead the people at the front of the caravan; she saw Mithra, who was riding around, speaking with people who were really excited to go. Ashvan ran to her.

Astyages was staring at caravan carefully to solve every little difficulty instantly. Mithra brought up the rear and stopped beside him.

"Is everything all right?" Mithra asked.

Astyages nodded. "The sooner we're gone, the better. We don't have time to wait," he said and ordered the soldiers. "Move around the people. Do not let anybody left behind."

Vanguards started moving, and the people followed them.

"Let's go," Astyages said.

"I have to back, looking for Nanny!" Mithra said.

Astyages looked surprised. "Why now?" He said.

Mithra grinned. "Nanny is not exactly popular, they know her as a sinister, so we were in a big problem if she had come earlier!" She said.

Astyages nodded. "We'll go after her!" He said as he swung his horse around.

"Wait. I'm coming with you!" Ashvan was rushing to them. "Nahira! I couldn't find her," she said worriedly.

Mithra glanced at Astyages. She looked worried, as well it might be.

"Do you know where she went?" Astyages asked.

"No, but I guess she is with Mahbod because I didn't find him too," Ashvan said.

"Don't worry, we are going after them," Astyages said.

Ashvan pleaded with him. "I want to come," she said.

Mithra bent from the horse and took her aunt's hand in her. "I won't go back without her." She promised.

Ashvan's intense anxiety appeared in her pale and agitated face, but she nodded. Mithra and Astyages galloped towards Diheh as fast as they could, and Ashvan's eyes escorted them.

"Look for them in Diheh," Mithra shouted, urging the horse to even greater speed. "I'll search around Diheh, all where they might be."

"No, we won't be separated," Astyages shouted. "Besides, going to Diheh is a waste of bloody time; the soldiers have done it already. We'll check the surrounding so we'll find them sooner." He put the spur on his horse and went more quickly. Mithra marched, following him.

*****

Mithra and Astyages were galloping forward rapidly in the forest. They spent too much time at places that Mithra thought they could find Nahira and Mahbod, but there was no sign of them. They had to take shortcuts and rode across the narrow trail to get Nanny's hut faster.

Thin branches of trees were lashing their faces, but they had no time for thinking about it. Gradually, the density of trees was reduced, and they could see a vast meadow among leafless trees. They had to cross the field to reach Nanny's hut. Astyages pulled the reins of the horse and stood up. Mithra followed him and stopped a few steps away. She looked with wonder at Astyages who was sliding down of the horse. They had not enough time, and his untimely stopping was very strange, but Astyages oblivious to her took the rein of the horse and walked to the edge of the forest slowly, where the trees were finished, and the meadow can be seen.

He glanced at Mithra. He would prefer to return and go to the old castle, but Mithra's waiting face showed that she would not go anywhere without her nanny. He stared at the meadows again. He should at least check everything and did not put themselves at risk. In the forest, they could hide in the shelter of the trees, if Assyrians chased them, they could go through the trails that Mithra knew them so well and they could escape, but in the meadow, there was no shelter to hide and no shortcut to run away, nothing!

Mithra was frustrated by Astyages' hesitate. She dismounted, went to the Astyages and stared at him. "Why are we stopping?" She asked.

Astyages still was looking at the meadow, the Nanny's hut was not so far from them, and if it was not in sheltered of a rocky cliff, it could be seen, but even at this short distance, their life could be in danger.

"You stay here! I take Nanny, but you must go as fast as you can to the old castle if I don't come back soon," Astyages said without looking at her.

Mithra chuckled. "Are you nuts? You're wasting our time here to tell me these nonsenses?" She said.

"If there was a danger, I can fight better without you. I can't put you in danger," Astyages said.

Mithra went to the horse. "Don't worry. I can take care of myself!" She said.

Astyages stepped forward and took Mithra's hand. "We must act wisely. We don't all have to die here," he said seriously.

Mithra mounted the horse regardless of Astyages. "So stay here, I'll go," she said stubbornly.

Astyages opened his mouth to give her an answer, but a savage yelling drew their attention. They both turned to the sound. An Assyrian giant man was galloping ahead, up the meadow way, and three soldiers were following him, shouting, and rotating their swords in the air. Mithra listened more carefully; several voices were crying at once, which mingled with a weak scream. She rushed forward; saw a dark mass was being dragged along on her stomach, trying desperately to get back on her feet.

Her nanny's body was stretching on the rocks of the mountain and Mithra could hear her screaming with pain.

"Mom…," Mithra shouted.

CHAPTER TEN

JAMASPA

Ancient Land of Mannaeans, 627 BC, Summer

Assyrians wedding customs and traditions was different. The ancient traditions of Assyrians demanded that the bride tied a big red scarf to her belt. This scarf had been decorated with lapis lazuli, one lapis lazuli per every day after the engagement, to keep the devil's eyes away from the bride, and some coins, gold or silver, gifts from the bride's family depending upon their financial situation, which sewed on the scarf too. On the wedding day, the scarf should be taken to the sanctum where the priests could sanctify it.

Nanny opened the door of the wardrobe, shoved the clothing aside, pulled out a red torn and faded scarf and opened it on her knees. Twenty lapis lazuli and a few bronze coins were sewed tidily on the scarf, two silver coins were seen on it too. Nanny sighed; once again the memories were alive for her.

*****

Nineveh, Assyria, 644 BC, winter

She was part of a poor family, the daughter of a farmer who achieved little more than a bare living. She had seven sisters; still, the same quiet life went on at their little cottage, at least until her father came home. He was earning almost nothing enough to live, but he cost the devil of a lot with his drinking with his friends in the pub. Jamaspa's mother was a maid in the royal palace, and Jamaspa and her sisters were eating the royal food every night, some of the leftovers of the court's table, if her mother was not a maid, they all starved. They were eating the foods hidden from her father, only when he was asleep. Her father said he would rather die than his children eat others left over, but without that food, they were going to die, not him.

*****

Father threw open the thin wooden door.

He took a step, and another, so drunk that his barefoot kept missing the stirrup. Jamaspa's seven sisters were in the back room, like always, took refuge in silence, didn't dare to come out, but Jamaspa had to be there to bring her father's supper. She prepared a table before him, beet, and boiled bulgur. She heard her father's growling curses in low, raspy voices. *Let him curse. One hour and it will be done.* Jamaspa thought. Her father cursed Jamaspa for her bland food, cursed her mother for staying with her lady until midnight, cursed himself for his damn life… he cursed everybody up and down until finished his meal. He pushed his plate away from him, cleared his throat as he got up, but fell back down on the couch in an unbalanced attempt to walk. He got up again, gripping on the table, "Help me!" He roared to Jamaspa. She came to help him. He leaned on her heavily. His body was heavy and threw her off balance, she had to hold him tight, and she could feel he had an erection, but fortunately, he was too tired to stay awake.

She rushed across the yard, took a long breath to keep the smell of wine, misery, and poverty well behind her. *He's always the same, lashing out at everyone, trying to make us all as miserable as he is,* she thought. She was feeling the same way as her father until the age of sixteen, until her breasts started growing when she realized that she looked so lovely, even in her raggedy dress! She had found a very private, personal sort of pleasure. Jamaspa leaned over the water well, took another deep breath and smiled at her own reflection, her flashing green-brown eyes and her gregarious smile. She drew others attention to herself each time she went to the river to wash clothes and bring water. There was no mirror in Jamaspa's house, but her reflection in the water showed that she was a stunning girl. She was enjoying the feeling of being pretty, making girls jealous, and watching the shine of admiration and desire in the boys' eyes. She combed her long, black hair, braided and left on her shoulder, washed her face with icy water to give a blush to her cheeks, pulled her fingers on her eyebrows to give them a beautiful shape and then she left the house. She took her head up with pride to show off her neck better as she carried the water pitcher upon her shoulder. She went to the river through the crowded market. Jamaspa's beauty was so stunning that her patched and threadbare clothes were not considered.

Her father came home at night, tired, drunk and angry and he never noticed any changes in his daughters but her mother had kept a close watch on her daughter's growing up, and Jamaspa's beauty did not make her happy. She knew that beauty is not a blessing for a poor girl, her beauty was her curse, a dangerous belong that attracted the robbers' eyes, who don't look at poor people usually. Her mother was looking for the right solution, and it would be best for her to send her to another house, another man's hands, another dominant, who can manage her, hopefully, better than her father!

*****

"You will marry, soon!" Her mother only told her. Jamaspa's father was pleased; for him, a girl less in his house meant more money in his pocket. Her mother was happy too, she did not hold the responsibility for her beautiful daughter anymore. Nobody asked Jamaspa if she is pleased with this marriage or not, but she would like to leave her father's home. She had never had big dreams or ambitions; she knew the groom was not a farmer like her father, so she was delighted.

Her engagement ceremony was very simple. Jamaspa took a quick peek over her shoulder at her fiancée. He was just a common man with a typical look, dark, tall, with black eyes that were always staring at the ground with shy. He did not look at Jamaspa, and she wondered if he had desired to see her, but when she wanted to turn her face suddenly their eyes met, and they stared at each other for a few seconds, her heart ran fast. She stared at the ground horribly, but she had a beautiful smile on her lips. *This is probably love,* she thought. Her fiancé tied the red scarf around Jamaspa's waist finally, without looking at her. Only twenty days, then they could start out on the road of life.

Jamaspa could not wait to show her red scarf to her friends. She went to the river afternoon. The girls surrounded her, laughing, greeting and asking about the groom. Who's he? What does he look like? What's his job? Their chatting was so sweet that she did not notice the time passing. She noticed she must go home when it was half-light. She had to hurry; her father was at home after the darkness. She picked up her things and ran through the narrow and crowded streets of Nineveh as if before a storm. She did not notice that a man was chasing her. She made the last turn at the down of the alley and sighed of relief, she had to cross three further lanes, each narrower than the one before, to be home but just at that moment, someone grabbed her from behind and hit her to the wall. The Jar fell and broke into the dozens of pieces.

A robust man in worn army uniform stood against Jamaspa and stared angrily at her, at the same time his big and strong hand pushed her skinny body on the wall, an old long scar was seen on his sour face that had divided his eyebrow into the half. Jamaspa looked at him like a caged, frightened rabbit, her eyes wide with terror. The man's round amber eyes remembered the eyes of hawks, his mouth that was almost stuck to Jamaspa's face smelt wine.

"What is it?" The man angrily shouted, pointing to her shawl.

Jamaspa did not expect such a question; her big green-brown eyes grew bigger. She did not answer, just stared wide-eyed at him. The man ripped apart her scarf. He looked into her fearful eyes. "You're mine," he said through his clenched teeth, took a deep breath, inhaled Jamaspa's body smell, and closed his eyes with pleasure for a second then looked at her with a smile that was showing his yellow teeth. "I have been watching you for days." His fingers were slipping on her neck's skin. "You're a beautiful woman." His hand stopped on her breast. "Very pretty." The tip of his finger touched her thin breast skin through the gap of her dress button, his breaths were shallow, and his voice scratched.

"Brazen! Hey Brazen! Where are you, man?"

A voice was heard from the distance. The stout man looked toward the sound.

"Remember that, no one... no one has the right to be your husband. You're just mine, understood? If anyone dares to marry you, I'll cut his throat with this," the man said as he brought a small steel dagger up in front of her eyes, then laughed aloud and walked away. When Jamaspa could move, a few minutes had passed. She picked up her shawl from the ground with a shaking hand and ran as fast as she could. She finally got home, when her father was there, so angry that he was shaking, cursing her and kicking on everything in the house. Jamaspa went to the kitchen and prepared the meal, shivering, too frightened even to cry. She gave her father the food and let him sleep. Midnight, when everyone was sleeping, she made her tears roll on her face, silent, hot and precipitous.

For the first time in her life, Jamaspa stayed in bed, three nights and four days, burning up with fever, but she was only nineteen years old and blessed to be young, she forgot the man. At a young age, the mind could create hope, and the heart could believe it completely. She decided to stay at home. *After the wedding ceremony that terrible man doesn't look after me again because he'll notice that I'm a married woman,* she told herself, her mother's tales always ended with blissfully married.

Day followed night and nights followed day. Jamaspa was getting married in two days. Every day, she was sewing a cheap lapis lazuli on her scarf. Her mother also brought a few bronze coins, which her lady gave her as a gift for her daughter's wedding, finding more coins seemed almost impossible. *Beyond that, I can do nothing,* she thought, *There is no miracle in my life.*

One day, Jamaspa's younger sister, who had gone to bring water from the river for her, rushed back home. She sat beside Jamaspa with joy and opened her fist in front of her face. Jamaspa saw two silver coins in her fist.

Jamaspa gave a cry of delight, hugged her sister tight and kissed her face. "Where did you get them from?" Jamaspa asked, staring at her in surprise.

"A man gave them to me in the market," her sister said excitedly.

"I have to believe in the miracle in my life," Jamaspa said, smiling. "I will stitch the coins in front of my scarf, where the groom's family could see it well." She was turning the shiny coins in her hand and looking at them with joy. "Why did he give these coins to you?"

"I was in the market, a young man in army uniform came forward, he told me he has heard my sister will soon be married, and I said, yes, only two days left in her wedding, then he gave me the coins," her sister said.

The coins fell through Jamaspa's fingers.

"This man had a scar on his face?" Jamaspa asked in horror.

"Yeah, that's him, a cut scar in one of his eyebrow!" Her sister said with excitement.

*****

Jamaspa's head held high, her pretty face hidden behind a bright red veil.

The Assyrians had a unique wedding custom, the bride and the groom had to go barefoot down the four stairs led them down the tower of the temple, slowly, with each step they took, the priest blessed their lives. The groom took his bride by the hand, and started toward the stairs, pulling her behind him.

Four; Jamaspa counted as her worried eyes were looking around. The priest asked from God Marduk, for the young couple: *A love that lasts a lifetime*. The priest was reading litanies aloud, asking for a love that did not form yet but he wanted to continue for lifelong.

Three; Jamaspa counted, and the priest said, loudly and clearly: *many children*. Suddenly those words drew her attention. *Oh no, please don't listen to him God Marduk,* Jamaspa thought.

Two; Jamaspa counted. Abundant wealth; the priest loudly said as he was pouring some harmala in the censer. Jamaspa was feeling her heart in her throat. *God Marduk, please do something the priest read the litanies faster*, Jamaspa murmured.

One and the last, she thought. Long life, she realized those words among the strange words of litanies that the priest was reading. *Yes*, that was which one she wanted for sure. *Please God Marduk, save him, give him a long life.*

It seemed the god had heard her pray, the ceremony had come to an end, nothing had happened, and she could go home her own home. Jamaspa sighed of relief, raised her head and smiled the groom sweetly, but above him, she saw the young commander figure on horseback. Jamaspa had no chance, even for a scream. The commander with the dagger that he had shown to Jamaspa ripped the groom's throat; wrapped his hand on Jamaspa's waist and cut her off from the ground. Brazen even did not decrease the speed of his horse. He was galloping quickly while he kept Jamaspa on his side. She could see the blood ran down of the groom's throat and his face grew visibly pale.

Images quickly got away from her. The groom was dead on the ground... His mother and sister cried... Jamaspa's mother's worried and frightened eyes were pinned at her... her mother's eyes were the last thing that she saw, and then she fainted.

*****

Jamaspa opened her eyes, hardly. The air was hot and heavy with the smell of wine, unclean oil lamp, and sweat of a man... a strange man. It made her dizzy. She sat with a groan and looked around. She could not remember where she was. There was a damp cellar, crowded with barrels of wine and she was on a bed of dried grass, completely naked. Her body felt painful, covered with bruises. She got up, feeling her head heavy. She saw her wedding dress in the corner of the cellar and remembered everything. Her husband ripped throat, his widened eyes in horror and his face that quickly lost the life. She remembered the long night... the terrible and very long night that had reached to the twilight with the smell of wine, sweat of a stranger body... and shame... and pain.

Jamaspa dragged herself to her clothes and put them on. No light could come in the cellar but a shallow light, coming through the gap of a gate at the top of the stairs. Jamaspa did not know what time of the day was. She went up the stairs, opened the gate and suddenly found herself in a smoky pub. She could feel the drunk men's eyes crawling over her as she went on. Jamaspa tried to cover up her torn collar as she passed through men with trembling steps. She went to the door, in the doorway; somebody grabbed the back of her skirt.

"Where do you think you're going? The commander will come soon!" A coarser voice shouted.

Jamaspa looked back fearfully. A short man, who was as tall as her legs, had taken her skirt, looking at her angrily. Jamaspa stepped back, pulling her skirt forcibly off his hands and then ran with all power that was left to her. It was evening. Out of the pub, Jamaspa suddenly knew where she was. She had seen this pub before; she was on the fringes of the bazaar, where Jamaspa had passed every day, with a straight neck and slow steps. She knew she needed to go home before it became too late. *Home*, she felt more power when she remembered that she would be at home just a few minutes later, in the loving arms of her mother and sisters. She tried to ignore stares and did not stop until she reached her home.

She pounded her fists onto the wooden door. "Open up, open," she yelled.

She heard voices, a low conversation, an argument. Her mother was begging and asking her father to let open the door for Jamaspa. Her sisters were moaning quietly, and her father was cursing. Jamaspa hit the door with her fists over and over until she heard the sound of her father's slap on her mother's face. Jamaspa's hands froze on the door for a few moments, but she could not give up. She pounded the door, stronger. She cried, tougher. Her father opened the door finally but stood in the doorway. He beat his fist on Jamaspa's chest, and she fell on the ground.

"What do you want? Huh? Go... head back to where you come from!" her father shouted.

Jamaspa had collapsed on the ground with pain and stared at her father in surprise. "Where? I have no place to go," she said.

"Go back...," he said, his drunk voice was trembling. "Go back to the man that clearly loves you!" Added quietly.

She crawled on the ground and grabbed her father's foot. "Please, I don't want to live that way."

Her father threw her back with the heel of his foot. "Then how would you live, huh? How could you live?" He shouted as he turned to walk inside.

"I hate you," Jamaspa said through her clenched teeth. "You don't care about me... you never cared about me."

Her father turned to her again, looked at her for a few moments. "You can't live here; you can't live like your past," he said finally. "The people won't let you! You have to stay with him... it's not my choice." He went inside horribly, without looking at her again.

Jamaspa sat on the dirty street and cried, soundless. She heard the sound of the opening door; neighbors came out to peek at her. Her mother and sisters were crying yet. When Jamaspa raised her head, it was quite dark. She got up, walked with wobbly steps to the bazaar, at the end of the alley she turned, looked at her home for the last time, a house that she had dreamed of leaving but now wished to live there so badly that her stomach hurt with the wanting.

In the pub, the short man looked at her angrily. "The commander was waiting for you," he said as he was drying the cups that he had washed up with a torn and dirty cloth. "Be careful! His anger is a terrible thing when rouse."

*****

She was spending her life in this cursed pub, washing the dirty cups, arranging the tables and wiping the floor that was always dirty of drunken men throwing mouth water. The short man, Forte, was still so harsh and angry but despite his appearances, he was not a bad guy. On the other hand, Jamaspa was a hard worker, never moaned, grumbled or complained, so Forte had no reason to kick her out.

Brazen, a lowly military officer, the man had made Jamaspa his mistress, spent most of his evenings in the pub. He drank wine until midnight, made love with Jamaspa till dawn and slept till noon. Although making love was a very ridiculous word for what Brazen was doing with her, what Jamaspa had heard about the sex was very different from his wild, brutal attitude.

Jamaspa had killed him in her mind many times. Every afternoon, she laid in bed, stared at the ceiling, and her mind feverish with thoughts of killing him, which had become an enjoyable hobby for her. Sometimes she decided to poison his wine and sometimes she wanted to provide a small dagger that she could dip it in his throat to handle. But each time she met him, the warmth of that magic dreams leave her as fear replaced it, a fear that filled her, worse than any fear she had ever felt before, so dazed with terror, obedient without question to whatever Brazen wanted.

Although her life was precisely terrible, she gradually learned a few things to ease her discomfort. She learned to prepare Forte's favorite food and wine, which pleased him, learned how to move through the tables far from the men's hands, and determined to add some ephedra poppy sap to Brazen's wine at nights to make him sleep faster.

We are remarkably adaptable, coping with all kinds of situations, it is human nature. We get used to the good things, so we do those but still not feeling joy and bad things become familiar enough that they are not hateful anymore but everything changes when we thought we are adapting well.

*****

Jamaspa was feeling chronically hungry; her life has become a whirl of fatigue and nausea. *That's my worst nightmare*, she thought miserably. Her body was showing in the early turns of pregnancy. She knew the signs of pregnancy very well; her mother was pregnant many times.

One morning, she had knelt on the ground, in back of the pub, bending her head into a bucket, throwing up viciously when somebody kicked the bucket. After a startled, she looked up.

"Great!" Forte shouted angrily. "Now I realize why you don't work as the same as before. Brazen has to find somewhere for you."

"Where?!" Jamaspa asked, her discomfort forgotten for a moment.

"Somewhere, anywhere," Forte said and went to the door.

Jamaspa ran toward Forte and grabbed him by the hand to hold him back, "Please, brother, don't talk to...," she said, unwilling even to say Brazen's name. "I'm begging you. Please let me stay here!"

Forte turned back to her. "I have no reason to keep you and your bastard. I'm not trying to get into any more trouble," he Shouted, pushing her hand aside.

"Please let me stay, and I'll be your wet nurse, I work for you harder than before, I swear... I do whatever you want," she said.

Forte spat, took another step.

"I'll eat one meal a day!"

Forte stepped faster, stubbornly, pulling the crying Jamaspa along.

"There is no place for me to go...please!" Jamaspa wailed.

Forte stood doubtfully, stared at her for a few moments. "Gods be damned... listen to me, make yourself of use. Do your work!" He finally said.

Jamaspa began to weep again, nodding fearfully. "I will; you are too kind. Thank you."

She knelt, shivering, put her hand on her belly and sighed. She knew she should let Brazen know. He is a human too, she thought, maybe he wants to have children, like other men. Perhaps if I give him a son, he treats me well enough...

"Hey bitch, come up here."

Jamaspa heard Brazen's harsh voice. She stood and stared fearfully at him as he sat in his wood-leather chair. She cleaned herself, trembling. She had never seen him in the hub before night. She went to the pub, wondering what awaited her.

Brazen was in a lively mood, he was entertaining Forte with the latest tales from the Assyrian army attack on Medes land. Jamaspa went in, shivering, hiding behind the pillar. Brazen saw her.

"No need to hide bitch, I'm your lover!"

The word of *Lover* that Brazen had just uttered, produced the effect of hate on Jamaspa's face. She stared at him in revulsion.

"Don't stare at me like that, bring me wine!" Brazen said. "Be happy! The war has raged right over our border in the north, and I'm going to whack that goddamn Medes king ass. Pray God Marduk, maybe I'll be dead before the war is done." He laughed, a snort of amusement.

Brazen's voice echoed in her ears. This news, only one month ago could be bloody good news to her, but now, with a baby in her belly... fear filled Jamaspa's gut like a meal she could not digest. *I have to say something; I cannot bear to wait another moment. He must know about his child,* Jamaspa thought. She swallowed twice, but she was unable to speak and stared at him in confusion.

Brazen looked at her and chewed his mustache. Jamaspa's gaze made him angry. He turned to Forte. "Why is she looking at me that way?" He shouted.

Jamaspa took a step backward slowly, and another, hiding again. Forte brought Brazen a bowl of hot fish stew, some warm fresh bread and a cup of wine as well. He dropped the bread on a table, annoyed. "What about her?" Forte said, pointing to Jamaspa with his head.

"What are you afraid of? She works for you hard enough, at least as much as her room rent and meals. What do you want else?" Brazen said. "Remember, when I come back, I'll keep an eye on your pub and make sure you stay safe."

"What if you don't return?" Forte gave him a hard stare, "your whore is pregnant! What am I supposed to do with her, and her bastard?" He said with a sullen face.

"Pregnant?!" Brazen asked, confused by what he was hearing. He looked at Jamaspa who chose to peer at him behind the pillar, then looked at Forte again. "I warn you man, that's not funny!"

"Do you hear me chuckling?" Forte said.

Brazen reached for his wine cup and took a swallow.

"I warned you this would happen, but you did not care to hear it," Forte said, standing on his toes and straining upward, he managed to pull himself up and seat on his high stand chair. "You need to find a shelter for her before going aboard. She lives here, as long as she can work for me."

Jamaspa took a quick peek at Brazen and began to tremble. Brazen poured wine into the cup, drank it in a breath. He did not seem in a good mood anymore, and he was looking into the distance with a frown. He suddenly stood up, went to the Forte, oblivious to the fearful look that Jamaspa gave him and poured a handful of silver coins in front of Forte. Brazen glanced at Jamaspa's face and said: "Keep her, keep her safe. The war would be over, and everyone would come back to Nineveh."

Forte gave him a sullen glance. "Many would be killed when the war is done if anything happens to you... I can't sit here waiting for a person that might or might not come back to Nineveh."

"Gods be damned!" Brazen roared in a bored tone. "If anything happens to me, keep her and her baby for yourself, a gift from me! A beautiful wife and a child, without any trouble, even fucking!" He gave a bark of laughter and left them.

Jamaspa stared at Forte, trying to guess what will happen next. "Bastard!" Forte said, his voice was thick and angry. He collected coins, counting carefully. It made her anxious. She lowered her eyes and tried to keep quiet. When his mood darkened, any chance word might set off one of his rages. Forte went up to his bedchamber to take his daily nap before the customers coming. Jamaspa was suddenly very frightened, found herself alone in the pub. Her body was shaking; *I don't know how long it's going be before Forte decides to throw me out?* She thought, *should I stay here, or run after Brazen and plead to stay in Nineveh?*

Yet she paused and stood.

*****

Next days were better than she expected. Not only Jamaspa would be pleased by the absence of Brazen, but she also had three meals and less work. On the other side, her swollen face and growing belly could defend her from the unwanted attentions of the drunken men.

She used to hide in the dark crypt of the pub every midnight when everyone had left. She lay down behind on a mass of dry grass that was her bed, stroked her belly gently, and whispered softly at her baby, sang the songs that she had learned from her mother. She closed her eyes to imagine what her daughter might look like. She believed she definitely welcome a baby girl to the world. She could feel it, carrying around the middle, craving sweets, excessive morning... she knows the signs well enough to have the idea, her mother had shown these signs several times before. Once Jamaspa started to feel her baby move, she grew strong enough to dare to dream of a life she might make. Every night she was whispering her baby the stories of a home, their home, a house bigger than that one she lived in, sat on top of the little hill. A house that had walls painted white with window frames of mahogany, a home that was the scent of lavender, the delicate blooms in one of her mother's old jam jars,... a home... often she fell asleep while she was whispering.

*****

Even during the final days of her pregnancy, Jamaspa had to work hard.

Jamaspa chewed her lip as she walked, led her big belly through the tables. *Just hang on a little longer*, she told herself as she moved among the tables, pouring wine, collecting dirty cups. One of the men slid a hand up under her skirts, she gasped to roars of laughter. She tried to move faster, panting, looking neither right nor left. She dared not to stop working beneath Forte's gaze. She stood next to a table and extended her hand to pick up the cups but a man's fingers wrapped around her wrist. Jamaspa looked at man's face. She was startled to see his eyes, gasped and dropped the cup. His face was thin, with a high forehead, massive jaw, and an eagle nose, like his brother... *the man who was my husband, only for a minute*, Jamaspa thought. The man stared at her, unblinking, his eyes glittered in the torchlight, dark and wet, his fingers had sunk into her flesh, like claws of an eagle but Jamaspa did not flinch or cry out, only seeing him through a veil of tears.

"I was traveling in the Medes, when I came home, my elder brother was dead. I was eager to see you since I came home." He smiled a sad smile. "My brother's killer..." He lowered his voice. "I vowed to kill you for what you did to my brother." He got up so quickly that overturned the table, the empty cups shattered into a thousand pieces across the stone floor. His hands grabbed Jamaspa's throat, five fingers hard as iron digging deep into her flesh. Jamaspa stared at the young man, effortless. The drunken men had gathered around them and made excited the young man to kill Jamaspa with their shouts.

"Hey young, leave her!" Forte shouted as he was pushing aside the men.

"Stay out of this, dwarf... she knows well that she deserves to die!" The man said through in his clenched teeth.

"Leave her; if you know me, you know I could put you in a dungeon for the rest of your life!" Forte roared again.

The young man spared a glance for Forte's serious face. "I'm not kidding!" Forte said sullenly. The young man's fingers relaxed, loosed his grip slowly, let her body could slide to the stone floor, coughing and shivering. He closed his fingers into a fist, stared at her for a few seconds. "There is no way to spare you, I swear!" He made a disgusted face and spat full in her face, leaving her with an unsightly pink sign on her throat.

Jamaspa's eyes escorted the man with sadness, then lowered her face to stare sullenly at the broken cups and plates. The men had stood around yet, staring at her; she could feel tears stinging her eyes. "He's absolutely right," she said in a choked voice, embarrassed. She rubbed her tears away angrily and dragged herself on the ground to go down the stairs. She laid on her bed, shivering in the darkness of the crypts, and pressed her face into her red wedding shawl, then the world turned into a blur. Jamaspa recalled she has never mourned for her husband.

She began to wail for her husband, painfully, for long minutes until her voice refused to utter any sound. She was gasping for air that simply was not there, her throat burned, forming a silent scream.

Forte stood at the top of the stairs, paused, sighed and then shut the door.

* * * * *

Jamaspa opened her eyes, afraid. She woke up, thinking surely this was some mad dream, a young man with her dead husband's face choked her, but she still felt pain in her throat. She heard some men footsteps as they rushed on the pub's wooden floor. They were almost running, but the steps stopped just when they were loudest, right outside the door. She sat on the bed; her face was puffy from all her crying, listened carefully. The sound of argument added. She could recognize Forte's voice, his voice growing sharp. Her shawl was beside the bed. Jamaspa slipped it on and went to the door. The door to the crypts was made of iron, old and heavy, she shoved it, but it was as if someone has put a heavy bulk on the door from the outside. Jamaspa pushed the door again, harder, and again. She struggled, but to no avail.

"Forte, Forte! Open the door! Forte, what's going on?" Jamaspa shouted.

She still was hearing Forte's obscure shouts from the pub, but the sound became gradually farther and farther and then a sudden silence fell upon the pub. Jamaspa did not know what was going on, but there was something wrong without a doubt. She smashed with full force on the door.

"Open the door! Forte! Nobody is there?" Jamaspa yelled.

Jamaspa heard a pounding behind her as someone hammering the ceiling. At once she stilled, fearing even to blink. She glanced from the corner of her eye, suddenly the wooden ceiling came crashing apart, and make a hole. Someone threw a flaming torch into the crypts through the hole. The flames leaped like an uncaged tiger into the darkness and ran onto the dry grasses on the floor. The fire roared for joy and consumed all in its path and heat beat against her face! She was pounding furiously at the door, screaming, eyes wide with horror. She cried more violently as she felt the fire licking against the back of her thighs, a scream of hysteria, disbelief, and terror.

"Heeeeeeeeeeeeeeeeeeeeeeeelp!"

It was a terrible scream, a wail of pain that seemed to burn the ears.

Over the roar of the flames, Jamaspa heard shouts. "Get the fuck her out of here." The door swung open, and somebody wrapped her in a blanket and brought her out of the fire. The smoke and screams and pain were making her feel faint.

*****

Jamaspa opened her eye, only one of her eyes could be opened. She realized a hand was brushing her hair back from her face in a gentle caress. It felt good. When she tried to move, she gave a sharp gasp of pain.

"Calm, close your eyes baby!" She heard her mother's voice, feeling her mother's lips close in her ear but her voice was weak and could be heard from a distance.

"How can I close my eyes, when I bloody wished to see your face again for months?!" She murmured in a voice thin and wispy and wracked by pain. "My mother." A tremulous smile touched her face as her hand groped for her mother. She stared at her mother with her only eye. A drop of tear slowly rolled out of the corner of her eye.

Her mother kissed her daughter's hair. "My own sweet baby," her mother said, so grief-stricken, seeing her through a veil of tears.

"Baby! My baby..." Jamaspa's fingers reached out and touched her belly fearfully. "Thank Gods!" She caressed her belly bomb and drew a breath of relief. "I can endure darkness as long as I can hope that my new sun will rise. My daughter is alive, so I could bear anything!"

Even the weight of a blanket could make her shudder of pain, but she bore the pain without complaint. "Silence is your only friend, no one must ever see or hear you," her mother had told her. "If you wish to survive, if you want to hold your child in your arms, you need to be strong!"

Jamaspa did not know what should she do in this situation, she hesitated, then nodded slowly nodded.

After a few days, she was strong enough to sit on the bed and explore her new home. They had left her alone in another crypt, on a bed of dry grass, again. Her mother brought food to her, steaming joints of meat and fruits from her lady's palace kitchen, the food which her father hated to eat. The feeling of the baby kick in her belly strengthened her to endure everything for the sake of her child. *Endure this for a little while longer, and it shall pass,* she comforted herself.

Her recovery had taken twenty-three days, her days were anxious, her nights restless, and every noise made her clench her teeth, remembering the crypts in the fire like a nightmare of burning in hell!

*****

Her mother opened the door with a loud creak; she came into the crypt along with a man who was strangers to Jamaspa. The man in his black clothes was looking at Jamaspa oddly; he glanced at Jamaspa, shook his head and walked away. Her mother rushed toward him, grabbed his arm, and began to speak. The man watched Jamaspa's mother as she spoke, his face was a mask, still and stern, betraying nothing. Jamaspa could not hear her mother, but it seemed like she was trying to convince the man. Finally, when the man nodded and left, a smile broke across her mother's face. Jamaspa's mother came to her, sat down beside her bed, and gave her a bitter smile.

Her mother leaned forward.

"Baby, you have to get away from here!" She whispered in her ear.

"No, no no, I'm not going anywhere mom, I want to stay here with you… I'm safe here," Jamaspa said, sobbing, although she was not sure.

"You're not safe. If you think hiding here will make that boy forget you, you are sadly mistaken."

Her mother's image became glazed with a glassy layer of tears. Jamaspa blinked, her tears dripped from her eyelids and slid down her cheeks.

Her mother lower lip quivered as words slowly made their way out of her mouth. "We have no choice," her mother murmured sadly "If they find you, they will kill you." She wiped her tears with the back of her wrinkled hand, pulled out a fistful of coins from her skirt pocket and pressed them into her daughter's palm. "My lady gave me them. Her sister is living in another land, Mannea! You have to go there," her mother said. "Amitira, my lady's sister, knows me well. She has grown up in my arms, I have no doubt that she will help you and won't leave you alone. No caravan goes from here to Mannea, but this man takes you to the border, you will find a way to reach there." She stroked her daughter's face and brushed back a loose strand of Jamaspa's hair. "You have a long journey ahead of you, it is not easy, I know. Just be patient," her mother added, putting her head down, she could not bear the misery in her daughter's eyes.

The man entered, helped Jamaspa to get up from the bed. Jamaspa had to climb a dozen stairs before step outside. The fierce sun beat down, when she stood again; it took her eyes a moment to adjust. There was no house, an uninhabited wasteland. Jamaspa looked around with wondering eyes, *why is there a crypt among nothing at all?* She thought. She walked with unsteady steps to a carriage that was ready outside the crypt. Her mother pulled a thick woolen scarf up over Jamaspa's shoulders.

"Hold it, it's cold up there, in Mannea lands, this scarf should help," her mother said in a loud voice.

Her mother took two steps and hesitated, full of grief and longing, then she turned and raced back in a rush. Her feet flew kicking up the wispy sand. It was tough to leave her daughter in the hands of life with an uncertain fate but at the last minute turned to see the end of it. The man was helping Jamaspa to mount, her eyes lingered on Jamaspa's face, and she looked at her mother, crying desperately. Her mother turned and left them, without hesitation.

*****

Jamaspa had been wandering the streets of Lakaran for hours, the last town on the border. It was too cold, too damp, too far away and she was cold, wet and fearful. The cold wind was blowing, bothering her damaged skin. The market square had been thronged with farmers selling vegetables, and their customers when Jamaspa crossed it. In the crowd, people were shoving, cursing one another, passing quickly, some oblivious to her and some turning face with disgust. She heard the voice of a farmer man who was selling fresh vegetables. He was yelling, but she could hear his voice from a distance. Jamaspa turned off the square, wandering alone through the streets. She followed winding path up a long hill, past grizzled ironmongers selling old blades and razors from their wagons and stood before a blacksmith, working at an open forge. A brisk wind made blacksmith's apron swirl and snap. An ugly dog was stretched out asleep beneath the wall. The blacksmith had not seen her, hammered out a new sword.

"Excuse me, master!" Jamaspa said loudly because she could not hear herself.

The blacksmith startled, looked at her and took a step back in disgust. "Go away, go away... I have nothing to give you," he shouted.

Jamaspa stepped back, so quickly she almost tripped over the rushes. "I'm not a beggar," she said. "I should find a convoy, I need caravans from Mannea."

The man said something, frowning, and pointed out an archway. Jamaspa did not hear him but followed the same direction, shivering in the mountain chill. The wind was gusting, cold as ice, and it was really hard to walk with her big belly, but the most horrible thing was people who turned their face in disgust when they saw her. She put her head down and tried to go faster.

She walked through the archway, soon found herself in a courtyard. On the east side, an old wooden inn stood with white walls. Even at this hour, it was crowded, noisy, and ablaze with light. *I could have anything I want on there: food and fire,* she thought, but she hesitated, continued down the courtyard to the stable, avoiding the people gaze.

In the inn's stable, a mule and three horses occupied the stalls. Jamaspa entered, stood near the horses, hoping to finds someone. Jamaspa liked one of the strange black-and-white ones; she made her way toward them to stroke the horse's mane. She sensed something beneath the horse and looked down. She saw her reflection in a bucket of water, staggered, and sank on both knees. It was as though she were looking at a stranger. The left side of her face was a ruin, her hair was burned, almost bald, her left eyelid had been burned and remained closed, and her face was a twisted mass of burned, pink flesh. It was difficult to believe, one-day Jamaspa was a beautiful girl who caught the eyes.

"Hey, what are you doing here?"

Jamaspa wiped her tears hurryingly and turned to the voice. There was a tall man, standing right behind her. He frowned when he saw her and Jamaspa raised her hands to cover her face. He does not seem like Assyrians. He was thin and swarthy, with black hair, big black eyes, and pale skin. He had an accent that was so strange to her.

"I want to go Mannea," Jamaspa said as she was pulling the scarf over her face quickly.

The man said something but Jamaspa did not hear him.

"Repeat it, louder please, I can't hear you," Jamaspa said.

Something flashed beneath the surface of his hardened expression, there was a pity in his look when he said loudly, "This is not a good time to travel…," the man pointed at her belly and added, "… We can't take you in this condition!" He shook his head. "Go back home."

He walked forward but not too close to her, to feed the horses.

"I have no home," Jamaspa said, her voice shivered with rage and grief.

He turned to stare at her, "Our journey through the mountain will be dangerous, no pregnant woman survives it."

"I'm strong, I had to be," Jamaspa said. "Mannea is my last hope, please brother."

"It is impossible," he said and turned his face immediately.

Jamaspa pulled out the coins that her mother had given to her. "I have money… look," Jamaspa said. The man looked first at coins and then at Jamaspa. "I'm begging you. I have nowhere to go," she said. "Please."

The man stared at Jamaspa, her face was so ugly it held a queer fascination for him, but at the same time, she seemed so innocent, helpless and desperate that he could not be indifferent to her. The man paused a moment. "What has happened to you, are you sick?" He asked.

Jamaspa pulled her scarf further over her face, as she was shaking her head vehemently "No, my… my face is burned," Jamaspa said, embarrassing.

"I'm taking a caravan up to Stentorian lands tomorrow," the man said as he grabbed four coins. "That's enough. Pull the rest in a place where others could not see them. Our convoy passes Lakaran Mountains and goes to Giles, but Mannea is my land. At the bottom of the mountain, if you would be still alive, I will tell you how you will get there," the man said.

Jamaspa's hand trembled as she hid the coins in her belt, but she nodded slowly.

"There's no woman in our convoy, all men, Assyrian men!" The man said. "You probably know your men, isn't it?" The man added, his tone was edged with malice.

"I know them!" Jamaspa murmured.

"They are harsh… sometimes dangerous," he said regardless of her answer. "You have to watch yourself, not me! Understood?"

Jamaspa nodded again.

"The inn is full of men and whores; you can just sleep here, in the corner of the stable tonight, all right? I'll bring you some food," the man said. "We'll go tomorrow morning, an hour before the sunrise."

*****

In two days of hard riding, Jamaspa was into the back of a mule cart. The ground was rough, the cart was shuddering on its wooden wheels, and with every movement, pain lanced through her belly, but she would not cry out.

The men erected shelters, a shield against the wind, tended the horses, and built a fire. The Mannaean man offered a hand to help her as she entered on foot. Her belly was cramping badly, and the camp was a welcome sight. She found a comfortable spot, beside the fire and sat on a stone. A big boulder provided shelter for her against the biting wind.

Jamaspa wrapped herself more in a blanket that the Mannaean man had given her and warmed her frozen bones against the night's chill. She stared into the flickering flames, lost in her thoughts. She had learned to make no unreasonable claims, but she expected to have an ordinary life, with small happiness. *My joys were like this swirl of fire sparks rose to meet the snowflakes coming down and die, and my sorrows are ashes, dark, cold and perennial.* Jamaspa wondered, *why am I escaping? What I'm afraid of? I have nothing to lose. Hope is like a precious, valuable pearl, for those who are invisible and forgotten by fate.* The child moved in her belly, gave a sharp gasp of pain. *My baby!* This reminded her of one incident in her mother's life when her only son was born dead. Jamaspa was greatly astonished at the words, which her mother had spoken, she said, "I have to rise up, I don't care how hard this is, I don't care how disappointed I am, I'm moving on with my life." She bit her blue lip with cold to stop the rush of bitter words, her fingers stroking her belly. "Too much to live for yet, right?" She whispered to her child.

The men sat around the fire, and one of them stared at Jamaspa with disgust. Jamaspa noticed the man, pulled her scarf further, did her best to hide her fear. The Mannaean man stewed some dried meat with some grain, and wild onions. An hour later, the savory smell of stew filled Jamaspa's nostrils. She dragged herself over to where the man was tending the stew pot. The Mannaean man handed everybody a pot of stew. Jamaspa tapped her wooden spoon against the edge of the bowl and downed it with pleasure. The warm food made her feel stronger, but suddenly she heard a shout from one of the Assyrian men.

"Do I have to bear her ugly face when I'm eating my food?" The Assyrian man said, loud enough for Jamaspa to hear it.

"She has paid for the food, more than you, so she can eat more than you," the Mannaean man said coldly, tearing apart a loaf of black bread to soak in his stew.

"I didn't say she doesn't eat, but she has to get out of my sight... I don't want to bear this evil bitch's ugly face," the man growled.

"You're as stupid as she is ugly, but I tolerate you." The Mannaean man glanced at him with disgust. "This woman is pregnant, she needs to eat food and warm herself, so just leave her alone."

Jamaspa felt the Assyrian man's eyes on her, chilly eyes, angry and unsympathetic. The Assyrian man rose. No one of other men dared speak to him, or try to bar his way as he made his way toward Jamaspa.

"Go to hell bitch. Go to hell!" The Assyrian man shouted as he kicked at the bowl of food in front of Jamaspa.

Jamaspa dragged herself back to keep herself out of his hands, but at that moment, the Mannaean man rested the tip of his dagger under the Assyrian man's chin with incredible speed before he could move.

"I told you to give her alone!" The Mannaean man said with a dour face.

That brought the Assyrian man lurching backward. The Mannaean man got the fear he wanted as he stared at the Assyrian man with his cold eyes and the Assyrian man backed away, until the darkness of night devoured him in.

"We'll reach Gizan two days later." The Mannaean man gave an angry sniff and said. "We have a long journey ahead of us go, long and dangerous. I don't want anybody gets lost among this snowy mountain so that your body will not found until the summer... unless you make me, so tell your friend, he must be careful...," he glanced over them

222

with a sullen face as sheathed the dagger, "… or you'll be in big trouble, all of you!"

Then he placed his bowl in front of Jamaspa who was looking at him with gratitude and squatted beside the fire.

*****

They had been riding since dawn, Jamaspa was cold, shaking, though they had passed the mountain path and the wind had died, and the sun was higher in the sky. She was sitting bleary-eyed into the cart, leaning heavily on barrels of oil that the Assyrian men had brought for sale, with an ashen face. She could feel the pain inside her like a worm, slowly but deliberately draining her life. Everything seemed to move in a dragged pace, all submerged into a hazy fuzz in her vision.

"We're here, Giles," the Mannaean man told her, he sounded concerned. "Here our paths will separate. I have to find someone to take you to Mannaeans land."

Jamaspa nodded weakly to show she has understood; she had no strength to answer. Her breath quivered in short, quick gasps every time she inhaled, her lungs having no choice but to painfully and rigidly take in the chilled air around her. She could not seem to stop shaking. The Mannaean man glanced toward her for the last time as he entered the inn and felt a stab of pity. He stood in the open door, glanced around carefully and suddenly he shouted with joy.

"Hey, Bliss!"

A robustness young man, sitting cross-legged on soft cushions, raised his head. He smiled, came before his friend to greet him pleasantly and two men hugged.

"Long time my old friend, what brings you home?" Bliss said.

The Mannaean man smiled. "Yeah, I'll tell you someday but now's not the time." He glanced back, saw Jamaspa's pale face. "I ask you to do me a favor," he said, smiled, his smile was wan and tired.

"I'll do as you've asked!"

"I need you to deliver a passenger, a pregnant woman, to Mannea. I think she's going to her relatives," the Mannaean man said.

"Mannea? Don't you know that your land has been involved in a war? Forget it, it's too dangerous."

The Mannaean man ran his fingers through his hair. "I didn't know," he said. "It is a dangerous thing to do, but it is probably her only chance to survive!" Then he looked back to the yard where Jamaspa was waiting for him. He rested his hand on Bliss's shoulder. "You know the ways better than anybody, if you take the shortcuts across the woods; I swear that you will arrive at the downhill village without any risks."

"She cannot bear that, you said she's pregnant, the road veered north by northeast through the wood with flint hills, rough and stony summits."

"She can not bear to be lost here as well... she would not survive, at least her relatives take care of her there," the Mannaean man said, hoping that was true. "I give four pieces of silver for he, I know it's not much, but I hope you accept that."

"I'll take her," Bliss said as he stretched forth his hand and grabbed two coins. "That's enough." He gave the Mannaean man's shoulder a squeeze. "Don't worry; I'll take care of her."

The Mannaean man moved to Jamaspa. "So there you go. I found one of my friends to take you, but..." Jamaspa raised her face, smiled a wan smile. The Mannaean man wanted to say Mannea was a war going on, but he looked at her face, Jamaspa seemed as pale as Ghost, and even though a cold wind was blowing out of the north, her face was damp with perspiration. He thought this poor woman had enough worries and sorrow, no need to add anything to it.

"Thank you for your help," she said in a barely audible voice. She pulled out her coin bag from her belt and stretched forth it towards him.

The Mannaean man pushed Jamaspa's hand aside gently. "Keep your coins. You will need them."

Bliss came with two stout horses.

"Wouldn't it be better if you prepare a cart for her?" The Mannaean man asked anxiously.

"That's not possible," Bliss said. "We must travel up, cross the hills, past the river, and turn north to the village, all goat paths, no carts can get through those!"

The Mannaean man nodded solemnly as he helped Jamaspa to climb to her feet. "Remember, this woman doesn't know our language, she is from Assyria," he said to Bliss.

"Assyria? It's strange, isn't it?" Bliss seemed puzzled.

"What's strange about that?" The Mannaean man asked as he was leading Jamaspa toward the horses.

"Well, they are enemies."

"During the war, your tribe's patriarchs encouraged their members to go to war, even if it meant killing people of their own religion but we're still friends. War is the dumbest thing that I've ever seen, especially in comparison with friendship!"

"You're damn right." Bliss was impressed.

The Mannaean man helped Jamaspa to mount on the huge black horse. She gave him a fade smile with her abnormal lips and wanted to return the blanket.

"Keep it," the Mannaean man said. "It's still pretty chilly." *And dangerous,* he thought.

Bliss stared at Jamaspa's strange face, shocked. He hesitated half a heartbeat, then gathered the reins in his hands and mounted.

"Do not worry, you're in good hands." The Mannaean man pointed to his friend. "He knows the roads like the back of his hand! You will be in a warm, comfortable place before night," he said loudly so that Jamaspa could hear him.

"I've never had to thank a man for anything before," Jamaspa said as she wrapped the blanket around herself. "If I didn't meet you, I couldn't imagine that a man will be kind enough to assist a woman without any expectation." Her pale lips promised, "I'll never forget your kindness, thank you!"

The Mannaean man only smiled a sad smile.

Bliss waved hand then put his spurs into his horse and galloped toward hills, holding the reins of Jamaspa's horse, who riding on the tall black horse that cradled her back and front. The Mannaean man stood on the road, gave them one last longing look with worried eyes.

"Hey, are you quite finish your flirtation with your beautiful mistress? Come on, we have to go," one of the Assyrian men shouted from behind him, the men were laughing.

*****

There was a way through the hills to the north, much tougher than the way that had brought her here.

They were riding in a narrow defile. Bliss glanced back, he saw Jamaspa, a little of her face that could be seen beneath her scarf was as colorless as a ghost, but her breath still puffed faintly from her nostrils whenever she exhaled. Bliss should return to the same place, which he had left, and it was a long way back in the dark, through the hazardous territory, so he spurred his horse to a gallop even though he could hear the sounds of Jamaspa's ragged and painful breath.

The red sun was going down behind the mountains in the west when Bliss led her through a steep, twisting trail toward a mountain cleft, where Dihe was. He looked at the sky; it was almost night. Bliss shuddered at the thought of getting lost in his own hometown. *It's already too late, I should go back now*, he thought. *She could go the rest of the way by foot, Dihe is near enough, and she has no problem.*

Bliss dismounted and stand beside other horse. Jamaspa lifted her head slowly to look at him. The stripes of light and darkness fell across her terrible burnt face. He took a step back unconsciously.

"I really have to get back," Bliss said meekly.

Jamaspa said nothing, did not seem to hear Bliss's words. She was still looking at this strange man, from land that she had never known when he placed a hand on her shoulder. "I have to go," he whispered as he helped her to dismount. "Go straight down this road." He gestured at the distant hills. "Do not be afraid! You almost there." He stared at her pale face and cracked lips. He knew that this woman did not understand any of this but added. "I just wish I could have found another way to help you." He ran his fingers through his hair, frustrated. "Go!" Bliss said again and showed her the road.

Jamaspa nodded silently, looked at the steep and rocky road, spotted with gnarled poplar trees, she stepped forward. Three quick steps and then she stood, turned her face to Bliss.

"Thank you, brother. Thank you!" Jamaspa said.

Bliss did not need to know the Assyrian language to understand what she said; he brought a smile to his face. He raised his hand. "Good luck sister, and Godspeed."

Jamaspa moved slowly. Bliss's eyes lingered on Jamaspa's wobbly steps. "You are definitely fighting fate, trying to keep your child alive… no one knows how this ends up, but if God wants it, even hell gets better, let alone a village in Mannea," he murmured before mounted and turned his horses toward home.

*****

Jamaspa fell to her knees, clutched at roots and rocks, every time another cramp took root inside her belly and twisted, she would cry out. Even inside the fur-lined blanket, Jamaspa's body had begun to throb with pain. The pain was so severe, and for half a heartbeat she feared this was as far as she could go. Her breath made a ragged white cloud. She crawled to her knees, reached a poplar tree, found a fallen branch just long enough to use as a crutch. Leaning heavily upon it, she staggered toward the village.

Just a little further, and everything will be all right, she told herself, for the millionth times, encouraged herself to walk. Her thoughts were almost as painful as her situation. *What will happen if Amitira doesn't shelter her under their roofs?*

"My mother was certain that Amitira doesn't leave me alone," she said herself loudly, hoping to assure herself that there is no need to be concerned. She closed her eyes, imagined herself, sinking into a warm feather bed, in front of a fireplace that was full of hot ash, with a hot orange heart burning within. Her infant daughter was on the breast; she began to caress her belly, sing a song that her mother was singing for her daughters, but the pain had been so fierce that caused her put aside any thoughts, gritting her teeth against the pain. The wind was rising, raindrops turned to crystals, slashing at her face as she struggled through the trails of razor-sharp rocks.

At the end of the road, after a steep slope, under the fading sunlight of a winter evening, Jamaspa saw the huts with its sod roof and thick walls of rough-hewn logs, among the leafless trees. This was the most beautiful sight. Lightning flashed, and thunder rumbled, at the same time, with a wave of intense pain in her belly, Jamaspa let out a raucous scream, and a warm liquid ran down her legs. She knew that she has only a few minutes of the baby's born.

*****

Jamaspa was walking, alone, through the streets.

She could not believe what she was seeing. *What the hell is going on in here?* Every building in the village she had passed had been burned and abandoned. Jamaspa had glimpsed no living man since she had entered the town. *It's impossible…. It is just impossible… somebody has to be here*, Jamaspa thought. Fear had overwhelmed her pains, she began to make her way upward, to the main street, shouting for help, but no one was there, there was a village with not a single living one!

Her steps took her to a marble temple. The wild roses spread their bare branches entire the central altar. A brass sculpture was placed on a marble base, a warrior, a goddess with ruby eyes, which seemed to look down at her. Jamaspa stopped to catch her breath and ease the pain in her belly. She felt her child movement inside her with sharp pain and fell heavily to her knees in mud. *This is the end*, she thought. Now that she had fallen, she could not seem to find the strength to rise again. She groped for a branch and clutched it tight. Thorn sank to her palm, but the pain in her belly was greater than she could notice that. *It would be so bad dying here*, she thought, *my baby needs to come out right now*. She sheltered under the altar and cried as a spasm of pain washed over her. "Oh, Gods forgive me, please..." She cried, grabbed two more branches, hissing in pain. "God Marduk... help me pleeeeeease."

She threw back her head, and after Jamaspa's last painful cry, the child was born. For a moment, she forgot her horrible situation, and smiled with relief then listened carefully, there was no sound but the wind that blew more vigorously. "Noooo," she shouted, her eyes opened to gaze up at the child. *Please, no, no, no...* She held the baby. In the child's black face was no sign of life.

No, no, it can't be true; this is not fair. This was just not fair, she had lost her husband, her virginity and honor, her family, her beauty, and at the end, her homeland. This child was her last belong, the only thing that was left for her in this world. *There is no sin so foul for me to take from me all I loved.*

"God, this is not fair!" Jamaspa cried, but the clash of thunder smothered her voice.

She glanced at the black and sullen sky overhead, then she fainted.

*****

Jamaspa heard a faint ringing of bells, and a child's cry, and suddenly felt a movement of an infant's tiny lips on her breast. She looked at the beautiful baby girl who was looking for her nipple eagerly. She positioned her breast correctly in her mouth, and the baby began to suck. Jamaspa stroked her hair. It was a miracle. She kept the child clutched to her chest nursed her at her breast as she was kissing and smelling her wholeheartedly.

*****

Ancient Land of Mannaeans, 627 BC, Summer

Brazen was marching north toward the hills, four Assyrian warriors behind him. They were Bannermen warriors, to recognize hostile defense strategies against them.

Brazen's hair had turned grey, he had borne other scars, more profound than the ones around his eyebrow and a mouth full of broken teeth, shattered by fighting, but he still was strong and muscular, with a barrel chest, thick arms, and bandy legs. He was known for his brute strength. He should be a chief commander now if he did not drink too much every day and did not have sticky fingers.

Brazen spurred forward at a hard gallop, and after a few minutes, he stood atop the rocks, gazed off toward the setting sun. He could see the light shimmering like hammered gold off the surface of Chichest Lake. In front of him, a series of bare stony hills rose high, giving way to the dense and wild forest. On the horizon, a large village had stood among two hills, the town surrounded by grey-green sentinels and tall blue soldier pines.

In fact, nobles' goods were the primary target for Brazen. Besides drinking wine, he had a gambling problem. He used to go to the largest slum in Nineveh, where the real cockfighting championship was going on, a blood sport between two giant cocks that held in a ring called a cockpit. The horned cocks inflicted on each other by attaching metal spurs to the cocks' natural spurs. Brazen loved this violent competition, also he was a betting man, would put his money on his cocks; unfortunately, he often lost his money for this, and hence he was in gambling debt. Of course, his creditors were not so brave to ask their money but until he did not pay his debt, no more bets were for him so Brazen had to spend the money to them to could take part in those tournaments.

"There's a sight I'd like to see! The downhill village, where the wealthiest Mannaeans live!" Brazen said, smiled through the grey of his beard. "So let's have it."

*****

Jamaspa put aside her faded wedding scarf. It was a pity that she had such a miserable fate but she was well contented with her life, she had a beautiful daughter, and she has been planning her daughter's wedding. Her daughter should be honored on her wedding night when the groom would sit beside her. She smoothed a red silk scarf down. The light of the afternoon was slanting down through thick windows, made the shimmering silken veil seem to glow. She always imagined her daughter in this scarf. Jamaspa pressed some coins in her palm, twenty gold coins, her whole life savings. She smiled a crooked smile and started to sew them on the scarf.

An Assyrian young warrior stepped into the house, slowly and cautiously, the frightened goats made a lot of noise but not high enough to hear by Jamaspa. She was sewing the coins on the scarf patiently. No one came out, so the man sheathed his sword, guessing the residences have left the hut. The soldier searched the hall for something of value and threw jars across the room. Jamaspa startled, dropped the coins and whirled toward the voice.

"Mithra, is that you?" Jamaspa asked quietly as she moved into the hall.

The soldier was taken by surprise. He turned to her, grabbed her hair and pushed her down to the ground savagely. Jamaspa dragged herself down to the floor; the fear went through her like a knife. The soldier just kept coming. He touched his sword, but suddenly he caught sight of the coins glinting in the sun. He bent over and gathered the coins quickly, peeking at Jamaspa.

"You rat bastard," a voice boomed suddenly from the gate.

The young soldier froze when he heard his commander's voice. Jamaspa had not listened to the Assyrian language for a long time; it struck her as strange.

The young soldier glanced at Brazen over his shoulder as the coins were pouring out from his fingers. "This old woman was hiding the coins," he said defensively.

Brazen pointed toward the door with his head. "Go out and have a GOOD look around," he said with a commanding tone.

The young soldier looked longingly at the coins and went out. Brazen waited until the soldier went out, then he glanced at Jamaspa. *She's not worth killing!* He thought, in his eyes, she was only an old woman with a hideous face. He stepped forward to pick up the coins off the ground, but Jamaspa had recognized him, even though Brazen had a helmet that had covered half of his face. Jamaspa knew those eyes very well; those were same eyes that scared her when she was living in Nineveh.

"Get your fucking hands off my coins before I kill you!" Jamaspa shouted.

Brazen glanced at her. She was speaking their tongue, *how could she possibly learn this in Mannea?* He thought, but more importantly, she was threatening him, and that was impossible to deal with. "What the hell did you just say, old hag?" He said, threatening.

"I'm not going to let you do this to me," Jamaspa said in disgust. "No, not anymore."

"What are you talking about?" Brazen sounded honestly puzzled.

"Don't you recognize me, huh? You're right... my face has changed a bit," Jamaspa said, sarcastically.

Brazen stepped forward and stared at her with curiosity, but he did not remember anything about this old woman.

"I am Jamaspa, who you ruined her life," she shouted, as she jumped over him, dug her nails into his eye sockets.

Brazen cried out in pain. He slammed into her chest and knocked her off. Jamaspa's jaws locked on his left arm as they fell, her teeth sinking through the leather and wool and soft flesh. She ground her teeth together, and Brazen grunted in pain. He grabbed her throat with one hand and slapped her with the other so hard that her lip tore open all over and all of a sudden she let him go, the taste of his blood and hers filled her mouth. He stared at her face, his strong fingers coiling around Jamaspa's throat. "You can't be Jamaspa," he whispered.

"You have to speak up, son of a bitch, I can't hear you," Jamaspa shouted.

For a few moments, Brazen looked shocked. Then a smile spread across his face. "You're Jamaspa, you really are... your only eye is the same eye that always stared at me with such hatred!" He said, laughing aloud.

"Yeah, you're looking at your masterpiece, almost bald, almost blind and deaf, with a grotesque, ugly face," Jamaspa said through clenched teeth.

"Yeah, you've changed so much! Ah, that's a pity!" Brazen said, laughing harder. "You are a hideous, ugly beast now!"

"And you are a filthy beast yet!" Jamaspa said and spat into his face with disgust.

Brazen seized her by the shoulder and slammed her down onto the stone floor so hard that Jamaspa heard her teeth crack.

"You've totally changed, Jamaspa, you look awful, and you've lost your mind!" Brazen screamed. He pushed his fingers into her hair, made an angry face. "But I'm going to start doing those horrible things again because I haven't changed." He moved toward the door, dragging Jamaspa by her hair. He peeled off his gloves, tucked them through his belt, and tied one end of his rope around Jamaspa's wrists, the other end around his horse saddle. Three Assyrian riders had emerged from behind the rocks, coming toward them at a slow trot.

"Let's go… have some fun friends," Brazen yelled. "Come on, I want to play!" He mounted, spurring to a gallop.

A QUEEN FOR HER ENEMIES

(DANCING WITH FATE - BOOK TWO)

www.ingramcontent.com/pod-product-compliance
Lightning Source LLC
Chambersburg PA
CBHW031107260626
47172CB00001B/262